Zara's

D0336814

RICHARD ADAMS'S

Favourite Animal Stories

RICHARD ADAMS'S
Favourite Animal Stories

octopus

Richard Adams was born in Berkshire in 1920 and studied history at Bradfield and at Worcester College, Oxford. He served in the Second World War and in 1948 joined the Civil Service. In the mid-1960's he completed his first novel, WATERSHIP DOWN, the story of which he originally told to his children to while away a long car journey. WATERSHIP DOWN was awarded both the Carnegie medal and the *Guardian* award for children's fiction for 1972.

In 1974 he retired from the Civil Service to devote himself to writing and in that year published his second novel, SHARDIK. His third novel, THE PLAGUE DOGS, followed in 1977 and his fourth, THE GIRL IN A SWING, in 1980.

Richard Adams lives in the Isle of Man with his wife Elizabeth, who is an expert on English ceramic history, and his two daughters, Juliet and Rosamond. His enthusiasms are English literature, music, chess, beer and shove-ha'penny, bird-song, folk-song and country walking.

This edition first published in Great Britain in 1981 by
Octopus Books Limited, 59 Grosvenor Street, London W1

ISBN 0 7064 1276 1

Reprinted 1982, 1983

Printed in Czechoslovakia
50445/3

CONTENTS

INTRODUCTION

Telling stories is the oldest form of entertainment on earth – unless, indeed, dancing is older; but dancing, like painting, probably began as a form of worship and magic rather than entertainment. No kind of story is older than the animal story. We know this because the folk tales of the most primitive peoples still inhabiting the world – such as the Australian aborigines – include a great many animal stories. Also, rock and cave paintings found all over the world – for example, at Altamira, Lascaux and in Central Africa – depict animals, sometimes together with men and sometimes in ways which suggest that they were regarded as divine. It is remarkable that mankind's interest in telling and hearing animal stories should have remained alive for untold centuries, continually coming up new, continually adapting itself to changing conditions of human life. To-day it is as strong as ever.

There are – or so it seems to me – four different kinds of animal story. The first is what is called 'anthropomorphic fantasy' – stories in which animals and birds are made to talk and behave like human beings. Nearly always, this involves some degree of social comment or satire. The animals represent different types of human being, e.g. the fox is a subtle, crafty villain, the bear is a big, heavy simpleton, the eagle is a noble, all-seeing aristocrat and so on. In primitive (and some not so primitive) societies one had to be careful how one told stories about other people. A man who openly made fun of the king or his henchmen was likely to find himself in trouble. But if he could make up a story about an animal who looked rather like the king, or behaved rather like him, he could make his point and it would be harder to pin anything on him. The king himself might even enjoy the joke. Again, if one is an ordinary person trying to attack a tyrant, mere indignation and resentment will get nowhere, for the tyrant holds all the aces. But if one can contrive to make the tyrant look a fool and everyone laugh at him, even he will have no defence. 'Animal Farm' has put Stalin in his place for good and all.

This kind of animal story – the fable – has gone on up-dating itself for century after century. One might have thought that human beings would have become too sophisticated for this sort of thing, but they have not. 'The Wind in the Willows', for example, is a story supposedly about animals who are really human beings. (Toad can drive motor cars and Mole can catch a horse in a field and put a bridle on it.) This book contains two or three examples of this kind of story. Uncle Remus's tales of Brer Rabbit and Brer Fox are very old and have counterparts in folk

7

tales all over the world. Joel Chandler Harris, who was a journalist in Atlanta, Georgia, about 110 years ago, simply wrote up and put into the mouth of the fictitious 'Uncle Remus' the folk tales that he had heard told by black people. Again, Beatrix Potter's animal stories contain a great deal of mild but very shrewd and amusing satire on the Lakeland society in which she herself lived during the first twenty years of this century. The extract, in this book, from 'The Fairy Caravan' is a good example. No doubt Beatrix Potter had herself often seen cheapjacks like Messrs. Ratten and Scratch at work on market days in the Lakeland. Anna Sewell, who had strong humanitarian views about the ill-treatment of horses in Victorian times, put her own opinions into the mouth of Black Beauty.

The second type of animal story is that which constitutes a kind of parable, and tells of the animal's dealings with God – or with a god, or with Providence. It is usually on the lines of 'How the Leopard Got His Spots', 'How the Giraffe Got His Long Neck', and so on. Sometimes the animal is blest by being given some splendid attribute. A particularly beautiful example (not in this book) is the story of how the nightingale received his voice when God touched his tongue with a paint-brush dipped in gold. Or conversely, the creature may be punished for having committed some evil deed: or it may once have been a human being who was turned into an animal or bird for wrong-doing, like the over-inquisitive old woman who was turned into a woodpecker and ever since flies about poking her nose into trees and holes, looking for insects. To my way of thinking, this kind of story is moving because it shows that human beings have always felt a kind of magical and numinous quality in animals. Nowadays, perhaps, children feel this more strongly than adults, but primitive people are like children in many ways. Yet all of us, I think, share a feeling that animals have something divine about them and that they form an important part of the mystery of life on earth. Many a man prefers dogs to humans: dogs don't tell lies. Since this book does not set out to include folk tales as such, there are no 'straight' examples of this kind of story here; but Rudyard Kipling's 'The Cat That Walked By Himself' is in this vein.

The third type of story is that in which the animal itself is represented as divine – either as being a god or as being in some way a representative of God. It is a curious fact that there is scarcely an animal or bird in the world which has not, somewhere and at some time, been worshipped. Some of these are rather surprising. Rats have been worshipped, for example, and so have scorpions and sparrows. Once again, there are no straightforward examples of that kind of story in this book, although it is one which has always held interest for me. (I have myself attempted it more than once – for example, in the El-ahrairah stories in 'Watership Down', in 'Shardik' and in Rowf's story of Man's Fall in 'The Plague Dogs'.) One might, however, stretch a point and include in this category 'Saki's' 'The Wolves of Cernogratz', in which the wolves are obviously the agents of some supernatural power.

Lastly, we have the perfectly plain animal story, which means no more than it says, without satire, parable or religious meaning. Such stories must be every bit as old as the other three kinds, going back to the days when the First Caveman told the Second Caveman about the mammoth he hunted last Wednesday. Most of the stories in this book are of that kind.

To-day Man's traditional relationship to the animals – his love and respect for them – which has always played so beautiful and important a part in his life on earth, is gravely threatened by our very power, supremacy and overwhelming numbers. Whereas in days gone by we used to share the world with the animals, we have now become so numerous and powerful that we have complete control and can diminish or destroy any other species – sometimes without even meaning to. Many we have. During the past 300 years, about 300 species of animal and bird have become extinct, due to the activities of the human race. The killing of animals, which used to be on a relatively small scale, carried out by few hunters, often at the risk of their lives, has now become big business. The animals no longer have a sporting chance. We are guilty of the near-extinction of the whale and the African elephant, and of the wicked and iniquitous Canadian harp seal slaughter, which involves the battering and disembowelling of 150,000 three-week-old seal pups every year, in the presence of their mothers, just so that a few men can make money out of the fur – which nobody needs. This miserable catalogue of cruelty for money could be extended to greater length, but this is not the place. The respect and love for animals which the human race has always felt – and which these stories illustrate – has never been in greater danger than to-day of being swamped and overwhelmed by our greed for gain.

I hope that as well as fulfilling its main intention, which is simply to amuse and entertain, this book will help to remind people of how much animals have always meant to us and how much poorer and uglier our imaginative lives would be if we were to allow our natural fellow-feeling for them to be blotted out of our hearts.

RICHARD ADAMS

9

The Cat that walked by Himself

RUDYARD KIPLING

This is the picture of the Cat that Walked by Himself, walking by his wild lone through the Wet Wild Woods and waving his wild tail. There is nothing else in the picture except some toadstools. They had to grow there because the Woods were so wet. The lumpy thing on the low branch isn't a bird. It is moss that grew there because the Wild Woods were so wet.

Underneath the truly picture is a picture of the cosy Cave that the Man and the Woman went to after the Baby came. It was their summer Cave, and they planted wheat in front of it. The man is riding on the Horse to find the Cow and bring her back to the Cave to be milked. He is holding up his hand to call the Dog, who has swum across to the other side of the river, looking for rabbits.

Illustration by Rudyard Kipling

THE CAT THAT WALKED
BY HIMSELF

Hear and attend and listen; for this befell and behappened and became and was, O my Best Beloved, when the Tame animals were wild. The Dog was wild, and the Horse was wild, and the Cow was wild, and the Sheep was wild, and the Pig was wild – as wild as wild could be – and they walked in the Wet Wild Woods by their wild lones. But the wildest of all the wild animals was the Cat. He walked by himself, and all places were alike to him.

Of course the Man was wild too. He was dreadfully wild. He didn't even begin to be tame till he met the Woman, and she told him that she did not like living in his wild ways. She picked out a nice dry Cave, instead of a heap of wet leaves, to lie down in; and she strewed clean sand on the floor; and she lit a nice fire of wood at the back of the Cave; and she hung a dried wild-horse skin, tail-down, across the opening of the Cave; and she said, 'Wipe your feet, dear, when you come in, and now we'll keep house.'

That night, Best Beloved, they ate wild sheep roasted on the hot stones, and flavoured with wild garlic and wild pepper; and wild duck stuffed with wild rice and wild fenugreek and wild coriander; and marrow-bones of wild oxen; and wild cherries and wild grenadillas. Then the Man went to sleep in front of the fire ever so happy; but the Woman sat up, combing her hair. She took the bone of the shoulder of mutton – the big flat blade-bone – and she looked at the wonderful marks on it, and she threw more wood on the fire, and she made a Magic. She made the First Singing Magic in the world.

Out in the Wet Wild Woods all the wild animals gathered together where they could see the light of the fire a long way off, and they wondered what it meant.

Then Wild Horse stamped with his wild foot and said, 'O my Friends and O my Enemies, why have the Man and Woman made that great light in that great Cave, and what harm will it do us?'

Wild dog lifted up his wild nose and smelled the smell of the roast mutton, and said, 'I will go up and see and look, and say; for I think it is good. Cat, come with me.'

'Nenni!' said the Cat. 'I am the Cat who walks by himself, and all places are alike to me. I will not come.'

'Then we can never be friends again,' said Wild Dog, and he trotted off to the Cave. But when he had gone a little way the Cat said to himself, 'All places are alike to me. Why should I not go too and see and look and come away at my own liking?' So he slipped after Wild Dog softly, very softly, and hid himself where he could hear everything.

When Wild Dog reached the mouth of the Cave he lifted up the dried horse-skin with his nose and sniffed the beautiful smell of the roast mutton, and the Woman, looking at the blade-bone, heard him, and laughed, and said, 'Here comes the first. Wild Thing out of the Wild Woods, what do you want?'

Wild Dog said, 'O my Enemy and Wife of my Enemy, what is this that smells so good in the Wild Woods?'

Then the Woman picked up a roasted mutton-bone and threw it to Wild Dog, and said, 'Wild Thing out of the Wild Woods, taste and try.' Wild Dog gnawed the bone, and it was more delicious than anything he had ever tasted, and he said, 'O my Enemy and Wife of my Enemy, give me another.'

The Woman said 'Wild Thing out of the Wild Woods, help my Man to hunt through the day and guard this Cave at night, and I will give you as many roast bones as you need.'

'Ah!' said the Cat, listening. 'This is a very wise Woman, but she is not so wise as I am.'

Wild Dog crawled into the Cave and laid his head on the Woman's lap, and said, 'O my Friend and Wife of my Friend, I will help your Man to hunt through the day, and at night I will guard your Cave.'

'Ah!' said the Cat, listening. 'That is a very foolish Dog.' And he went back through the Wet Wild Woods waving his wild tail, and walking by his wild lone. But he never told anybody.

When the Man woke up he said, 'What is Wild Dog doing here?' And the Woman said, 'His name is not Wild Dog any more, but the First Friend, because he will be our friend for always and always and always. Take him with you when you go hunting.'

Next night the Woman cut great green armfuls of fresh grass from the water-meadows, and dried it before the fire, so that it smelt like new-mown hay, and she sat at the mouth of the Cave and plaited a halter out of horse-hide, and she looked at the shoulder-of-mutton bone – at the big broad blade-bone – and she made a Magic. She made the Second Singing Magic in the world.

Out in the Wild Woods all the wild animals wondered what had happened to Wild Dog, and at last Wild Horse stamped with his foot and said, 'I will go and see and say why Wild Dog has not returned. Cat, come with me.'

'Nenni!' said the Cat. 'I am the Cat who walks by himself, and all places are alike to me. I will not come.' But all the same he followed Wild Horse softly, very softly, and hid himself where he could hear everything.

When the Woman heard Wild Horse tripping and stumbling on his long mane, she laughed and said, 'Here comes the second. Wild Thing out of the Wild Woods, what do you want?'

Wild Horse said, 'O my Enemy and Wife of my Enemy, where is Wild Dog?'

The Woman laughed, and picked up the blade-bone and looked at it, and said, 'Wild Thing out of the Wild Woods, you did not come here for Wild Dog, but for the sake of this good grass.'

And Wild Horse, tripping and stumbling on his long mane, said, 'That is true; give it me to eat.'

The Woman said, 'Wild Thing out of the Wild Woods, bend your wild head and wear what I give you, and you shall eat the wonderful grass three times a day.'

'Ah!' said the Cat, listening. 'This is a clever Woman, but she is not so clever as I am.'

Wild Horse bent his wild head, and the Woman slipped the plaited-hide halter over it, and Wild Horse breathed on the Woman's feet and said, 'O my Mistress, and Wife of my Master, I will be your servant for the sake of the wonderful grass.'

'Ah!' said the Cat, listening. 'That is a very foolish Horse.' And he went back through the Wet Wild Woods, waving his wild tail and walking by his wild lone. But he never told anybody.

When the Man and the Dog came back from hunting, the Man said, 'What is Wild Horse doing here?' And the Woman said, 'His name is not Wild Horse any more, but the First Servant, because he will carry us from place to place for always and always and always. Ride on his back when you go hunting.'

Next day, holding her wild head high that her wild horns should not catch in the wild trees, Wild Cow came up to the Cave, and the Cat followed, and hid himself just the same as before; and everything happened just the same as before; and the Cat said the same things as before; and when Wild Cow had promised to give her milk to the Woman every day in exchange for the wonderful grass, the Cat went back through the Wet Wild Woods waving his wild tail and walking by his wild lone, just the same as before. But he never told anybody. And when the Man and the Horse and the Dog came home from hunting and asked the same questions same as before, the Woman said, 'Her name is not Wild Cow any more, but the Giver of Good Food. She will give us the warm white milk for always and always and always, and I will take care of her while you and the First Friend and the First Servant go hunting.'

Next day the Cat waited to see if any other Wild Thing would go up to the Cave, but no one moved in the Wet Wild Woods, so the Cat walked there by himself; and he saw the Woman milking the Cow, and he saw the light of the fire in the Cave, and he smelt the smell of the warm white milk.

Cat said, 'O my Enemy and Wife of my Enemy, where did Wild Cow go?'

The Woman laughed and said, 'Wild Thing out of the Wild Woods, go back to the Woods again, for I have braided up my hair, and I have put away the magic blade-bone, and we have no more need of either friends or servants in our Cave.'

Cat said, 'I am not a friend, and I am not a servant. I am the Cat who walks by himself, and I wish to come into your Cave.'

Woman said, 'Then why did you not come with First Friend on the first night?'

Cat grew very angry and said, 'Has Wild Dog told tales of me?'

Then the Woman laughed and said, 'You are the Cat who walks by himself, and all places are alike to you. You are neither a friend nor a servant. You have said it yourself. Go away and walk by yourself in all places alike.'

Then Cat pretended to be sorry and said, 'Must I never come into the Cave? Must I never sit by the warm fire? Must I never drink the warm white milk? You are very wise and very beautiful. You should not be cruel even to a Cat.'

Woman said, 'I knew I was wise, but I did not know I was beautiful. So I will make a bargain with you. If ever I say one word in your praise, you may come into the Cave.'

'And if you say two words in my praise?' said the Cat.

'I never shall,' said the Woman, 'but if I say two words in your praise, you may sit by the fire in the Cave.'

'And if you say three words?' said the Cat.

'I never shall,' said the Woman, 'but if I say three words in your praise, you may drink the warm white milk three times a day for always and always and always.'

Then the Cat arched his back and said, 'Now let the Curtain at the mouth of the Cave, and the Fire at the back of the Cave, and the Milk-pots that stand beside the Fire, remember what my Enemy and the Wife of my Enemy has said.' And he went away through the Wet Wild Woods waving his wild tail and walking by his wild lone.

That night when the Man and the Horse and the Dog came home from hunting, the Woman did not tell them of the bargain that she had made with the Cat, because she was afraid that they might not like it.

Cat went far and far away and hid himself in the Wet Wild Woods by his wild lone for a long time till the Woman forgot all about him. Only the Bat – the little upside-down Bat – that hung inside the Cave knew where Cat hid; and every evening Bat would fly to Cat with news of what was happening.

One evening Bat said, 'There is a Baby in the Cave. He is new and pink and fat and small, and the Woman is very fond of him.'

'Ah,' said the Cat, listening. 'But what is the Baby fond of?'

'He is fond of things that are soft and tickle,' said the Bat. 'He is fond of warm things to hold in his arms when he goes to sleep. He is fond of being played with. He is fond of all those things.'

'Ah,' said the Cat, listening. 'Then my time has come.'

Next night Cat walked through the Wet Wild Woods and hid very near the Cave till morning-time, and Man and Dog and Horse went hunting. The Woman was busy cooking that morning, and the Baby cried and interrupted. So she carried him outside the Cave and gave him a handful of pebbles to play with. But still the Baby cried.

Then the Cat put out his paddy paw and patted the Baby on the cheek, and it cooed; and the Cat rubbed against its fat knees and tickled it under its fat chin with his tail. And the Baby laughed; and the Woman heard him and smiled.

Then the Bat – the little upside-down Bat – that hung in the mouth of the Cave said, 'O my Hostess and Wife of my Host and Mother of my Host's Son, a Wild Thing from the Wild Woods is most beautifully playing with your Baby.'

'A blessing on that Wild Thing whoever he may be,' said the Woman, straightening her back, 'for I was a busy woman this morning and he has done me a service.'

That very minute and second, Best Beloved, the dried horse-skin Curtain that was stretched tail-down at the mouth of the Cave fell down – *woosh!* – because it remembered the bargain she had made with the Cat; and when the Woman went to pick it up – lo and behold! – the Cat was sitting quite comfy inside the Cave.

'O my Enemy and Wife of my Enemy and Mother of my Enemy,' said the Cat, 'it is I: for you have spoken a word in my praise, and now I can sit within the Cave for always and always and always. But still I am the Cat who walks by himself, and all places are alike to me.'

The Woman was very angry, and shut her lips tight and took up her spinning-wheel and began to spin.

But the Baby cried because the Cat had gone away, and the Woman could not hush it, for it struggled and kicked and grew black in the face.

'O my Enemy and Wife of my Enemy and Mother of my Enemy,' said the Cat, 'take a strand of the thread that you are spinning and tie it to your spindle-whorl and drag it along the floor, and I will show you a Magic that shall make your Baby laugh as loudly as he is now crying.'

'I will do so,' said the Woman, 'because I am at my wits' end; but I will not thank you for it.'

She tied the thread to the little clay spindle-whorl and drew it across the floor, and the Cat ran after it and patted it with his paws and rolled head over heels, and tossed it backward over his shoulder and chased it between his hind legs and pretended to lose it, and pounced down upon it again, till the Baby laughed as loudly as it had been crying, and scrambled after the Cat and frolicked all over the Cave till it grew tired and settled down to sleep with the Cat in its arms.

'Now,' said the Cat, 'I will sing the Baby a song that shall keep him asleep for an hour.' And he began to purr, loud and low, low and loud, till the Baby fell fast asleep. The Woman smiled as she looked down upon the two of them, and said, 'That was wonderfully done. No question but you are very clever, O Cat.'

That very minute and second, Best Beloved, the smoke of the Fire at the back of the Cave came down in clouds from the roof – *puff!* – because it remembered the bargain she had made with the Cat; and when it had cleared away – lo and behold! – the Cat was sitting quite comfy close to the fire.

'O my Enemy and Wife of my Enemy and Mother of my Enemy,' said the Cat, 'it is I: for you have spoken a second word in my praise, and now I can sit by the warm fire at the back of the Cave for always and always and always. But still I am the Cat who walks by himself, and all places are alike to me.'

Then the woman was very very angry, and let down her hair and put more wood on the fire and brought out the broad blade-bone of the shoulder of mutton and began to make a Magic that should prevent her from saying a third word in praise of the Cat. It was not a Singing Magic, Best Beloved, it was a Still Magic; and by and by the Cave grew so still that a little wee-wee mouse crept out of a corner and ran across the floor.

'O my Enemy and Wife of my Enemy and Mother of my Enemy,' said the Cat, 'is that little mouse part of your Magic?'

'Ouh! Chee! No indeed!' said the Woman, and she dropped the blade-bone and jumped upon the footstool in front of the fire and braided up her hair very quick for fear that the mouse should run up it.

'Ah,' said the Cat, watching. 'Then the mouse will do me no harm if I eat it?'

'No,' said the Woman, braiding up her hair, 'eat it quickly and I will ever be grateful to you.'

Cat made one jump and caught the little mouse and the Woman said, 'A hundred thanks. Even the First Friend is not quick enough to catch little mice as you have done. You must be very wise.'

That very minute and second, O Best Beloved, the Milk-pot that stood by the fire cracked in two pieces – *ffft!* – because it remembered the bargain she had made with the Cat; and when the Woman jumped down from the footstool – lo and behold! – the Cat was lapping up the warm white milk that lay in one of the broken pieces.

'O my Enemy and Wife of my Enemy and Mother of my Enemy,' said the Cat, 'it is I: for you have spoken three words in my praise, and now I can drink the warm white milk three times a day for always and always and always. But *still* I am the Cat who walks by himself, and all places are alike to me.'

Then the Woman laughed and set the Cat a bowl of the warm white milk and said, 'O Cat, you are as clever as a man, but remember that your bargain was not made with the Man or the Dog, and I do not know what they will do when they come home.'

'What is that to me?' said the Cat. 'If I have my place in the Cave by the fire and my warm white milk three times a day I do not care what the Man or the Dog can do.'

That evening when the Man and the Dog came into the Cave, the Woman told them all the story of the bargain, while the Cat sat by the fire and smiled. Then the Man said, 'Yes, but he has not made a bargain with *me* or with all proper Men after me.' Then he took off his two leather boots and he took up his little stone axe (that makes three) and he fetched a piece of wood and a hatchet (that is five altogether), and he set them out in a row and he said, 'Now we will make *our* bargain. If you do not catch mice when you are in the Cave for always and always and always, I will throw these five things at you whenever I see you, and so shall all proper Men do after me.'

'Ah!' said the Woman, listening. 'This is a very clever Cat, but he is not so clever as my Man.'

The Cat counted the five things (and they looked very knobby) and he said, 'I will catch mice when I am in the Cave for always and always and always; but *still* I am the Cat who walks by himself, and all places are alike to me.'

'Not when I am near,' said the Man. 'If you had not said that last I would have put all these things away for always and always and always; but now I am going to throw my two boots and my little stone axe (that makes three) at you whenever I meet you. And so shall all proper Men do after me!'

Then the Dog said, 'Wait a minute. He has not made a bargain with *me* or with all proper Dogs after me.' And he showed his teeth and said, 'If you are not kind to the Baby while I am in the Cave for always and always and always, I will hunt you till I catch you, and when I catch you I will bite you. And so shall all proper Dogs do after me.'

'Ah!' said the Woman, listening. 'This is a very clever Cat, but he is not so clever as the Dog.'

Cat counted the Dog's teeth (and they looked very pointed) and he said, 'I will be kind to the Baby while I am in the Cave, as long as he does not pull my tail too hard, for always and always and always. But *still* I am the Cat who walks by himself, and all places are alike to me.'

'Not when I am near,' said the Dog. 'If you had not said that last I would have shut my mouth for always and always and always; but *now* I am going to hunt you up a tree whenever I meet you. And so shall all proper Dogs do after me.'

Then the Man threw his two boots and his little stone axe (that makes three) at the Cat, and the Cat ran out of the Cave and the Dog chased him up a tree; and from that day to this, Best Beloved, three proper Men out of five will always throw things at a Cat whenever they meet him, and all proper Dogs will chase him up a tree. But the Cat keeps his side of the bargain too. He will kill mice, and he will be kind to Babies when he is in the house, just as long as they do not pull his tail too hard. But when he has done that, and between times, and when the moon gets up and night comes, he is the Cat that walks by himself, and all places are alike to him. Then he goes out to the Wet Wild Woods or up the Wet Wild Trees or on the Wet Wild Roofs, waving his wild tail and walking by his wild lone.

Pussy can sit by the fire and sing,
    Pussy can climb a tree,
Or play with a silly old cork and string
    To 'muse herself, not me.
But I like *Binkie* my dog, because
    He knows how to behave;
So, *Binkie's* the same as the First Friend was,
    And I am the Man in the Cave!

Pussy will play Man Friday till
    It's time to wet her paw
And make her walk on the window-sill
    (For the footprint Crusoe saw);
Then she fluffles her tail and mews,
    And scratches and won't attend.
But *Binkie* will play whatever I choose,
    And he is my true First Friend!

Pussy will rub my knees with her head
    Pretending she loves me hard;
But the very minute I go to my bed
    Pussy runs out in the yard,
And there she stays till the morning-light;
    So I know it it only pretend;
But *Binkie*, he snores at my feet all night,
    And he is my Firstest Friend!

Lobo, The King of Currumpaw

ERNEST THOMPSON SETON

LOBO
THE KING OF CURRUMPAW

Currumpaw is a vast cattle range in northern New Mexico. It is a land of rich pastures and teeming flocks and herds, a land of rolling mesas and precious running waters that at length unite in the Currumpaw River from which the whole region is named. And the king whose despotic power was felt over its entire extent was an old grey wolf.

Old Lobo, or the king, as the Mexicans called him, was the gigantic leader of a remarkable pack of grey wolves, that had ravaged the Currumpaw Valley for a number of years. All the shepherds and ranchmen knew him well, and, wherever he appeared with his trusty band, terror reigned supreme among the cattle, and wrath and despair among their owners. Old Lobo was a giant among wolves, and was cunning and strong in proportion to his size. His voice at night was well known and easily distinguished from that of any of his fellows. An ordinary wolf might howl half the night about the herdsman's bivouac without attracting more than a passing notice, but when the deep roar of the old king came booming down the cañon, the watcher bestirred himself and prepared to learn in the morning that fresh and serious inroads had been made.

Old Lobo's band was but a small one. This I never quite understood, for usually, when a wolf rises to the position and power that he had, he attracts a numerous following. It may be that he had as many as he desired, or perhaps his ferocious temper prevented the increase of his pack. Certain is it that Lobo had only five followers during the latter part of his reign. Each of these, however, was a wolf of renown, most of them were above the ordinary size, one in particular, the second in command, was a veritable giant, but even he was far below the leader in size and prowess. Several of the band, besides the two leaders, were especially noted. One of those was a beautiful white wolf that the Mexicans called Blanca; this was supposed to be a female, possibly Lobo's mate. Another was a yellow wolf of remarkable swiftness, which, according to current stories had, on several occasions, captured an antelope for the pack.

It will be seen, then, that these wolves were thoroughly well known to the cowboys and shepherds. They were frequently seen and oftener heard, and their lives were intimately associated with those of the cattlemen, who would so gladly have destroyed them. There was not a stockman on the Currumpaw who would not readily have given the value of many steers for the scalp of any one of Lobo's band, but they seemed to possess charmed lives, and defied all manner of devices to kill them. They scorned all hunters, derided all poisons and continued, for at least five years, to exact their tribute from the Currumpaw ranchers to the extent, many said, of a cow each day. According to this estimate, therefore, the band had killed more than two thousand of the finest stock, for, as was only too well known, they selected the best in every instance.

The old idea that a wolf was constantly in a starving state, and therefore ready to eat anything, was as far as possible from the truth in this case, for these freebooters were always sleek and well-conditioned, and were, in fact, most fastidious about what they ate. Any animal that had died from natural causes, or that was diseased or tainted, they would not touch, and they even rejected anything that had been killed by the stockmen. Their choice and daily food was the tenderer part of a freshly killed yearling heifer. An old bull or cow they disdained, and though they occasionally took a young calf or colt, it was quite clear that veal or horseflesh was not their favourite diet. It was also known that they were not fond of mutton, although they often amused themselves by killing sheep. One night in November, 1893, Blanca and the yellow wolf killed two hundred and fifty sheep, apparently for the fun of it, and did not eat an ounce of their flesh.

These are examples of many stories which I might repeat, and show the ravages of this destructive band. Many new devices for their extinction were tried each year, but still they lived and throve in spite of all the efforts of their foes. A great price was set on Lobo's head, and in consequence poison in a score of subtle forms was put out for him, but he never failed to detect and avoid it. One thing only he feared – that was firearms, and knowing full well that all men in this region carried them, he never was known to attack or face a human being. Indeed, the set policy of his band was to take refuge in flight whenever, in the daytime, a man was descried, no matter at what distance. Lobo's habit of permitting the pack to eat only that which they themselves had killed, was in numerous cases their salvation, and the keenness of his scent to detect the taint of human hands or the poison itself, completed their immunity.

On one occasion, one of the cowboys heard the too familiar rallying-cry of Old Lobo, and stealthily approaching, he found the Currumpaw pack in a hollow, where they had 'rounded up' a small herd of cattle. Lobo sat apart on a knoll, while Blanca with the rest was endeavouring to 'cut out' a young cow, which they had selected; but the cattle were standing in a compact mass with their heads outward, and presented to the foe a line of horns, unbroken save when some cow, frightened by a fresh onset of the wolves, tried to retreat into the middle of the herd. It was only by taking advantage of these breaks that the wolves had succeeded at all in wounding the selected cow, but she was far from being disabled, and it seemed that Lobo at length lost patience with his followers, for he left his position on the hill and, uttering a deep roar, dashed towards the herd. The terrified rank broke at his charge, and he sprang in among them. Then the cattle scattered like the pieces of a bursting bomb. Away went the chosen victim, but ere she had gone twenty-five yards Lobo was upon her. Seizing her by the neck he suddenly held back with all his force and so threw her heavily to the ground. The shock must have been tremendous, for the heifer was thrown heels over head. Lobo also turned a somersault, but immediately recovered himself, and his followers, falling on the poor cow, killed her in a few seconds. Lobo took no part in the killing – after having thrown the victim, he seemed to say, 'Now, why could not some of you have done that at once without wasting so much time?'

The man now rode up shouting, the wolves as usual retired, and he, having a bottle of strychnine, quickly poisoned the carcass in three places, then went away, knowing they would return to feed, as they had killed the animal themselves. But the next morning, on going to look for his expected victims, he found that, although the wolves had eaten the heifer, they had carefully cut out and thrown aside all those parts that had been poisoned.

The dread of this great wolf spread yearly among the ranchmen, and each year a larger price was set on his head, until at last it reached $1,000, an unparalleled wolf-bounty, surely; many a good man has been hunted down for less. Tempted by the promised reward, a Texan ranger named Tannerey came one day galloping up the cañon of the Currumpaw. He had a superb outfit for wolf-hunting – the best of guns and horses, and a pack of enormous wolf-hounds. Far out on the plains of the Panhandle, he and his dogs had killed many a wolf, and now he never doubted that, within a few days Old Lobo's scalp would dangle at his saddle-bow.

Away they went bravely on their hunt in the grey dawn of a summer morning, and soon the great dogs gave joyous tongue to say that they were already on the track of their quarry. Within two miles, the grizzly band of Currumpaw leaped into view, and the chase grew fast and furious. The part of the wolf-hounds was merely to hold the wolves at bay till the hunter could ride up and shoot them, and this usually was easy on the open plains of Texas; but here a new feature of the country came into play, and showed how well Lobo had chosen his range; for the rocky cañons of the Currumpaw and its tributaries intersect the prairies in every direction. The old wolf at once made for the nearest of these and by crossing it got rid of the horseman. His band then scattered and thereby scattered the dogs, and when they reunited at a distant point of course all of the dogs did not turn up, and the wolves no longer outnumbered, turned on their pursuers and killed or desperately wounded them all. That night when Tannerey mustered his dogs, only six of them returned, and of these, two were terribly lacerated. This hunter made two other attempts to capture the royal scalp, but neither of them was more successful than the first, and on the last occasion his best horse met its death by a fall; so he gave up the chase in disgust and went back to Texas, leaving Lobo more than ever the despot of the region.

Next year, two other hunters appeared, determined to win the promised bounty. Each believed he could destroy this noted wolf, the first by means of a newly devised poison, which was to be laid out in an entirely new manner; the other a French-Canadian, by poison assisted with certain spells and charms, for he firmly believed that Lobo was a veritable 'loup-garou,' and could not be killed by ordinary means. But cunningly compounded poisons, charms, and incantations were all of no avail against this grizzly devastator. He made his weekly rounds and daily banquets as aforetime, and before many weeks had passed, Calone and Laloche gave up in despair and went elsewhere to hunt.

In the spring of 1893, after his unsuccessful attempt to capture Lobo, Joe Calone had a humiliating experience, which seems to show that the big wolf simply scorned his enemies, and had absolute confidence in himself. Calone's farm was on a small tributary of the Currumpaw, in a picturesque cañon, and among the rocks of this very cañon, within a thousand yards of the house, Old Lobo and his mate selected their den and raised their family that season. There they lived all summer, and killed Joe's cattle, sheep, and dogs, but laughed at all his poisons and traps, and rested securely among the recesses of the cavernous cliffs, while Joe vainly racked his brain for some method of smoking them out, or of reaching them with dynamite. But they escaped entirely unscathed, and continued their ravages as before. 'There's where he lived all last summer,' said Joe, pointing to the face of the cliff, 'and I couldn't do a thing with him. I was like a fool to him.'

This history, gathered so far from the cowboys, I found hard to believe until, in the fall of 1893, I made the acquaintance of the wily marauder, and at length came to know him more thoroughly than anyone else. Some years before, in the Bingo days, I had been a wolf-hunter, but my occupations since then had been of another sort, chaining me to stool and desk. I was much in need of a change, and when a friend, who was also a ranch-owner on the Currumpaw, asked me to come to New Mexico and try if I could do anything with this predatory pack, I accepted the invitation and, eager to make the acquaintance of its king, was as soon as possible among the mesas of that region. I spent some time riding about to learn the country, and at intervals, my guide would point to the skeleton of a cow to which the hide still adhered, and remark, 'That's some of his work.'

It became quite clear to me that, in this rough country, it was useless to think of pursuing Lobo with hounds and horses, so that poison or traps were the only available expedients. At present we had no traps large enough, so I set to work with poison.

I need not enter into the details of a hundred devices that I employed to circumvent this 'loup-garou'; there was no combination of strychnine, arsenic, cyanide, or prussic acid, that I did not essay; there was no manner of flesh that I did not try as bait; but morning after morning, as I rode forth to learn the result, I found that all my efforts had been useless. The old king was too cunning for me. A single instance will show his wonderful sagacity. Acting on the hint of an old trapper, I melted some cheese together with the kidney fat of a freshly killed heifer, stewing it in a china dish, and cutting it with a bone knife to avoid the taint of metal. When the mixture was cool, I cut it into lumps, and, making a hole in one side of each lump, I inserted a large dose of strychnine and cyanide, contained in a capsule that was impermeable by any odour; finally I sealed the holes up with pieces of the cheese itself. During the whole process, I wore a pair of gloves steeped in the hot blood of the heifer, and even avoided breathing on the baits. When all was ready, I put them in a raw-hide bag rubbed all over with blood, and rode forth dragging the liver and kidneys of the beef at the end of a rope. With this I made a ten-mile circuit, dropping a bait at each quarter of a mile, and taking the utmost care, always, not to touch any with my hands.

Lobo, generally, came in to this part of the range in the early part of each week, and passed the latter part, it was supposed, around the base of Sierra Grande. This was Monday, and that same evening, as we were about to retire, I heard the deep bass howl of his majesty. On hearing it one of the boys briefly remarked, 'There he is, we'll see.'

The next morning I went forth, eager to know the result. I soon came on the fresh trail of the robbers, with Lobo in the lead – his track was always easily distinguished. An ordinary wolf's forefoot is $4\frac{1}{2}$ inches long, that of a large wolf $4\frac{3}{4}$ inches, but Lobo's, as measured a number of times, was $5\frac{1}{2}$ inches from claw to heel; I afterwards found that his other proportions were commensurate, for he stood three feet high at the shoulder, and weighed 150 pounds. His trail, therefore, though obscured by those of his followers, was never difficult to trace. The pack had soon found the track of my drag, and as usual followed it. I could see that Lobo had come to the first bait, sniffed about it, and finally had picked it up.

Then I could not conceal my delight. 'I've got him at last,' I exclaimed; 'I shall find him stark within a mile,' and I galloped on with eager eyes fixed on the great broad track in the dust. It led me to the second bait and that also was gone. How I exulted – I surely have him now and perhaps several of his band. But there was the broad paw-mark still on the drag; and though I stood in the stirrup and scanned the plain I saw nothing that looked like a dead wolf. Again I followed – to find now that the third bait was gone – and the king-wolf's track led on to the fourth, there to learn that he had not really taken a bait at all, but had merely carried them in his mouth. Then having piled the three on the fourth, he scattered filth over them to express his utter contempt for my devices. After this he left my drag and went about his business with the pack he guarded so effectively.

This is only one of many similar experiences which convinced me that poison would never avail to destroy this robber, and though I continued to use it while awaiting the arrival of the traps, it was only because it was meanwhile a sure means of killing many prairie wolves and other destructive vermin.

About this time there came under my observation an incident that will illustrate Lobo's diabolic cunning. These wolves had at least one pursuit which was merely an amusement, it was stampeding and killing sheep, though they rarely ate them. The sheep are usually kept in flocks of from one thousand to three thousand under one or more shepherds. At night they are gathered in the most sheltered place available, and a herdsman sleeps on each side of the flock to give additional protection. Sheep are such senseless creatures that they are liable to be stampeded by the veriest trifle, but they have deeply ingrained in their nature one, and perhaps only one, strong weakness, namely, to follow their leader. And this the shepherds turn to good account by putting half a dozen goats in the flock of sheep. The latter recognize the superior intelligence of their bearded cousins, and when a night alarm occurs they crowd around them, and usually are thus saved from a stampede and are easily protected. But it was not always so. One night late in last November, two Perico shepherds were aroused by an onset of wolves. Their flocks huddled around the goats, which being neither fools nor cowards, stood their ground and were bravely defiant; but alas for them, no common wolf was heading this attack. Old Lobo, the wer-wolf, knew as well as the shepherds that the goats were the moral force of the flock, so hastily running over the backs of the densely packed sheep, he fell on these leaders, slew them all in a few minutes, and soon had the luckless sheep stampeding in a thousand different directions. For weeks afterwards I was almost daily accosted by some anxious shepherd, who asked, 'Have you seen any stray OTO sheep lately?' and usually I was obliged to say I had; one day it was, 'Yes, I came on some five or six carcasses by Diamond Springs'; or another, it was to the effect that I had seen a small 'bunch' running on the Malpai Mesa; or again, 'No, but Juan Meira saw about twenty, freshly killed, on the Cedra Monte two days ago.'

At length the wolf-traps arrived, and with two men I worked a whole week to get them properly set out. We spared no labour or pains, I adopted every device I could think of that might help to ensure success. The second day after the traps arrived, I rode around to inspect, and soon came upon Lobo's trail running from trap to trap. In the dust I could read the whole story of his doings that night. He had trotted along in the darkness, and although the traps were so carefully concealed, he had instantly detected the first one. Stopping the onward march of the pack, he had cautiously scratched around it until he had disclosed the trap, the chain, and the log, then left them wholly exposed to view with the trap still unsprung, and, passing on, he treated over a dozen traps in the same fashion. Very soon I noticed that he stopped and turned aside as soon as he detected suspicious signs on the trail and a new plan to outwit him at once suggested itself. I set the traps in the form of an H; that is, with a row of traps on each side of the trail, and one on the trail for the cross-bar of the H. Before long, I had an opportunity to count another failure. Lobo came trotting along the trail, and was fairly between the parallel lines before he detected the single trap in the trail, but he stopped in time, and why or how he knew enough I cannot tell, the Angel of the wild things must have been with him, but without turning an inch to the right or left, he slowly and cautiously backed on his own tracks, putting each paw exactly in its old track until he was off the dangerous ground. Then returning at one side he scratched clods and stones with his hind feet till he had sprung every trap. This he did on many other occasions, and although I varied my methods and redoubled my precautions, he was never deceived, his sagacity seemed never at fault, and he might have been pursuing his career of rapine today but for an unfortunate alliance that proved his ruin and added his name to the long list of heroes who, unassailable when alone, had fallen through the indiscretion of a trusted ally.

Once or twice, I had found indications that everything was not quite right in the Currumpaw pack. There were signs of irregularity, I thought; for instance there was clearly the trail of a smaller wolf running ahead of the leader at times, and this I could not understand until a cowboy made a remark which explained the matter.

'I saw them to–day,' he said, 'and the wild one that breaks away is Blanca.' Then the truth dawned upon me, and I added, 'Now, I know that Blanca is a she-wolf, because were a he-wolf to act thus, Lobo would kill him at once.'

This suggested a new plan. I killed a heifer, and set one or two rather obvious traps about the carcass. Then cutting off the head, which is considered useless offal, and quite beneath the notice of a wolf, I set it a little apart, and around it placed two powerful steel traps properly deodorized and concealed with the utmost care. During my operations I kept my hands, boots, and implements smeared with fresh blood, and afterwards sprinkled the ground with the same, as though it had flowed from the head; and when the traps were buried in the dust I brushed the place over with the skin of a coyote, and with a foot of the same animal made a number of tracks over the traps. The head was so placed that there was a narrow passage between it and some tussocks, and in this passage I buried two of my best traps, fastening them to the head itself.

Wolves have a habit of approaching every carcass they get the wind of, in order to examine it, even when they have no intention of eating it, and I hoped that this habit would bring the Currumpaw pack within reach of my latest stratagem. I did not doubt that Lobo would detect my handiwork about the meat, and prevent the pack approaching it, but I did build some hopes on the head, for it looked as though it had been thrown aside as useless.

Next morning, I sallied forth to inspect the traps, and there, oh joy! were the tracks of the pack, and the place where the beef-head and its traps had been was empty. A hasty study of the trail showed that Lobo had kept the pack from approaching the meat, but one, a small wolf, had evidently gone to examine the head as it lay apart and had walked right into one of the traps.

We set out on the trail, and within a mile discovered that the hapless wolf was Blanca. Away she went, however, at a gallop, and although encumbered by the beef-head, which weighed over fifty pounds, she speedily distanced my companion who was on foot. But we overtook her when she reached the rocks, for the horns of the cow's head became caught and held her fast. She was the handsomest wolf I had ever seen. Her coat was in perfect condition and nearly white.

She turned to fight, and raising her voice in the rallying cry of her race, sent a long howl rolling over the cañon. From far away upon the mesa came a deep response, the cry of Old Lobo. That was her last call, for now we had closed in on her, and all her energy and breath were devoted to combat.

Then followed the inevitable tragedy, the idea of which I shrank from afterward more than at the time. We each threw a lasso over the neck of the doomed wolf, and strained our horses in opposite directions until the blood burst from her mouth, her eyes glazed, her limbs stiffened and then fell limp. Homeward then we rode, carrying the dead wolf, and exulting over this, the first death-blow we had been able to inflict on the Currumpaw pack.

At intervals during the tragedy, and afterward as we rode homeward, we heard the roar of Lobo as he wandered about on the distant mesas, where he seemed to be searching for Blanca. He had never really deserted her, but knowing that he could not save her, his deep-rooted dread of firearms had been too much for him when he saw us approaching. All that day we heard him wailing as he roamed in his quest, and I remarked at length to one of the boys, 'Now, indeed, I truly know that Blanca was his mate.'

As evening fell he seemed to be coming toward the home cañon, for his voice sounded continually nearer. There was an unmistakable note of sorrow in it now. It was no longer the loud, defiant howl, but a long, plaintive wail: 'Blanca! Blanca!' he seemed to call. And as night came down, I noticed that he was not far from the place where we had overtaken her. At length he seemed to find the trail, and when he came to the spot where we had killed her, his heartbroken wailing was piteous to hear. It was sadder than I could possibly have believed. Even the stolid cowboys noticed it, and said they had 'never heard a wolf carry on like that before.' He seemed to know exactly what had taken place, for her blood had stained the place of her death.

Then he took up the trail of the horses and followed it to the ranch-house. Whether in hopes of finding her there, or in the quest of revenge, I know not, but the latter was what he found, for he surprised our unfortunate watchdog outside and tore him to little bits within fifty yards of the door. He evidently came alone this time, for I found but one trail next morning, and he had galloped about in a reckless manner that was very unusual with him. I had half expected this, and had set a number of additional traps about the pasture. Afterward I found that he had indeed fallen into one of these, but such was his strength, he had torn himself loose and cast it aside.

I believed that he would continue in the neighbourhood until he found her body at least, so I concentrated all my energies on this one enterprise of catching him before he left the region, and while yet in this reckless mood. Then I realized what a mistake I had made in killing Blanca, for by using her as a decoy I might have secured him the next night.

I gathered in all the traps I could command, one hundred and thirty strong steel wolf-traps, and set them in fours in every trail that led into the cañon; each trap was separately fastened to a log, and each log was separately buried. In burying them, I carefully removed the sod, and every particle of earth that was lifted we put in blankets, so that after the sod was replaced and all was finished the eye could detect no trace of human handiwork. When the traps were concealed I trailed the body of poor Blanca over each place, and made of it a drag that circled all about the ranch, and finally I took off one of her paws and made with it a line of tracks over each trap. Every precaution and device known to me I used, and retired at a late hour to await the result.

Once during the night I thought I heard Old Lobo, but was not sure of it. Next day I rode around, but darkness came on before I completed the circuit of the north cañon, and I had nothing to report. At supper one of the cowboys said, 'There was a great row among the cattle in the north cañon this morning, maybe there is something in the traps there.' It was afternoon of the next day before I got to the place referred to, and, as I drew near, a great grizzly form arose from the ground, vainly endeavouring to escape, and there revealed before me stood Lobo, King of the Currumpaw, firmly held in the traps. Poor old hero, he had never ceased to search for his darling, and when he found the trail her body had made he followed it recklessly, and so fell into the snare prepared for him. There he lay in the iron grasp of all four traps, perfectly helpless, and all around him were numerous tracks showing how the cattle had gathered about him to insult the fallen despot, without daring to approach within his reach. For two days and two nights he had lain there, and now was worn out with struggling. Yet, when I went near, he rose up with bristling mane and raised his voice, and for the last time made the cañon reverberate with his deep bass roar, a call for help, the muster call of his band. But there was none to answer him, and, left alone in his extremity, he whirled about with all his strength and made a desperate effort to get at me. All in vain, each trap was a dead drag of over three hundred pounds, and in their relentless fourfold grasp, with great steel jaws on every foot, and the heavy logs and chains all entangled together, he was absolutely powerless. How his huge ivory tusks did grind on those cruel chains, and when I ventured to touch him with my rifle-barrel he left grooves on it which are there to this day. His eyes glared green with hate and fury, and his jaws snapped with a hollow 'chop', as he vainly endeavoured to reach me and my trembling horse. But he was worn out with hunger and struggling and loss of blood, and he soon sank exhausted to the ground.

Something like compunction came over me, as I prepared to deal out to him that which so many had suffered at his hands.

'Grand old outlaw, hero of a thousand lawless raids, in a few minutes you will be but a great load of carrion. It cannot be otherwise.' Then I swung my lasso and sent it whistling over his head. But not so fast; he was yet far from being subdued, and, before the supple coils had fallen on his neck, he seized the noose and, with one fierce chop, cut through its hard thick strands, and dropped it in two pieces at his feet.

Of course I had my rifle as a last resource, but I did not wish to spoil his royal hide, so I galloped back to the camp and returned with a cowboy and a fresh lasso. We threw to our victim a stick of wood which he seized in his teeth, and before he could relinquish it our lassos whistled through the air and tightened on his neck.

Yet, before the light had died from his fierce eyes, I cried, 'Stay, we will not kill him; let us take him alive to the camp.' He was so completely powerless now that it was easy to put a stout stick through his mouth, behind his tusks, and then lash his jaws with a heavy cord which was also fastened to the stick. The stick kept the cord in, and the cord kept the stick in, so he was harmless. As soon as he felt his jaws were tied he made no further resistance, and uttered no sound, but looked calmly at us and seemed to say, 'Well, you have got me at last, do as you please with me.' And from that time he took no more notice of us.

We tied his feet securely, but he never groaned nor growled, nor turned his head. Then with our united strength were just able to put him on my horse. His breath came evenly as though sleeping, and his eyes were bright and clear again but did not rest on us. Afar on the great rolling mesas they were fixed, his passing kingdom, where his famous band was now scattered. And he gazed till the pony descended the pathway into the cañon, and the rocks cut off the view.

By travelling slowly we reached the ranch in safety, and after securing him with a collar and a strong chain, we staked him out in the pasture and removed the cords. Then for the first time I could examine him closely, and proved how unreliable is vulgar report when a living hero or tyrant is concerned. He had *not* a collar of gold about his neck, nor was there on his shoulders an inverted cross to denote that he had leagued himself with Satan. But I did find on one haunch a great broad scar that tradition says was the fang-mark of Juno, the leader of Tannerey's wolf-hounds – a mark which she gave him the moment before he stretched her lifeless on the sand of the cañon.

I set meat and water beside him, but he paid no heed. He lay calmly on his breast, and gazed with those steadfast yellow eyes away past me, down through the gateway of the cañon, over the open plains – his plains – nor moved a muscle when I touched him. When the sun went down he was still gazing fixedly across the prairie. I expected he would call up his band when night came, and prepared for them, but he had called once in his extremity, and none had come; he would never call again.

A lion shorn of his strength, an eagle robbed of his freedom, or a dove bereft of his mate, all die, it is said, of a broken heart; and who will aver that this grim bandit could bear the threefold brunt heart-whole? This only I know, that when the morning dawned he was lying there still in his position of calm repose, his body unwounded, but his spirit was gone – the old King-wolf was dead.

I took the chain from his neck, a cowboy helped me to carry him to the shed where lay the remains of Blanca, and, as we laid him beside her, the cattleman exclaimed: 'There, you *would* come to her, now you are together again.'

Flip

GEOFFREY MORGAN

FLIP

It was very still in the dawn light. The night shadows glided silently away before the widening streaks across the eastern sky, leaving a thin white vapour of mist over the marsh. Already the geese had left the tidelines to flight in and settle on the stubbles behind the sea wall. As the light grew over the sea the creeks, twisting into the dark green vegetation of the marsh, began to stir with the flood, and isolated flocks of waders gathered to feed along the moist flats of mud and sand at the edge of the tide. From the distant stalk edges, across grey gullies and silvery pools that patterned a cloak of emerald samphire, sea aster and sedge, the faint call of a curlew reached the sea wall.

As the lonely cry died away two figures reached the top of the embankment from the farm track below. The man was tall, broad, with a mop of unruly dark hair that he shook from his eyes with irritated jerks of his head; his knuckles gleamed white through the brown weathered skin of his hands clenching the bundled lip of the bulging corn sack across his back. The boy was slender, his thin legs lost in thigh waders which seemed as big and cumbersome as those worn by the man. Despite the thick jersey and stained anorak the boy was cold, but it was a coldness born of apprehension; the bleak scene was reflected in the round face, the pallor relieved only by the cloud of freckles that climbed the bridge of his nose and spattered his forehead beneath the quiff of auburn hair. His eyes, usually large, alive with interest, were deadened by the look of resignation as he glanced again at the burden on his companion's back.

'He's quietened now,' he said.

'I told you he'd settle.'

They stood for a moment peering across the saltings as the light strengthened. The mist was thinning, withdrawing towards the sea, leaving faint shapeless contours of vapour above the still pools dotting the green. At the edge, where broad rinds of mud stretched into the saltings, the wide curve of Mallard Creek identified itself.

'It seems a long way,' the boy said.

'You've been out there before.'

The boy glanced at the bundle again. 'It's different this time.' He put out his hand, gently touching the bulging shape of the sack.'Flip . . .' The quiet murmur of his voice was meant as a comforting sound.

The man stepped forward impatiently. 'Don't disturb him,' he said sharply. 'Let's get on with it.'

They moved slowly down the steep seaward side of the grass-covered bank, the boy following the man's steps, ready to support the burden if his companion should slip. They reached the narrow plateau, pausing again on the brink of the gaping dyke of mud and water that separated the marsh from the sea wall. It was deep but as yet held no more than a trickle of brackish water; the sides sloped in broken shelves of mud and clay to rise again on the further side in shallow ledges to the fringe of the crab grass.

They descended slowly, their rubbered feet sinking to the ankles in the ooze. At the bottom of the channel water and mud rose almost to their knees. The man shifted the load, adjusting his grip, and then they were climbing, slipping, swaying, their boots stabbing a hold, up the serried mud slope of the other side until they were standing on firmer ground.

'That's the worst over with,' the man said grimly, and, hunching the sack into a more comfortable position, turned seaward. They moved off, side by side, their pace quickening over the soggy crab grass, following the way by instinct rather than by any defined path.

By the time they reached the creek the sun was rising into a red-rimmed sky that patterned the rippled underbelly of the night clouds with fiery colours. The mist had gone, driven before the faint off-shore breeze to the far reaches of the sea. The flooding surface of the creek mirrored the world above so that the grey swirling water of the incoming tide was shot with streaks of colour. But there was no warmth in the scene; it was as cold as the feeling that gripped the boy.

They paused on a small plateau of firm ground above a gully that marked the outer edges of the vegetation. Beyond, the creek carved its way between sloping shoulders of mud that were shiny naked but for faint patches of crab grass cresting the western banks; beyond, the green stalks gave way to mudflats that stretched monotonously towards the sea until they were lost with the course of the creek beneath the approaching tide.

'Where're you going to leave him?' the boy asked.

'Further down – that spit of sand.' The man moved off along the lip of the gully seeking the easiest crossing. After a hundred yards they reached a section where the banks had collapsed to form a shallow barrier across the gut that was fast filling with the tide. They splashed down, the water swirling the knees of their boots, but the bottom was firm. Once they topped the other side, the going was easier, and a few minutes later they were standing on the long spit of tawny sand.

The man swung round, bending as he gently lowered his burden to the sand. The boy was already on his knees as the sack was laid full length, and a head appeared through the open end.

'Flip ...' he said softly.

The seal pup stared at him. His round eyes were large, luminous, under the half circle of silver-grey body fur that formed a peak below the forehead. The long whiskers trembled, quivering the moustachial pads from which they sprouted, as the nostrils flared. The boy and the man were the only presence he knew. He trusted them. But he was confused. He did not move. Not even when the sack was withdrawn, exposing the plump silver-grey body.

The boy knew the creature was bewildered and afraid. He wanted to reassure him – but how could he reassure him of the unknown? He stroked the head, the hairs so dry the coat was like a warm muff into which his cold fingers sank. 'Flip ... you're on your own now ... It's the only way ...' His voice was hollow, strained with the effort of mustering a confidence he did not feel. He fingered the narrow circle of pure white hair that was like a collar of identification around the thick neck. 'I'll know you, Flip,' he said quietly. 'I'll watch for you. I promise ...'

'Come on. Don't make a fuss. It'll do no good.' The man stood a few paces away, folding the sack. 'The tide'll be cutting us off back there.'

The boy rose slowly, reluctantly, lingering, unable to take his eyes from the upturned face at his feet.

'You've got to leave him.' The man, retracing his steps, had turned impatiently. 'He won't move if you stay. Come on, you can watch from the marsh.'

It was another ten minutes before they had re-crossed the flooded gully and lay full length in the green stalks on the little plateau above the creek, watching the still form on the sloping sandspit. And the boy, Jamie, was near to tears. The pretence of having left the pup alone and vanished from the marsh was even worse than if they had returned direct to the sea wall without a backward glance. But neither his companion, nor Jamie himself, could have left the scene without knowing what the pup would do, even if they had to wait until the marsh was awash and the tide had floated the seal away.

'He's too frightened to move,' Jamie whispered miserably. 'It doesn't seem right – just leaving him ...'

'You know it's right, Jamie. He was born free. No wild creatures should be confined. All along you knew we had to return him to the sea.' Slade's tone had changed. His voice was gentle, patient. The tension of the outward journey had gone and he felt relief that their responsibility was over; now his mood was more related to the boy's. He felt the poignancy of the occasion, too. But not as deeply as the boy. Jamie was losing something that had been the most important thing in his life during the past three months of summer. Slade wanted to comfort him, but at the same time to emphasize the need to be practical, to re-affirm the inevitability of the action they had been preparing to take during the past few hectic days before he, himself, went away. 'Even if it was wrong to put him back – what would you have done with him?'

'I don't know.'

'You've never told your father?'

Jamie shook his head sullenly. 'You know my father. He'd kill him.'

'Well, then ...'

'If only you weren't going, too.'

'We should still have returned him to the sea.' Slade spoke with a finality that did not disguise his sympathy, shielding his eyes from the increasing glare of the climbing sun, as he stared again down the creek.

The pup remained exactly where they had left him; only his head stirred, turning slowly from side to side, his muzzle raised, as if attempting to analyse the strange scents his nostrils registered.

'He hasn't moved,' Jamie said quietly.

'He will.'

'But he's lost. He doesn't know what to do. How can he fend for himself after all we've done?'

'He'll have time to adapt. Wasn't that the idea of filling him with fish? Of building him up? Give him time to learn to hunt?'

'That's what you said.'

'He's fit. Over sixty pounds now. He can afford to lose twenty-five or more while he learns. Don't you worry about his welfare, Jamie. He's every chance of survival. He'd have had no chance at all if you hadn't found him.'

'No,' Jamie said. The choking feeling in his throat was still there. He seemed to have to keep swallowing to get his breath. There were prickles behind his eyes as he squinted over the fronds of a cluster of sea aster down the creek. He remembered the morning he found him. A small, wasted, helpless creature, left by the tide on Shoalend Marsh. Jamie had set his gill net there. He hadn't caught any fish, but he had found the seal pup in a nest of crab grass not fifty yards from the net. He had found other creatures, too, on occasion, like the widgeon with the injured wing, the pair of brent grazed with wildfowler's shot, the pinioned Canada goose who had eventually been returned to her owner. None could he have deserted. He had taken them home, nursing them in the garden shed, until they could be returned to the wild again.

His father had no patience with such sentimental diversions, although he suffered them under protest. Faced with Jamie and his mother, he had no valid reason to destroy the birds. But seals were different. They were enemies that ruined his nets. You couldn't wonder about the hostility, not when you remembered that 'Lucky' Joe Holt had earned his nickname by the fact that he was the most successful fisherman along the coast. But it wasn't so much luck as intuition, born from a family who had fished off the north Norfolk coast and across the sandstrewn basin of the Wash for generations. Jamie wanted to follow the family tradition. He should have been proud of his father. Instead, for so much of the time, he hated him.

The morning he had found the pup on Shoalend marsh his father was in Lowestoft seeking a new trawl winch, so Jamie had carried the survivor home and, with the connivance of his mother, hidden him in the shed and cycled at breathless speed to Philip Slade . . .

Flip had moved at last. He had turned to face the creek, but the creeping tide submerging the sandspit appeared to hold no temptation for him. His head turned constantly towards the marsh, to where he had last seen their upright figures; but Slade was sure he could not see them now.

'Keep your head down,' he whispered. 'He thinks we've gone. He can't resist the water much longer.' He knew what Jamie was feeling and he was anxious that nothing should go wrong. He had no more idea than the boy how the seal would react in returning to his own element. But there was no withdrawing now; nothing more they could do, except wait. At least Flip was getting a favourable start. He was in the peak of condition. He'd always been healthy. Unlike Slade's first experience. Then, the pup had died within a month of rescue; congestion of the lungs had been the vet's verdict.

But it was because of that first pup he had met Jamie and his father. In his brief off-duty periods Slade took the dinghy with a drift net in the hope of supplementing the food supplies he had to buy for his charge. But he seldom caught anything, except, on occasion, a mullet or two. That particular Saturday, over towards the Lynn Channel, was no different from any other attempt, and he was stowing the net when he saw Holt's boat. Holt obliged his request and sold him some of the poorer specimens from his catch, and it was after the transaction, when Slade lightly mentioned what an expensive business it was bringing up a seal, that he saw the dark scowl on Holt's face. It was much later that Slade learned from Jamie that his father wouldn't have sold him a sprat if he'd known it was to keep a seal alive. He learned, too, just how desperately opposed to his father the boy was on that score, for after that first encounter Jamie became a frequent visitor to Decoys, Slade's rented cottage not a mile from the sea wall, where marsh and sand stretched endlessly out into the Wash from the Lincolnshire coast.

So it had been no surprise to Slade when Jamie had arrived excitedly one morning with the news of the pup he'd found at Shoalend. They had gone back in the van, collected the survivor, and nursed him into the fine specimen they were now observing on the edge of Mallard Creek. But Jamie had been the mainstay of the pup's upbringing. As the company he worked for neared the end of its contract Slade had less and less time. He was, after all, an engineer, not a naturalist, although during the two years he had been at Decoys he had become increasingly concerned with the wildlife on the marsh. But he had a living to earn. The company were starting a new contract in the West Country, and he had to go where the work was. His leaving was inevitable. And Jamie's reluctance to let Flip go had driven the climax of their work together to the eve of Slade's own departure. Now the pup seemed as reluctant to go as Jamie was in parting with him ...

It was the sudden, shallow leap of fish that finally set Flip in motion. The flash of silver, the gentle splash on the surface was a loud alarm in the silence. The pup stared with rising curiosity at the widening circles of ripples spreading across the creek, and then he was hauling himself down the sand slope in the awkward humping motion that made his movement on land such an ungainly contrast to the graceful, gliding symmetry of his course through the water. One final heave into the shallows and he was out in the tide. He swam effortlessly to and fro, from one bank to the other, suddenly diving then surfacing almost at once to stand on his hindflippers with his head clear of the water, staring wide-eyed at his surroundings from this new yet strangely familiar vantage point.

'He's still looking for us,' Jamie murmured.

Slade shook his head, smiling. 'Just sizing up his new environment. He'll soon feel at home.'

Jamie didn't say anything. He didn't share Slade's confidence. But he couldn't argue. What was the use? Whatever Flip's feelings were, whatever became of him, was no longer Jamie's concern. All the nursing and affection he'd lavished on the pup he knew must end this way, yet still he could not accept it. Why couldn't he grow up, be sensible? He'd saved the pup's life, now he must let him live it. It was no use moaning over losing him like some silly girl who'd lost her doll. Everyone had to leave home, every bird the nest; some time. All the risks he'd taken, all the lies he'd told, the fish he'd filched, now left him with nothing at all. He must accept that. But it was not so much these things that contributed to the emptiness he felt; it was the bond that had grown between them from those very early days when they had sweated to keep him alive. The force feeding, the diet carefully blended with eggs, evaporated milk and vitamins, and the struggle it had been to get the frequent feeds down through the stomach tube; getting rid of the sea lice, coaxing him on to fish; the continuous cleaning and re-filling of the makeshift pool at the end of the cottage garden, and the repairs to the wire enclosure he was often breaking down . . . So much to do in those early days that with Slade at his job, there were times when Jamie had to play truant from school. But it was an exciting time, and watching him grow, playing with him, having him follow when Jamie called, it was easy to forget tomorrow.

Now tomorrow had come and Jamie knew the future would be a lonely place . . .

A formation of brent swept in over the marsh to the east, their calls a gaggle of sound on the still October air. The white and black flash of a pair of oyster-catchers caught the sunlight as they swooped low over the creek, and somewhere behind them a lapwing rose lazily from the marsh and began to cry. Down the creek, where it merged with the incoming sea, gulls were squabbling above a waterlogged fish box drifting in with the tide.

Flip was down there now. Swimming strongly against the current, his head a dark, glistening blob on the surface, his wake a rippling mirror reflecting the sunlight.

Slade stirred. 'He's on his way. Time we were, too, or we'll be up to our waists across the dyke.' He rose slowly, stiffly, from his damp bed of sea twitch and crab grass.

Jamie remained motionless, staring down the creek.

'Come on. You've given him a flying start.'

'I know.' Jamie got up at last, turning his face to the creek again. 'I just wanted a last glimpse.'

'Who said it's your last?'

The boy looked at his companion, a glimmer of hope livened his face. 'D'you think he'll come back?'

Slade shrugged. 'Who can tell? But you'll come down and see?'

'Yes,' Jamie said. 'I'll come down and see.'

Adopting an Anteater

GERALD DURRELL

ADOPTING AN ANTEATER

Making a collection of two hundred birds, mammals and reptiles is rather like having two hundred delicate babies to look after. It needs a lot of hard work and patience. You have to make sure their diet suits them, that their cages are big enough, that they get neither too hot in the tropics nor too cold when you get near England. You have to de-worm, detick and de-flea them; you have to keep their cages and feeding-pots spotlessly clean.

But above all, you have to make sure that your animals are *happy*. However well looked after, a wild animal will not live in captivity unless it is happy. I am talking, of course, of the adult, wild-caught creature. But occasionally you get a baby wild animal whose mother has perhaps met with an accident, and who has been found wandering in the forest. When you capture one of these, you must be prepared for a good deal of hard work and worry, and above all you must be ready to give the animal the affection and confidence it requires; for after a day or two you will have become the parent, and the baby will trust you and depend on you completely.

This can sometimes make life rather difficult. There have been periods when I have played the adopted parent to as many as six baby animals at once, and this is no joke. Quite apart from anything else, imagine rising at three o'clock in the morning, stumbling about, half-asleep, in an effort to prepare six different bottles of milk, trying to keep your eyes open enough to put the right amount of vitamin drops and sugar in, knowing all the time that you will have to be up again in three hours to repeat the performance.

Some time ago my wife and I were on a collecting trip in Paraguay, that country shaped like a boot-box, which lies almost in the exact centre of South America. Here, in a remote part of Chaco, we assembled a lovely collection of animals. Many things quite unconnected with animals happen on a collecting trip, things that frustrate your plans or irritate you in other ways. But politics, mercifully, had never before been among them. On this occasion, however, the Paraguayans decided to have a revolution, and as a direct result we had to release nearly the whole of our collection and escape to Argentina in a tiny four-seater plane.

Just before our retreat, an Indian had wandered into our camp carrying a sack from which had come the most extraordinary noises. It sounded like a cross between a cello in pain and a donkey with laryngitis. Opening the sack, the Indian tipped out one of the most delightful baby animals I had ever seen. She was a young giant anteater, and she could not have been more than a week old. She was about the size of a corgi, with black, ash-grey and white fur, a long slender snout and a pair of tiny, rather bleary eyes. The Indian said he had found her wandering in the forest, honking forlornly. He thought her mother might have been killed by a jaguar.

The arrival of this baby put me in a predicament. I knew that we would be leaving soon and that the plane was so tiny that most of our equipment would have to be left behind to make room for the five or six creatures we were determined to take with us. To accept, at that stage, a baby anteater who weighed a considerable amount and who would have to be fussed over and bottle-fed, would be lunatic. Quite apart from anything else, no one as far as I knew, had ever tried to rear a baby anteater on a bottle. The whole thing was obviously out of the question. Just as I had made up my mind the baby, still blaring pathetically suddenly discovered my leg, and with a honk of joy shinned up it, settled herself in my lap and went to sleep. Silently I paid the Indian the price he demanded, and thus became a father to one of the most charming children I have ever met.

The first difficulty cropped up almost at once. We had a baby's feeding-bottle, but we had exhausted our supply of teats. Luckily a frantic house-to-house search of the little village where we were living resulted in the discovery of one teat, of extreme age and unhygienic appearance. After one or two false starts the baby took to the bottle far better than I had dared hope, though feeding her was a painful performance.

Young anteaters, at that age, cling to their mother's back, and, since we had, so to speak, become her parents, she insisted on climbing on to one or the other of us nearly the whole time. Her claws were about three inches long, and she had a prodigious grip with them. During meals she clasped your leg affectionately with three paws, while with her remaining paw held your finger and squeezed it hard at intervals, for she was convinced that this would increase the flow of milk from the bottle. At the end of each feed you felt as though you had been mauled by a grizzly bear, while your fingers had been jammed in a door.

For the first days I carried her about with me to give her confidence. She liked to lie across the back of my neck, her long nose hanging down one side of me and her long tail down the other, like a fur collar. Every time I moved she would tighten her grip in a panic, and this was painful. After the fourth shirt had been ruined I decided that she would have to cling to something else, so I filled a sack full of straw and introduced her to that. She accepted it without any fuss, and so between meals she would lie in her cage, clutching this substitute happily. We had already christened her 'Sarah', and now that she developed this habit of sack-clutching we gave her a surname, and so she became known as 'Sarah Huggersack'.

Sarah was a model baby. Between feeds she lay quietly on her sack, occasionally yawning and showing a sticky, pinky-grey tongue about twelve inches long. When feeding-time came round she would suck the teat on her bottle so vigorously that it had soon changed from red to pale pink, the hole at the end of it had become about the size of a matchstick, and the whole thing drooped dismally from the neck of the bottle.

When we had to leave Paraguay in our extremely unsafe-looking four-seater plane, Sarah slept peacefully throughout the flight, lying on my wife's lap and snoring gently, occasionally blowing a few bubbles of sticky saliva out of her nose.

On arriving in Buenos Aires our first thought was to give Sarah a treat. We would buy her a nice new shiny teat. We went to endless trouble selecting one exactly the right size, shape and colour, put it on the bottle and presented it to Sarah. She was scandalized. She honked wildly at the mere thought of a new teat, and sent the bottle flying with a well-directed clout from her paw. Nor did she calm down and start to feed until we had replaced the old withered teat on the bottle. She clung to it ever after; months after her arrival in England she still refused to be parted from it.

In Buenos Aires we housed our animals in an empty house on the outskirts of the city. From the centre, where we stayed, it took us half an hour in a taxi to reach it, and this journey we had to do twice and sometimes three times a day. We soon found that having a baby anteater made our social life difficult in the extreme. Have you ever tried to explain to a hostess that you must suddenly leave in the middle of dinner because you have got to give a bottle to an anteater? In the end our friends gave up in despair. They used to telephone and ascertain the times of Sarah's feeds before inviting us.

By this time Sarah had become much more grown up and inde-pendent. After her evening feed she would go for a walk round the room by herself. This was a great advance, for up till then she had screamed blue murder if you moved more than a foot or so away from her. After her tour of inspection she liked to have a game. This consisted in walking past us, her nose in the air, her tail trailing temptingly. You were then supposed to grab the end of her tail and pull, whereupon she would swing round on three legs and give you a gentle clout with her paw. When this had been repeated twenty or thirty times she felt satisfied, and then you had to lay her on her back and tickle her tummy for ten minutes or so while she closed her eyes and blew bubbles of ecstacy at you. After this she would go to bed without any fuss. But try to put her to bed without giving her a game and she would kick and struggle and honk, and generally behave in a thoroughly spoilt manner.

When we eventually got on board ship, Sarah was not at all sure that she approved of sea-voyages. To begin with, the ship smelt queer; then there was a strong wind which nearly blew her over every time she went for a walk on deck; and lastly, which she hated most of all, the deck would not keep still. First it tilted one way, then it tilted another, and Sarah would go staggering about, honking plaintively, banging her nose on bulkheads and hatch-covers. When the weather improved, however, she seemed to enjoy the trip. Sometimes in the afternoon, when I had time, I would take her up to the promenade deck and we would sit in a deck-chair and sunbathe. She even paid a visit to the bridge, by special request of the captain. I thought it was because he had fallen for her charm and personality, but he confessed that it was because (having seen her only from a distance) he wanted to make sure which end of her was the front.

I must say we felt very proud of Sarah when we arrived in London Docks and she posed for the Press photographers with all the unselfconscious ease of a born celebrity. She even went so far as to lick one of the reporters – a great honour. I hastily tried to point this out to him, while helping to remove a large patch of sticky saliva from his coat. It was not everyone she would lick, I told him. His expression told me that he did not appreciate the point.

Sarah went straight from the docks to a zoo in Devonshire, and we hated to see her go. However, we were kept informed about her progress and she seemed to be doing well. She had formed a deep attachment to her keeper.

Some weeks later I was giving a lecture at the Festival Hall, and the organizer thought it would be rather a good idea if I introduced some animal on the stage at the end of my talk. I immediately thought of Sarah. Both the zoo authorities and the Festival Hall Management were willing, but, as it was now winter, I insisted that Sarah must have a dressing-room to wait in.

I met Sarah and her keeper at Paddington Station. Sarah was in a huge crate, for she had grown as big as a red setter, and she created quite a sensation on the platform. As soon as she heard my voice she flung herself at the bars of her cage and protruded twelve inches of sticky tongue in a moist and affectionate greeting. People standing near the cage leapt back hurriedly, thinking some curious form of snake was escaping and it took a lot of persuasion before we could find a porter brave enough to wheel the cage on a truck.

When we reached the Festival Hall we found that the rehearsal of a symphony concert had just come to an end. We wheeled Sarah's big box down long corridors to the dressing-room, and just as we reached the door it was flung open and Sir Thomas Beecham strode out, smoking a large cigar. We wheeled Sarah into the dressing-room he had just vacated.

While I was on stage, my wife kept Sarah occupied by running round and round the dressing-room with her, to the consternation and horror of one of the porters, who, hearing the noise, was convinced that Sarah had broken out of her cage and was attacking my wife. Eventually, however, the great moment arrived and amid tumultuous applause Sarah was carried on to the stage. She was very short-sighted, as all anteaters are, so to her the audience was non-existent. She looked round vaguely to see where the noise was coming from, but decided that it was not really worth worrying about. While I extolled her virtues, she wandered about the stage, oblivious, occasionally snuffling loudly in a corner, and repeatedly approaching the microphone and giving it a quick lick, which left it in a very sticky condition for the next performer. Just as I was telling the audience how well-behaved she was, she discovered the table in the middle of the stage, and with an immense sigh of satisfaction proceeded to scratch her bottom against one of the legs. She was a great success.

After the show, Sarah held court for a few select guests in her dressing-room, and became so skittish that she even galloped up and down outside in the corridor. The we bundled her up warmly and put her on the night train for Devon with her keeper.

Apparently, on reaching the zoo again, Sarah was thoroughly spoilt. Her short spell as a celebrity had gone to her head. For three days she refused to be left alone, stamping about her cage and honking wildly, and refusing all food unless she was fed by hand.

A few months later I wanted Sarah to make an appearance on a television show I was doing, and so once again she tasted the glamour and glitter of show business. She behaved with the utmost decorum during rehearsals, except that she was dying to investigate the camera closely, and had to be restrained by force. When the show was over she resisted going back to her cage, and it took the united efforts of myself, my wife, Sarah's keeper and the studio manager to get her back into the box – for Sarah was then quite grown up, measuring six feet from nose to tail, standing three feet at the shoulder and with forearms as thick as my thigh.

We did not see Sarah again until quite recently, when we paid her a visit at her zoo. It had been six months since she had last seen us, and quite frankly I thought she would have forgotten us. Anteater fan though I am, I would be the first to admit they are not creatures who are overburdened with brains, and six months is a long time. But the moment we called to her she came bounding out of her sleeping den and rushed to the wire to lick us. We even went into the cage and played with her, a sure sign that she really did recognize us, for no one else except her keeper dared enter.

Eventually we said good-bye to her, rather sadly, and left her sitting in the straw blowing bubbles after us. As my wife said: 'It was rather as though we were leaving our child at boarding school.' We are certainly her adopted parents, as far as Sarah is concerned.

Yesterday we had some good news. We heard that Sarah has got a mate. He is as yet too young to be put in with her, but soon he should be big enough. Who knows, by this time next year we may be grandparents to a fine bouncing baby anteater!

Koko the
Thingumabob

ANTHONY ARMSTRONG

KOKO THE THINGUMABOB

Once upon a time a dusty messenger was shown into the Council Hall of the King of Sparmania. He carried with him a small wooden box which he handed to the King together with a letter. Then he looked round to see if there was any chance of a drink.

There wasn't. Everyone was far too busy trying to edge near enough to see what the box contained and yet not near enough to get hurt in case it was anything dangerous. In those days one never knew; people – particularly fairies – had queer ideas as to exactly what constituted a good practical joke.

The King, after one nervous peep into the box for dignity's sake, remarked quickly that he couldn't possibly see without his spectacles, and handed the box to the Court Chamberlain. The Court Chamberlain instantly said it was a very peculiar thing but he too had left his glasses behind, and popped the box into the Vizier's arms. The Vizier was just pretending to fumble in his pocket when the King, the box being now at a safe distance, told him very sharply that his unaided eyesight was perfectly adequate. Thereupon the Vizier with a resigned expression gingerly opened the box.

In it upon a nest of straw was an extraordinary little creature. It had the head of a cock with extremely bright, beady eyes, small almost embryo wings, and a long tail with little hackles on it. It possessed sharp claws, and occasional feathers grew in unexpected places. On seeing the light, it opened its beak and gave vent to a feeble chirping. Whatever it was, it was quite young.

'Bless my soul,' said the King, who had now conveniently found his spectacles. 'What is it?'

'I don't know!' replied the Chamberlain, equally puzzled.

'Well, I don't believe it's true,' pronounced the King, emphatically after a prolonged scrutiny. 'There's *no* such thing!'

'It's quite true!' interposed the Vizier, advancing a finger and withdrawing it a little too late, as the animal made a nasty peck.

The Chamberlain ventured upon a humorous remark about things off cheeses, but the King only stared at him coldly for two minutes and then opened the accompanying letter:

MEMO (he read)

'*From H.I.M. The Emperor of Granada,*
'*To H.M. The King of Sparmania.*
'*Dear old boy,*
'*Am sending herewith this little thing we hatched out unexpectedly the*

other day in our Farm Yard. Something got among the hens and killed them all and the only thing we had handy to hatch out what eggs had not been trodden on was a serpent. Only one came out and, as you will see, the result is rather peculiar. The Empress thinks the egg must have been a foreign one but I say there's magic in it somewhere. Anyway, I'm sending it to you because I know you are fond of animals.

'*Yours,*
'Granada.'

'P.S. – *His pet name is Koko, we think.*

'P.P.S. – *I hope you will keep him safely.*'

'Hm!' said the King thoughtfully to himself, while the Court was crowding round the novelty. He had a worried look. For the Emperor of Granada was an extremely powerful rival, and indeed was only looking for an excuse to invade Sparmania. In those days they were a little more punctilious about the opening stages of a war than we are now, but so far the King and his ministers had steered a safe and tactful course in the face of all provocations. 'I wonder what Granada is up to now?' mused the King, taking a closer look at the gift.

'Isn't he a *darling?*' cried an enthusiastic lady-in-waiting. 'Koko! Koko! Oh the little diddums.' ...

'Shut up, fathead!' said the King testily. 'I'm thinking.'

The young lady shut up. Privately she considered the King rather a rude man, even for a King.

'I don't like that postscript,' at last said the Vizier to his master.

'Eh? Why not? Koko seems all right as a name.'

'No, I meant the other postscript. ... Here! You!' he added to the messenger, who was still looking as thirsty as he could. 'Was there any verbal message?'

'Only this, Sire: That His Imperial Majesty has given you a present and that he will consider it a serious matter, and one for *personal* investigation, should you lose or destroy it.'

'Oh!' said the King apprehensively. 'Well, that'll do, thank you.'

The messenger bowed. 'Would there be anything else?' he inquired tactfully. He hoped the answer would be a stoup of wine.

'Not for you,' snapped the King, who was an outspoken man.

The messenger went. 'And I hope your whatzit *dies*,' he added vindictively; but not till he was well outside the door. The King of Sparmania had a reputation for enterprising forms of punishment.

That evening the King, with the Vizier and the Court Chamberlain, held a solemn inspection of Koko. They had never seen anything like him before. He had such a malevolent stare in his beady eyes that it actually made the recipient feel rather strange about the middle of the chest.

'I suppose there's a catch somewhere!' said the King at last, 'but it looks fairly harmless at the moment. Compared, of course, to what he might have sent,' he added hastily as the animal flapped its unformed wings and pecked viciously.

'Well, if we don't want war with Granada, we'll have to keep it,' pointed out the Vizier. 'That's flat.'

'I wish we had a magician to tell us what this thingumabob really is,' complained the King. 'It's just our luck his not being here.'

The Court had been without a magician for some days now. There was of course one on the strength, but he had vanished suddenly during some experiments, and to avoid friction a successor had not yet been appointed, in case he got over his slight disappearance – for they were by no means always fatal.

'Never mind,' continued the King briskly. 'We'll have to do without him. Send Ali to me!'

Ali was keeper of the royal stables. His job was no sinecure, for in those days a horse was about the last animal to be found in a royal stables. Dragons, snakes, seven-legged wolves, practically everything that came along, were parked in the royal stables under Ali's charge, and there was no lack of supply. One only needed a malicious witch or an inventive-minded magician with a passion for creating new animal types, such as jellyhocks or blue-rumped gnurgles, and so on, to keep the 'stalls full' boards out nearly the whole year round.

'Oh, Ali,' said the King airily when the keeper of the royal stables entered, chewing a straw – for he was a privileged person, and anyway, it was royal straw. 'Just take charge of this, will you?'

'Any name?' queried Ali, who was too experienced to ask what it was. It might be anything from the latest fashion in Court Fauna, to one of the ladies-in-waiting who had had words with a fairy.

'Well, not as yet,' replied the King. 'Its *pet name* though is Koko!'

'Don't look much of a pet to me! He's going to *grow* that's what he's going to do! Grow!'

'You must look after it very carefully. Nothing must happen to it. It's a matter of – of. . . .'

'Peace and War?' suggested the Vizier.

'Life and death?' added the Chamberlain.

'Both!' said the King candidly. 'The latter for you, Ali. So you'd better be careful! In fact, I've just thought of a new death. In my bath this morning. . . . Not, of course, that you'll let anything happen to Koko, Ali, will you?' he finished, smiling a pleasant, open smile.

'You bet I won't,' said Ali with some feeling. He picked up Koko with the practised grasp of the true animal lover who has been bitten before, and departed.

Time went on and beyond an occasional inquiry the King began to forget the Thingumabob, as the little stranger had now been officially named. Ali had reported that the animal was being fed on coal, for which he had shown a marked partiality, and that he looked very healthy and, as he himself had prophesied, was growing. Now and then the Vizier sent off a tactful letter with a bunch of flowers and a few diamonds to the Emperor of Granada to say how well Koko was looking and what fun it was having him about the place, and everyone felt a difficult situation was being adroitly handled.

Then after some months the King one day paid an official visit of inspection.

Koko the Thingumabob certainly had grown. In fact, he was now nearly as high as a man. His wings were large and leathery and a sheeny iridescence was beginning to show on his scaly feathers. His beak had a razor edge and the hackles of his tail were spiked. But his eyes were the most impressive thing about him. They had a penetrating and freezing quality which almost seemed to dry up the blood in the veins of those he looked at. The King gave one quick glance and turned away.

'Makes me quite ill,' he said. 'I suppose we've got to keep him, or Granada will invade. . . . Ali! What on earth's wrong with that man?' He pointed to a groom who was crossing the yard in a lethargic manner and with slow dragging steps.

Ali looked worried. He seemed a bit lethargic himself. 'That's one of the fellows that helps feed the Thingumabob, Your Majesty,' he replied. 'As a matter of fact, we're all getting a bit like that. It's the way that Thingumabob *looks* at you, *I* think?'

The King peered at Koko and looked away again.

'I knew there'd be a catch,' he said fretfully. 'I wish we had our magician back and could find out what the creature really is. . . .'

At this moment Koko suddenly opened his beak and yawned. A hot breath as of fire reached out towards them.

'Great Talismans!' ejaculated the King drawing back. 'He's got a touch of the dragon in him.'

'He ain't true-bred by *no* means,' agreed Ali. 'I'd like to see *his* pedigree, I would.'

'He's *very* nearly breathing fire,' continued the King, still keeping his face averted.

'Worst case of *halitosis* I've ever seen,' remarked the Chamberlain judicially.

'It's from eating all that coal,' supplemented Ali. 'And he's *growing*.'

The King left the stables thoughtfully. He considered the Emperor of Granada was no gentleman.

One morning next week there was consternation in the Palace. For Ali came running in to the Royal Presence in a great state of mind.

'Your Majesty!' he gasped.

'What is it? Is the Thingumabob dead?' demanded the King sharply. 'In that case, remember what I said. You'll be for my latest punishment. It's most ingenious, a kind of . . .'

'No no. Koko's all right. But he's suddenly taking to breathing real fire. . . .'

'Well, call the fire brigade!' snapped the King. 'It's no good telling *me*.'

'Worse still,' continued Ali. 'I daren't let him look at me.'

'Why not? It won't hurt him.'

'Two of the grooms *have* looked at him.'

'Well?'

'Come and see, Your Majesty!'

When they arrived a faint cloud of smoke hung over Koko's den at the far end of the yard, the result, Ali explained, of his breathing. And just outside the cage someone had apparently erected a new stone statue, a most life-like group of two grooms holding a bucket of coal between them.

'I – I don't understand,' said the King. 'Have you taken to sculpture? It's most lifelike. I congratu . . .'

'No . . . no . . .' stammered Ali. 'It's . . . it's the Thingumabob. *Those* are the two grooms who feed him. They've been getting slower and slower, and this morning, that Koko suddenly looked straight at them and they *turned into stone*.'

'Merciful Amulets!' gasped the King; and then they caught a glimpse of a beak showing in the smoke cloud. . . .

They were outside the place in record time. Ali didn't have to bother about letting royalty take precedence; the King had him beat by yards.

'I simply can't understand it,' the King said to the Vizier that night for the twentieth time. 'What *is* this Thingumabob?'

'The Court Chamberlain is still looking it up in the Library of Magic, Your Majesty. But it doesn't matter very much what it *is*. We can see for ourselves.'

'Oh, can we?' said the King. 'Not without catching a pretty bad spell.

And, anyway, the Books may tell us how to kill it.'

'But we can't *kill* it.'

'Why not?'

'Because of Granada. As long as we keep the thing here he won't make war on us.'

'True! I'd forgotten. . . . But we might put a charm on it to make it harmless. I mean, something must be done. I can't have the fire brigade standing by all day and my grooms slowly changing into a sculpture gallery. By the way, where are those two? Perhaps, I should say, where is The New Statue?'

The Vizier coughed discreetly.

'I've disposed of it,' he said at last with some confusion.

'Where is it?' repeated the King pointedly.

'Well . . . I – er – I have a nice lawn at home which just wanted something in the centre to set it off; a sundial or fountain or what-not. . . . And so I. . . .'

'Oh,' said the King grimly. 'Well, they're *my* grooms!'

'I'm sorry, Your Majesty, I thought under the circumstances. . . .'

'Have them returned at once to the Royal Palace!' commanded the King coldly.

'To the Dutch Garden,' he added after a moment's thought.

At this point the Court Chamberlain burst excitedly into the room with a large book.

'I've got it, Your Majesty,' he announced proudly. 'It's a *Basilisk!*'

'Basilisk? Never heard of it.'

'I have,' said the Vizier, anxious to instal himself in favour once more. 'But I thought they were extinct. . . .'

'Well, this one isn't,' snapped the King. 'Be quiet!'

The Vizier, who was having no luck, subsided into silence, while the Court Chamberlain read out long extracts about '*Ye Basiliske, sommetymes called ye Cockatrice,*' and which described perfectly the appearance and attributes of Koko the Thingumabob. '*Hys brethe,*' he read, '*burneth with fyre, and whoso meeteth ye glance of his eyes is straighteway turned to stone, and so too all livynge thynges save onlie ye wesle. . . .*'

'What's a wesle?' asked the King.

The Vizier opened his mouth and then shut it again. He was not taking any chances.

'Wesle! Wesle!' repeated the Chamberlain thoughtfully. 'I don't know. Some witch's invention I should think.'

The King reached up for a large tome on *The Fauna of Sparmania,*

Indigenous and Magical, edited by a local naturalist. With some annoyance he discovered that a Wesle was not mentioned and so turned to Basilisk. Under Basilisk he found 'See Cockatrice.' When he reached Cockatrice and discovered 'See Basilisk', he threw the book across the room and ordered the Vizier to have the author arrested next day for Lèse Majesté and Imbecility.

The Chamberlain then returned to his reading and disclosed the fact that a Basilisk could be killed by the crowing of a cock.

'But we daren't *kill* it,' objected the King very angrily. 'In fact, we'd better have all cocks near the Palace destroyed.' He swore to himself with feeling, and began to run over a few of the deaths he would like the Emperor of Granada to die, most of them preceded by lingering and loathsome diseases.

He was just feeling better when a servant was shown in and with many stammerings reported that some slight carelessness in the stables had again resulted in a fire in Koko's cage. It had, of course, been at once extinguished, but Ali, while helping, had been unfortunately immobilised and was now a statue.

'Ali a statue?' ejaculated the King, momentarily overcome.

'Yes, Your Majesty. He was just holding a squirter when the Thingumabob. . . .'

The King suddenly brightened. Then he slapped his knee.

'The Sunk Garden!' he cried. 'Instead of the fountain.'

The servant stared for a moment in uncomprehending surprise, then added:

'And one of the firemen, Your Highness, also ventured too close and got looked at.'

The King turned to the Vizier. He felt perhaps he had been a little harsh to him lately. 'You can have the fireman for that lawn of yours,' he said graciously. 'He ought to do well as a sprinkler. . . .'

By the end of a further fortnight the situation in Sparmania's Royal Palace had become strained. The Basilisk was now in an uninflammable cage made of metal, so that the risk of fire had been considerably minimised, but his glance was as deadly as ever. A chute for the daily ration of coal had been built out at the back, or blind side of his den, but notwithstanding this, the grooms had struck on three occasions for increased wages to make up for the risks of their employment, and there was great difficulty in filling the places of those who had, so to speak, inadvertently caught Koko's eye.

From the King's point of view, too, the novelty of the situation was wearing off. Every available lawn and path in the Royal Gardens now had its central stone figure, and the Vizier and Court Chamberlain and other favoured officials had several of their own. The groom *motif*, of course, predominated in all the sculpture, but there was one very fine group of seven firemen which the King had graciously had erected at his own expense in the square outside the municipal fire station.

He had also, at the Vizier's statesmanlike suggestion, invited a number of unsuspecting courtiers, of whom he disapproved or who were suspected of intriguing, to a fine meat tea, to be followed by a private view of his new pet. The Court Chamberlain, being of an economical turn of mind, had suggested that it would be cheaper if the meat tea came after the private view, but the King – nothing if not royally magnanimous – had refused to hear of it. The party was a great success, and a new wing of the Palace was opened up as a sculpture gallery.

But after that everything began to fall a little flat. To begin with, one could not go a yard anywhere without coming up against a stone animal; and the King never dared kick a cat – in case it had ceased to be a cat and had been just put there as a joke. Even the satisfaction of being able to write to the Emperor of Granada and say that Koko was still there was wearing off, and occasionally the King found himself thinking he had better import a cock, kill this Koko nuisance, and take the consequences of war and invasion.

In the middle of this delicate state of affairs the Court Magician one day suddenly reappeared. His reappearance caused a certain amount of confusion, firstly, because he materialised in the centre of the dinner table, and secondly, because he could not be made to understand for some while that he had been away longer than ten minutes.

The King, however, was desperately glad to see him and showed it so openly that the Magician, being a shrewd fellow, seized the opportunity to demand successfully a grant of money to the purchase of some new spell-weaving apparatus he had long set his heart upon. When this had been put in writing (the Magician's idea), the excited King dragged him off to his private room and told him the whole story.

'And you must devise some plan,' he concluded, 'by which we can keep this Basilisk here to satisfy that dirty Granada hound' – the King had got a little worked up during his narrative – 'and yet can avoid this infernal inconvenience. Why, only to-day I spent hours trying to think of a place for the statues of four small boys in a climbing attitude at the top of a fence. A most difficult position to. . . .'

'Your Majesty,' said the Court Magician, withdrawing, 'I'll see what I can do to-morrow.'

'Good-night!' said the King and added: 'Er – by the way, you'll be *here* to-morrow, won't you? I mean. . . .'

'Why, yes.'

'I mean, you're quite well? You don't feel another disappearance coming on or anything. Better take a spot of quinine, or . . .'

'No, I'm all right.'

'Splendid, and you *will* be careful with this Basilisk yourself, won't you? I mean I shan't know where to put *you*, if you make a slip. Every niche is full; unless' – he grew thoughtful – 'unless I put you on a pedestal at the foot of the main staircase. You could hold a torch and . . .'

The Magician felt that the conversation was becoming slightly morbid.

'Basilisks are child's play to me,' he remarked coldly and departed. The King slept better that night than he had done for days.

Next morning the Magician had an interview with the King and the Vizier.

'I shall visit the Basilisk this afternoon,' he began importantly. 'I am just making a little – er – gadget which will completely settle the matter.'

'Good!' The King rubbed his hands. Then he recollected something. 'Er – by the way, what is a Wesle?' he asked.

'It is old spelling for weasel. I shall need one of them too.'

'Weasel! Of course! What a fool I was! Vizier! A bag of gold for the man who brings a weasel to the Palace by lunch!'

Lunch was considerably delayed that day owing to the presence in the Palace courtyard of seventy-two peasants each with a bag containing a weasel. Considerable disorder prevailed when the Royal Treasurer refused to pay out seventy-two bags of gold, and many of the disappointed peasants freed their weasels in the courtyard as a protest. The Palace was full of stray weasels for some weeks afterwards, which were continually popping out of unexpected corners and frightening the ladies-in-waiting. In fact, the Court Poet composed a rhyme about it, which you may hear, in a garbled version, to this day.

Towards the middle of the afternoon a small but excited group assembled outside the gate leading into the stable yard, which now, by the way, wore a very neglected appearance. The party was composed of the King, the Vizier, the Chamberlain, a boy holding a weasel, the Magician with a large sort of shield covered with sacking, another boy holding a bag, and two highly nervous firemen.

'But we aren't going *in*, are we?' objected the King at this point. 'I mean, *I'm* valuable. I can get another Vizier, of course,' he looked meditatively at the Vizier, who glanced nervously at the Chamberlain, 'but I feel, myself, I. . . .'

'You'll all be quite safe with these,' said the Magician shortly, and from the big bag he handed the King, the Vizier and the Chamberlain each a large bundle of a herb, which he explained was called rue, and a piece of smoked glass.

'There, I never thought of smoked glass,' chatted the King. 'I say,' he added in a whisper. 'What about the two boys? They haven't got anything. I've been having trouble enough with parents as it is and I . . .'

'I'm not a complete fool,' retorted the Magician angrily. 'They're both orphans.'

'Oh,' said the King, and very gingerly he and the Vizier with their protective herbs and their smoked glass crept into the stable yard, which was littered with little statuettes of dogs, cats and other incautious animals. The Chamberlain, who was not nearly such a fool as he looked, stopped unobserved at the last moment to tie up his shoe lace.

'Go nearer, if you can't see properly,' said the Magician kindly to the others, as he, too, entered with his covered shield and his weasel and his small boys.

Both the King and the Vizier were understood to say they could see beautifully from where they were.

The Magician advanced slowly towards the fiery glow of the Basilisk's den. Through their smoked glass the King and the Vizier could just make out the Basilisk, now grown to terrifying proportions and shining with internal heat. From its beak leapt flames of fire and its eyes seemed to dart arrows at the Magician. In fact, he lost his small boys almost at once.

Quickly he released the weasel, which made straight for the cage, miraculously unharmed, while to the two onlookers' amazement the Basilisk quailed, its breath died down and it retired into a corner.

Under cover of this attack the Magician advanced and when in front of the cage drew the sacking off his shield and held it up in front of the Basilisk, giving tongue to a weird exclamation which the Vizier subsequently said was a spell, but which the King stoutly maintained was simply foul language.

There was a sudden crowing shriek from the Basilisk as it glared at the Magician and then silence. The smoke and flames died away completely; the Basilisk remained motionless, crouching in a dark corner of its den.

'It's all right now,' called the Magician. After a lot of hesitation the Vizier advanced – under a direct royal command.

'What's happened?' gasped the King when he had looked timorously at the Basilisk, watched the Vizier narrowly, felt his own arms, and looked again at the motionless Basilisk with increased confidence.

'A little trick,' explained the Magician and displayed his uncovered shield for the first time. 'My shield is a looking-glass. He's turned *himself* to stone!'

'B – but . . .' quavered the King, not understanding, 'then you've done him in . . .'

'N – no, not exactly, because he's still there in his cage and you can write every month to the Emperor of Granada and say so. But he's quite safe now.'

The King got the idea.

'Wonderful!' he ejaculated. 'Wonderful! You deserve a public vote of thanks and a . . . I know what I'll do, I'll erect a *statue* to you!'

Enter Emma

SHEILA HOCKEN

ENTER EMMA

I was, if the truth be known, ashamed of being blind. I refused to use a white stick, and hated asking for help. After all, I was a teenage girl, and I couldn't bear people to look at me and think I was not like them. Looking back, I must have been a terrible danger on the roads. Motorists probably had seizures; suddenly coming across me wandering vaguely through the traffic, they would have to step rapidly on their brakes. Apart from that, there were all sorts of disasters that used to strike on the way to and from work.

On the evening that made such a difference to my life, I got off the bus just about half-way home where I had to change buses, and as usual I was walking gingerly along to the right stop. Almost immediately I bumped into something. 'I'm awfully sorry,' I said and stepped forward only to collide again. When it happened a third time, I realized I had been apologizing to a lamp standard. This was just one of the idiotic things that constantly happened to me, and I had long since learnt to put up with them or even to find them faintly amusing. So I carried on and found the bus stop, which was a request stop. No one else was there and I had to go through the scary business of trying to estimate when the bus had arrived. Generally in this situation, because I loathed showing I was blind by asking for help, I tried to guess at the sound. Sometimes I would stop a petrol tanker or a big lorry and as it drew away would stand there feeling stupid, and in the end usually managed to swallow my pride and ask someone at the stop for help.

But on this particular evening no one joined me at the stop; it was as if everyone in Nottingham had suddenly decided not to travel by bus. Of course I heard plenty of buses pass, or thought I did, but because I had given up hailing them for fear of making a fool of myself I let them all go by. I stood there alone for half an hour without stopping one, then I gave up. I decided to walk on to the next stop, hoping there would be people there.

I got along the pavement as best I could – and that is another frightening experience difficult to describe to anyone who has not been blind, because although you are surrounded by noise you have no coherent mental picture of what is around you, and are guided only by sounds. The sounds were of traffic, and people's footsteps, and sometimes I could tell by the particular quality of the sounds that I was near buildings or passing an open space. But I had absolutely no visual conception of what the road might be like, still less what might be on the other side of it – the houses, the shops, the people and so on: this might well have been the edge of the world, or another universe for all I knew. Were there children playing, people gossiping, women buying bread or potatoes; what did they look like, who were they? I had simply no idea. I walked along in an enclosed grey little world, a box of sounds, two foot by two foot square, around me.

Eventually I reached the next bus stop. But once again there was nobody there, and no buses stopped. So I went on to the next, and then the one after that, and the one after that. By this time I was utterly lost, and simply did not know whether I was waiting at a bus stop or a telegraph post. In the end, I found myself walking about five miles back to the terminus in the city, because I knew if I got there I would be bound to catch the right bus. And this is what happened, but I was between two and three hours late getting home, and felt pretty miserable and out of sorts when I did get there.

I am a great believer in Fate. It has been the greatest single influence on my life, and I feel certain that Fate had decreed that my home teacher was there when I finally reached home that evening. Home teachers visit the blind. They come regularly to help, to talk over any problems, and to supply various aids such as braille paper, braille clocks, egg-timers that ring and so on. Mr Brown, who used to visit my family (since we were all registered as blind people), was quite a feature of life while I was growing up. He was a nice man, rather like an uncle. Mother used to order wool, which could be bought more cheaply through him than at a shop. When I was young he used to bring little presents, and one of these, a doll with separate sets of clothes, I had treasured very much.

Mr Brown had been waiting for me for about an hour. I explained why I was so late, and gave all the details of my nightmare journey. He immediately asked, 'Why on earth don't you have a guide-dog?'

They were the nine most important words of my life up to that time. Yet the suggestion was an astonishing one. The idea of having a guide-dog had simply never occurred to me, which is strange considering my previous attachment to dogs, and my hopes of finding work with them. Perhaps it was because my sight had gone very gradually, and I had always pretended to myself that it was not really going at all, and that I could still see if I tried. I did not want to admit to being blind. In fact, I couldn't believe Mr Brown when he suggested I should apply for a guide-dog. I imagined then that people had somehow to be very special to qualify for guide-dogs, that only a select few had them, and, as a result I suppose, it had never crossed my mind to consider the idea at all. But Mr

Brown went on, 'You quite obviously need a guide-dog, and you're just the right sort of age for one.'

I really could not take the idea in. Its impact was tremendous, as if someone had taken hold of the world and completely reversed its direction. 'What do I do about applying?' I said.

He replied very firmly, and in a voice full of encouragement, 'Well, I'll tell you. I'll get the forms, and I'll come down with them, and we'll fill them in together. I'll do the writing for you.'

When he'd gone, I sat back and thought about it. I thought of the books I had read about guide-dogs. I realized it would mean I'd never again have to face the kind of terrifying business I had been through that day, blundering from bus stop to bus stop in anonymous darkness with no idea where I was. And I'd be able to go out in the evening: I could be independent!

A few days later Mr Brown was back with the forms: sheet after sheet of questions. How tall was I? What did I do for a living? What sort of house did I live in? What were my hobbies? They even wanted to know how much I weighed. We sent the forms off, and a reply came from the training centre at Leamington Spa to say that they would send a guide-dog trainer to assess my personality and match me to a suitable dog. I was excited, but nervous too, because at the back of my mind I was wondering, 'What if they find I'm not suitable after all?' The prospect was heartbreaking. When the trainer came, he went along with me to see where I worked and what I did. We went for a walk together so that he could test my walking pace, and see I had no odd characteristics, such as skips and hops and so on when I went round corners. He examined the house we lived in, which had virtually no back garden and no fencing, and said, when I explained we were hoping to move to a council house, 'You must have a garden well fenced-off for your dog.' Lastly, he told me that there was a waiting-list for guide-dogs, and it would be about nine months to a year before I finally had a dog of my own.

This was in November, 1965. The waiting period was an agony of frustration. Every time a letter came I seized it, and tried to find someone to read it to me as quickly as possible. During these months I had plenty of time to find out about the Guide-Dog Association. It was started in 1934, but the original idea of using dogs to lead blind people was born in Germany during the 1914–18 war, when a doctor in charge of some men blinded at the front one day left his Alsatian to look after a soldier, and was struck by the way the dog carried out his task. The idea spread across the Atlantic and back to England. Yet, unbelievably, the use of guide-dogs was opposed here at first because people thought it unnatural, cruel even, for dogs to be put to work in this way. Fortunately, the Association flourished through a lot of hard work and voluntary effort. Today there are four centres for training guide-dogs and their owners, at Bolton, Exeter, Forfar, and Leamington Spa, as well as headquarters at Ealing near London, and a Breeding and Puppy-Walking Centre near Warwick.

I also learned that some blind applicants had to be rejected for various reasons, and this worried me. But the letter I wanted so much came more quickly than I had thought possible. It arrived towards the end of the following May, and I had only five more weeks to wait. Would I be at the training centre, Leamington Spa, on 1 July? Would I? I was prepared to camp on their doorstep so as not to miss the day.

At last, 1 July arrived. It was, as I thought only proper, glorious weather – bright and sunny. Obviously I could not have got from Nottingham to Leamington Spa on my own. But I was very lucky. Geoff, one of the reps at the firm where I worked, had offered to take me in his car. I was up with my cases packed and ready long before he called for me at nine o'clock. We took the M1 south from Nottingham, Geoff doing his best to describe the scenery to me as we went. I disliked travelling, as there was nothing to occupy me except the business of going from A to B. Geoff's descriptions at least stopped the boredom. Yet I couldn't really imagine all the things he was telling me about. I had no mental picture of what fields looked like because I couldn't remember ever seeing one, much less a cow. I remember him saying to me, 'What do you think I look like? You must have an *idea* of what I look like.'

'Yes, I get an image when I hear people, just as you must get an image of what people look like in your imagination when you hear them on the radio. But,' I added, 'if you later see a photograph of what they're really like, the two images don't match up, do they?'

'No, you're right. They don't,' he said.

'Well, don't blame me if I've got the wrong idea of you ... I think you've got dark, curly hair, and I know that you're about five foot seven because I can judge that when you're standing up and you talk.'

'Mm,' he replied, non-committally. The he went on, 'Do you ever feel people's faces to get an image of them?' I told him I didn't, but not the reason. It would have been like telling everyone I couldn't see.

About half-way to Leamington, Geoff asked if I'd like to stop for a coffee. I did not really want to. For one thing I wanted to get to Leamington as quickly a possible. For another, I hated going into strange places where I knew there would be lots of people, because I always felt so embarrassed. But we did stop, mainly because I thought Geoff deserved a coffee. We drew off the motorway, and into a big car park. Geoff wanted to be helpful, and he grasped my arm, not realizing how unnerving it was for me being dragged along in this way. As he was taking me from the car park, he said, 'Steps here, Sheila.' That was fine, as far as it went. But he didn't say whether the steps went up or down. I assumed they went up. I was wrong. I suppose I ought to have asked, to make sure. Then he led me, or more accurately propelled me, through some doors. I got the impression we were in a very large room, full of women, all talking. I could smell their perfume, and the coffee. I imagined it was about eleven o'clock, and they were all in there for the coffee break.

Left alone while Geoff got the coffee, I panicked. I felt desperately cut off, and wanted to run. Then another embarrassment presented itself. I wanted to go to the lavatory. But I did not want to have to ask Geoff. Although the situation was not new to me, I always found it humiliating. Unfailingly, it took me right back to primary school, my hand sawing the air, 'Please teacher, can I leave the room?' When I did summon up the courage to mention my predicament Geoff was very good and said immediately, 'Oh, of course. I'll get someone to take you.' Either he didn't notice my embarrassment, or covered up very well. He left the table and went to speak to someone. As it turned out, he must have picked the biggest and strongest woman in the room. I had the bruises on my arm the next day to prove it. She got hold of me and hauled me out of my seat by brute force. 'Come along, my dear,' she boomed, 'I'll take you. You poor thing, not being able to see.' And she literally pushed me through the room. I crashed into everything possible on the way: tables, chairs, even an occasional cup and saucer, they all went flying. I felt like a red-faced bull in a china shop. Even when I was in the Ladies, she insisted on standing guard outside the door, enquiring from time to time, 'Are you all right, dear?' and 'You're sure you don't need any help?' I didn't know whether to laugh or cry. I could not wait, once released from the grip of this Amazon, to be back in the car and driving the last lap to Leamington.

The training centre, Geoff told me when we arrived, was a large, Tudor-style house, with trees all round it, standing in a great expanse of grounds. While we waited for someone to come and look after me, I had a sudden moment of misgiving. 'What,' I thought, 'if I go through the course, and I can't do whatever they teach, and they say I'm not good enough to have a guide-dog. What then?' It was a cold, alien feeling and I was shaking slightly when the receptionist arrived.

She instantly dispelled my momentary panic. 'Hello, Sheila, we were expecting you round about this time. If you'd like to take my arm, I'll show you to your room.' No pushing or dragging here, I thought. Geoff said goodbye, and the receptionist took me through a lot of corridors and up several staircases. It seemed an enormous place as she guided me along, explaining the layout of the centre, and the way to the dining-room, the lounge, the bathroom and toilets, and so on. Then we reached my room. 'Here we are,' said the receptionist, 'Number Ten.' She stopped and told me to put my hand up to the door. To my utter amazement I felt 'Number Ten' in Braille. 'All the doors are numbered or marked like this,' she said, 'so you won't have any trouble finding your way about.' I was quite staggered. At last a place where they really understood the business of being blind. I felt better just at the touch of the 'Number Ten' on my door. Imagine, I thought, as I felt the outline through my fingers, they actually *expect* you to feel your way about.

Then the receptionist took me into my room, and described the layout. I, of course, had to 'picture' it through my sense of touch and my estimation of the distance between obstacles. Directly behind the door was an easy chair and then a fitted wardrobe. I felt along the wall and found my bed, and along the bed to the radio and the table. In the corner was a hand-basin with hot and cold taps, and on the same wall was the dressing table. I discovered a looking-glass on the dressing table, and the receptionist must have noticed my expression. 'Ah yes,' I heard her say, 'the looking-glass. You want to know why. Well; the reason is that if we didn't have normal fittings such as mirrors and lamps in the rooms it would be very odd to the sighted, particularly to those who work here. We expect you to fit into a sighted world, and accept these sorts of things.' Wonderful, I thought – integration ...

There was just one more item of furniture left to examine, and it was the most important. Next to the dressing table was the dog-bed. It seemed massive, and I felt its interior-sprung mattress and blanket. It was so obviously comfortable I fancied it myself. When I'd finished identifying it by touch the receptionist said, 'Well that's it, Sheila. I'll leave you to unpack. The midday meal will be in half an hour.' I heard the door close behind her, and started unpacking my suitcase. On the way to the wardrobe I had to keep passing the dog-bed. Every time I did so I stopped and felt it. I wondered longingly what sort of dog would soon be sleeping in it.

The sound of knocking interrupted my thoughts. When I opened the door, a voice said, 'Hello, I'm Brian Peel. I'm your trainer.' He not only trained the dogs, but also taught people how to use them. His handshake felt firm and friendly; I was sure we would get on well. 'If you'd like to come down with me,' he went on, 'I'll show you exactly where the dining-room and lounge are.' We went down to the lounge, and he explained the geography of the room. 'We meet here each morning to begin the day's training. There are chairs round the outside. If you follow them round to the right, you'll find the radio and television. On the opposite side are braille books and games ... mind that coffee table ... if you remember that table stands where the carpet ends, you won't walk into it.'

As we went on to the dining-room, the prospect of a familiar ordeal loomed up in my mind. I hated eating meals with sighted people. It always led to some kind of embarrassment. They usually wanted to cut my meat up, and imagined it would be better if I ate with a spoon instead of with a knife and fork. Or they said, 'Oh dear, if only I'd *known* you couldn't see, I would have made sandwiches.' I would become so demoralized and nervous I could hardly eat at all when a plate of food was eventually put in front of me. Not knowing what was on it, much less exactly where the food was, I would stab away, usually missing potatoes or meat or whatever, and ending up bringing my teeth together on the metal of an empty fork.

At the training centre it was totally different. Brian sat next to me and put the plate in front of me. 'Here we are,' he said, 'Fish, chips and peas. Chips at twelve o'clock, peas at three o'clock, and fish between nine and six.' So I not only knew what I was going to eat, but where to find it. We talked during the meal. 'Are there any other people here for training?' I asked.

'You're the first to arrive,' said Brian, 'we've three more coming this afternoon.'

Then, before many more chips and peas had disappeared, I asked the question which was burning in my mind: 'When do we get our dogs?'

'In a day or two, when we know a little bit more about you and you know more about the dogs. You know, a lot of the people we get for training have never had even a pet dog before they come here, and they wouldn't know how to look after a guide-dog. So first we teach the business of actually looking after a dog. Then, of course, you can't work with a dog unless you know how she's been trained, and what commands she will respond to.'

'I see,' I said. There was a pause. Then I asked, 'Have you chosen the dog, I'm going to have?'

'I think so,' said Brian, 'but over the next two days I shall make absolutely sure. You see, I know the dogs, but I don't know the students properly yet, even though you've all filled in your questionnaires. The thing is, we match the dog to the future owner as far as possible. For instance, if an owner is young and can move quickly, we want a dog that can move quickly. If the owner's older, we want a dog that will slow down a bit, and, generally, we try to match characteristics. Your dog – or the one I *think* you're going to have – was puppy-walked by a woman who had no men living in the house; she's obviously a woman's dog – she gets on with them better than with men. She's quite sensitive, too, and because you've handled dogs before, we think you might suit one another. But even so, like everyone on the course, you'll have to get used to her.'

After the meal, we went back to the lounge, and met the other students who had arrived in the meantime. Two of them I got to know very well. There was Dotty (Dorothy, officially), who was about thirty-four. She had come for her second guide-dog. And there was Harry, a man of forty-nine who had been blinded during the war. He had come for his third guide-dog.

During the afternoon, Brian began to tell us what to expect in the month ahead. He told us how he trained the dogs, and how we would be trained to use them. With two people present who had already had guide-dogs, I felt a very raw recruit, and slightly uneasy. But I need not have. Brian explained that even for people who had had a guide-dog before, it was necessary to come back to the centre, and re-train with their new dog. Techniques of handling were constantly being improved, and a dog had to have a month with its new owner to transfer its allegiance and affection away from the trainer.

In the evening, Dotty and Harry told me about their previous dogs, and it was exciting to hear them. But when the time came to go to bed, and I went upstairs to my room, I felt very lonely. In the next room to mine, I heard Dorothy's radio and decided to knock on her door.

'It's Sheila, may I come in?'

'Of course, the chair's behind the door. Sit down.'

I sat down and tried to make conversation, but Dotty didn't seem very communicative. In fact, she sounded rather upset.

'Would you rather I went?'

'Oh no, please don't.'

So I tried to cheer her up. 'Aren't you looking forward to getting your new dog? I can't wait to get mine.' At this, to my amazement, she burst into tears. 'Oh dear,' I said, 'whatever's the matter? What have I said?'

'It's all right,' she sobbed, 'I shall be all right. But I don't want another dog.'

I was utterly at a loss. 'Don't want another dog? I don't understand.'

'Well,' she said, 'you'd understand if you'd left a dog behind.' And it emerged that Paddy, her old dog, had had to be retired early because of illness, and had gone to friends near Dotty's home. 'It's so *awful*,' she went on, 'to have left Paddy behind, and to come for another dog. I feel I've betrayed her.'

I tried to console her. 'But if Paddy couldn't go on working, I'm sure she'll be glad to see another dog in her place ...'

'I don't know ...'

'But *surely*, for your own sake you must try to transfer your affection.'

'Yes, I know you're right. But it's easier said than done. At the moment I just don't feel able to love another dog.'

There was nothing more I could do to help. I said 'Goodnight' in as kindly a way as I could.

Next morning, all the gloom was swept away. At about half-past seven I was woken by a great chorus, nor far away, of barking dogs. It was the sweetest music I had heard for years. Which one, I wondered lying there half-awake, is going to be mine? Which bark is hers? I hurried through breakfast. I wanted to get down to the instruction as soon as possible. When we had all assembled in the lounge, we were each issued with a white harness for our dogs, and, so we would get the hang of using it, there was a life-size plastic model of a guide-dog. We called him Fred.

'Your dogs,' Brian began, 'are used to working with experienced sighted trainers. They won't take kindly to you blundering round them like blind people, trying to find out where to put the harness on. This is where Fred comes in. You can practise on him first.'

After we had all, in turn, found the correct end of Fred, Brian continued to instruct us on how to position ourselves by the dog: the dog always being on the left. 'These exercises,' Brian went on, 'may seem trivial. But you will be getting a fully-trained dog. The least you can do is to try to give the impression that you are a fully trained owner.'

Positioned at Fred's side, I was told how to instruct him. 'Let's pretend you are telling your dog to go forward. Always indicate with your right arm which direction you want. This will help the dog.' My first effort was unbelievably feeble. Brian started laughing. 'Well, if you were going to start off in the direction you were pointing you'd be leaping over your dog's head. Now have another go. No. Don't stand behind him, you'll step on his tail.' And so on. It was as well we had Fred to practise on. At least his plastic tail was not so sensitive to my foot.

Our next lesson was to learn how to follow the dog. Brian played the part of the dog, because Fred had not yet been fixed up with wheels. With dummy harness, and Brian in the lead, we set out in the grounds of the training centre. It was very difficult to follow, and to stop and go when he did. I was sure I had two left feet, and by the end of the first day's training I was convinced I would never make a guide-dog owner. But I was determined to improve and already the feel of the harness had come to be important to me.

In the lounge after breakfast the following day there was tremendous expectancy and excitement because we all knew we were going to meet our dogs for the first time. Brian gave us a final briefing, and then asked us to go back to our rooms. 'There'll be less distraction there,' he said, 'and you'll get to know your dog, and vice versa, with a bit of peace and quiet.'

I went up to Number Ten – able to find my way now unaided. I sat on the edge of the bed waiting, with the door open, and with enough time to have a stray, disturbing thought: what if my dog doesn't like me? What if she stands growling at me? Then I heard Brian's footsteps approaching along the corridor, and with them I heard the clicking patter of a dog's paws.

'Here we are, Sheila,' said Brian as he came into the room, 'here's your dog. She's called Emma, and she's a chocolate-coloured Labrador.'

At the same time I heard a tail swishing in the air, and Brian leaving, closing the door behind him. 'Emma,' I called. Immediately she came bounding across the room, and suddenly I was nearly bowled off the bed. Then I was licked all over. 'Hello, Emma,' I said, 'hello.' I could hardly believe it. She kept licking me, and pushing her cold nose into my hands. I knew then we were going to get on together. She likes me, I thought. She *likes* me. I could have danced round the room.

I tried to feel the shape of her head, but she would not stop bouncing up and down in front of me, twisting, turning and making snuffling noises in my hands. Every now and then I got a wet nose in my face. But at last she settled and sat by my feet, and I was able to feel what she was like. Her coat was very thick and rough, reminding me of a Teddy bear's. She was smallish for a Labrador, not fat, but thickset. She had a very thick tail, and ears that were as soft as velvet. And she was so lively.

Emma did not give me long to run my hands over her. She started to fetch me things. Under the dressing table I kept my shoes. She began rushing after them, and bringing them to me one by one. The message was quite clear. 'Here I am. I'm Emma. I'm your new dog, and this is your gift, a shoe.' I could not remember ever being so happy before. And from those first few moments of greeting, Emma's affection has never wavered. From then on she was never to leave my side, and I, in turn, took on the responsibility for her every need.

My first walk with Emma came that afternoon, and it was immediately evident why we had to have a month's training with the dogs. Although

Emma took to me, and we got on well together, she would not do a thing I told her. She would obey no one but Brian. Attachment and obedience to me would clearly come only with training.

I put Emma's harness on, and we started off down a quiet road near the centre. Brian was standing next to us. He gave the command to go forward, but before he even got the '-ward' bit out we were off, several miles down the road it seemed, and I was galloping along, hanging on grimly to the harness.

'I'll never keep this up,' I managed to gasp.

'Oh, you'll soon get used to it,' said Brian. 'You'll get fitter as you go along. The trouble is you've been accustomed to walking so slowly.'

A guide-dog's pace apparently averages about four miles an hour. This compares with an ordinary sighted person's two to three miles an hour. So what kind of speed I used to achieve before I have no idea, but it was obviously not competitive even with that of the snail population. At last I began to settle down to the fast rhythm, and was just beginning to think I might enjoy it after all, when, without any warning whatsoever, Emma stopped. I was off the pavement before I could pull up. Emma had sat down on the kerb, and I heard Brian laughing.

'Don't go without your dog, that's Lesson Number One,' Brian said. 'If you go sailing on when she stops at the kerb, you'll get run over. She stops, you stop.'

'Well, I didn't know she was going to stop, did I? And you didn't tell me.'

'No, you're right. But you've got to learn to follow your dog.'

Brian was about twenty-eight at the time, very pleasant and with a great sense of humour. I imagined him good-looking with fair hair and glasses. I liked him especially because he refused to make concessions to our blindness. He expected us to be independent. Rather than mop us up, and say, 'There, there,' when we fell off the kerb, he would turn it into a joke, which was the best medicine. At least it was for me. It certainly made me get up and think, 'Right. I'll show you who can be a good guide-dog owner.'

So on this occasion I got back behind Emma, took up the harness again, and said, 'What next?'

'You've got to cross this road. First you listen for any traffic. If it's quiet, you give Emma the command to go forward.'

When I could hear no traffic, this is what I did. But nothing happened.

Brian said, 'She knows that you're behind her and not me. You've got to encourage her, to make her want to take you over the road.'

'Good girl, Emma,' I said, 'there's a clever dog.' And after a little more of this persuasion, and the word 'Forward', thrown in from time to time, she finally took me across the road.

Crossing the road with a guide-dog is a matter of team-work: whatever you do, you do it together. I have met sighted people with such weird ideas about this. Either they think the dogs are not very clever, but just wear the harness to show their owner is blind – a sort of plea for help – or they think the dogs are superhuman, and the blind people idiots who are being taken round for a walk as other people take their dogs. The importance of partnership, or even its existence, never seems to occur to most people. My job when crossing a road was to listen and Emma's was to look. Only when I could hear nothing should I give her the command to cross. But if I was wrong in my assessment of the traffic, and she could see something coming, she would wait until it was clear.

Guide-dogs are taught to stop and sit down at every kerb and wait for the next command. The four basic commands are, 'Right', 'Left', 'Back', and 'Forward'. And you have to position yourself with your dog so that you give her every opportunity to obey the right command. For instance, when the command to go forward is given, it is accompanied by an indication in that direction with the arm. It is also important to keep on talking to the dog, and Brian reminded me of this on our first walk, just after we had crossed the road.

'Don't stop talking, or Emma'll think you've fallen asleep.'

'What do I say?' I asked rather stupidly.

'It doesn't matter, as long as you make it interesting. Tell her what you had for breakfast if you like.'

So there I was, galloping along a street in Leamington discussing bacon and eggs with a chocolate-coloured Labrador. Brian went on, 'You're working together, and if you stop talking, she'll stop working. You've got to keep her interest. She's a dog, and there are lots of nice, interesting smells all round, and things passing that you can't see. So unless you talk to her, she'll get distracted, and stop to sniff a lamp post.' I was quite hoarse by the time we had finished our first walk together.

I owe a great deal to Brian, not only for his training, but also for matching Emma and me together. His assessment of all he knew about us resulted in an inspired pairing, as time was to prove.

One day I remember asking him where Emma came from. What I really meant was, how did the centres come by the guide-dogs? Brian explained that they came to Leamington, or one of the other centres, after being puppy-walked. The Guide-Dog Association has a big breeding and puppy-walking centre at Tollgate House, near Warwick. They own a number of brood bitches and stud dogs that are let out to people as pets, because, naturally, a permanent kennel life is not desirable, and living with a family is a much happier arrangement. At the same time the Association controls which dog should mate with which. When the litters come along, it picks the dogs or bitches required for training. At about eight weeks old, a puppy undergoes various tests to see if it is basically bold and friendly, and capable of being trained as a guide-dog. Dogs bred in this way form about sixty per cent of the total, and there are now about two thousand guide-dog owners in the country. The remaining forty per cent come to the Association either by purchase or donation from breeders or private individuals. But the rejection rate is high. Dogs are kept on approval for about three weeks to see if they are suitable. If they're not, they're returned to their owners. In all cases the dogs chosen are usually female, because the male dog has a rather different outlook and nature, including a territorial instinct, and is not as tractable as the female, who in any case is spayed for the purposes of being a guide-dog. About seventy per cent of the breeds used are Labradors, like Emma – though I prefer to think she is unique, even among Labradors – and the remainder Alsatians, Collies, Golden Retrievers, and crosses from all of these.

Once the selection is made, the puppies go to people called puppy-walkers, who live around the training centres, and give homes to potential guide-dogs for about a year. In this time they have to teach the dog the basics. The dogs learn how to be well-mannered and clean in the house, to keep off furniture, not to beg for food, and to obey commands such as 'Sit', 'Stay', 'Down', 'Come', and so on. They are taught to walk on a lead, but not at heel, because of course they will eventually be required to walk in front of a blind man or woman. In general, the puppy-walkers are expected to take the dog everywhere with them, so that the dog is not shy of traffic, buses or trains, or the sort of sudden noises that sometimes occur in the street, such as pneumatic drills. They are also specifically instructed to take the dogs shopping. During this phase the puppy grows up and becomes used to urban life, and at the same time should remain bold and friendly.

At this point, Brian told me, they come to the centres for guiding training, which lasts about five months. The puppy-walkers do a wonderful job. I couldn't do it myself: have a dog for a year, then part with it; then have another, and see it go, and so on, and I really admire those who do so much to forge the first essential link between dog and blind person.

Naturally, when Brian told me all this, I wanted to know who had puppy-walked Emma, and he said, 'Someone called Paddy Wansborough. She's a marvellous woman. She's given nine or ten dogs to the Association after puppy-walking them. In fact, Emma, wasn't bred by the Association. She was bought by Paddy as a puppy, given her basic year, and then donated to the Association.'

I determined that one of the first things I would do when I got home would be to contact Paddy Wansborough.

Next day, I was out with Emma again. As the training progressed I gradually got more used to her. We used a mini-bus to get us about Leamington, and this played a big part in the training, because it taught us how to use public transport. When we were on the bus and the dogs under the seats, I heard a great bellow from Brian, 'I can see two brown paws sticking out.' Brown paws, I thought, that must be Emma.

He went on, 'Do you want somebody to stand on her?'

'No, of course I don't.'

'Well, do something about it.'

I began to wonder if my first impressions of Brian had been wrong. But though he was shouting at me a lot, he must have guessed what I was thinking.

'No one else is going to tell you these things, Sheila. If you don't learn here, Emma'll be the one that suffers, not you.'

My trust in Emma grew daily, but I really knew she had transferred her affections from Brian to me on about the tenth day of my stay at the centre. Up to then, she had always slept until morning in her dog-bed on the other side of the room. But on this particular evening, she refused to go to her bed. Instead, she curled up on the floor as near to my pillow as she could get. I felt then that we had made it. We were a team, each needing the other's company. I woke the following morning with an odd sensation. It felt as if there were a steam-roller on my chest. Emma was sitting on top of me, pushing with her nose, telling me, I have no doubt at all, that it was time for us both to get up. She was full of life and exuberance, and could not wait to start the day. When I did get up, I could hear her shake herself in anticipation, and stand wagging her tail near the door.

One of the centre's ingenious ways of familiarizing us with the day's programme was by using tactile maps. Pavements, buildings, and so on were raised on a wooden map of Leamington, so we could feel our way over the routes beforehand, right down to the zebra crossings and the bus stops. Emma would find these things for me, but I had to be in the right road, and the map helped enormously to make sure we did not miss our way. Our walks became more and more complicated, and Brian would try to find places where there were road works, to ensure we had mastered the business of getting round them, as well as other obstacles. Bus trips and shopping expeditions were also in the curriculum, and I really enjoyed shopping with Emma. She would not only find the shop, but also take me up to the counter. I began to forget I was blind. No one fussed round me any longer. They were all too interested in Emma.

But things did not always go smoothly. I was not keen on the obstacle course we had to practise. Emma always reacted very quickly, and usually I was not fast enough to follow. She would see the obstacle, assess it, and take a snap decision which way to go. Before I knew what was happening she would have changed course to one side or the other, and I would be left in a trail of harness and confusion. Brian always seemed to be on hand when I made mistakes, even if I thought he was following some other student. I would suddenly hear a great shout: 'When your dog jumps, you jump.'

It was easier said than done. On occasions like this, Emma would lose her confidence and sit down immediately. It was almost as if she were saying, 'It's no good me doing my bit, if all you can do is to trail behind and finish up in a heap.' Literally the only way I could get her back to work again was to apologize and promise to do better next time.

It was while we were doing the obstacle course that I learned one of Emma's aversions. It came to our turn and we were going through the obstacles fairly well. All at once Emma shot off like a rocket, and I felt myself being taken at right angles up a steep grass bank. As we went, I heard Brian hysterical with laughter. When we finally came to a stop, I said rather breathlessly, 'What was all that about? Whatever did she do that for?'

'Oh, it's Napoleon.'

'Napoleon? What do you mean, Napoleon?' I thought Brian had suddenly gone out of his mind.

'You know,' he said, 'the cat. Napoleon, the cat.'

'Oh,' I said. But I still did not know why Emma had shot up the bank.

Brian, still laughing, explained that Emma could not stand cats. She knew better than to chase them, but if she saw one, she would take off in the opposite direction – the opposite direction in this case having been the steep grassy bank. Still, Brian did congratulate me on my alacrity and speed in following, and promised to keep us in mind if there was ever a guide-dog expedition to Everest. At the same time, I thought the only way to cure Emma of her dislike of cats would be to get one, and I put that on my list of resolutions for when I got home.

That evening as we were sitting in the lounge, Brian came in and we laughed again about Emma and the cat. Then I asked him something that fascinated me more and more the longer the course went on. How did they train the dogs to accomplish the amazing things they did for us? I knew a little about dog training from the experience I had had with them, but I could not fathom some of the dog's abilities. After all, it is a fairly simple matter to train a dog to sit at a kerb every time, but how to you train them to disobey you? I asked Brian, 'For instance, I told Emma to go forward yesterday, when I hadn't heard a car coming, and she wouldn't go because she'd seen one. How on earth do you train them to do that?'

Brian replied, 'Once you've got a dog basically trained, and you're waiting to cross the road, you see a car coming and tell the dog to go forward. The dog, naturally, obeys immediately, but you don't move, and the car – other trainers drive them for these exercises – hoots, and makes a lot of noise, and the dog comes back on the pavement; by repetition of this sort of thing it is conditioned to associate the moving vehicle with danger, and therefore, despite all instinct to obey, refuses to move even when the command is given. Of course, only fairly intelligent dogs will respond like this, and that's why we have to be very stringent with our tests of character and aptitude to begin with.'

'What about obstacles?' I asked.

Brian explained that the principle behind teaching dogs not to walk their owners into obstacles was to get the dog to associate an obstacle with displeasure – to use a mild word – and also distress. A start is made with something simple such as a post. The dog walks the trainer into the post, is immediately stopped, the post is banged to draw attention to it, and the right way, allowing room, is shown. The next time a forceful 'NO' is shouted when the post is collided with, and the right way is shown again. So by repetition the dog eventually gets the message, and at the same time, the range of obstacles is extended to include the most frequent pavement obstacles of all, people.

It sounded simple in a way, but I knew a lot of hard work and talented training went into all this. The trainers, Brian told me, worked with a blindfold on when they considered the dogs had reached a certain standard of proficiency. They did this for about a fortnight to create real working conditions for the dogs, and give them confidence through working with someone they knew.

It was interesting to hear Brian explain it all, and particularly, in the light of what followed in the last stage of the course, the disobedience part. We were nearing the end of our month at Leamington, and went out once more in the mini-bus. Emma's paws, by now, were always well tucked away. Brian told us we were going to the station as a final test.

I have always loathed railway stations because of the noise, the hundred and one different obstacles, and the general sense of bustle which, if you are blind, is scaring. I got to dislike them so much I would never go into one, still less travel by train, even if there were a sighted person to take me. But Brian was adamant. 'Well, you know, you've got to get used to it. You might want to go by rail one day, or meet somebody off a train, and you've got Emma to guide you now. She knows her way around. There's nothing to it.'

I was not convinced. We got to the station, and I put Emma's harness on. Brian said, 'Right. I'll just go and park. You go in; Emma knows the way. I'll be with you in a minute or two.'

Emma took me through the doors, down a couple of flights of steps, in and out between people on the platform and sat down. I had no idea where I was. I just stood and waited for Brian. He was there within a couple of minutes. 'Right,' he said, 'Emma's been sitting bang on the edge of the platform. There's about a six-foot drop in front of you to the railway line. Now tell her to go forward.'

I was petrified, and my spine tingled. 'You must be joking,' I said. 'No, go on. Tell her to go forward.'

I stood there, not knowing what to do. This really was a terrible test. Dare I do it? I was so scared, I felt sick. In that moment I really did not want a guide-dog. Everything I had heard about them, all the training we had done, all I felt about Emma flashed through my mind, and it meant nothing. I just wanted, there and then, to lay the harness handle on Emma's back, and leave, get out, escape, anything. But, in a sort of hoarse whisper, I heard myself saying, 'Forward.'

Immediately, up she got, and almost in the same motion pushed herself in front of my legs. Then she started pushing me back, right away from the edge of the platform.

I have never felt so ashamed in all my life. I felt about an inch tall. How could I possibly have been so doubting, so unworthy of Emma? I was utterly humiliated. Brian said, 'There you are, I told you Emma would look after you, whatever you do. Whatever you tell her to do, if there's any danger in front of you, she'll push you away.'

So that was it. We had made it. The sense of freedom was incredible. I got over my awful feelings of shame, because I sensed that Emma understood and forgave. That afternoon I walked with her down the Parade in Leamington, the busy main road, crowded with shoppers. I walked with a great big smile on my face, weaving in and out of all those people, and feeling: I don't care if you can *see* I'm blind. I can see too: I've got Emma, and she's all I need.

All too soon the day came when we were to go home, Emma and I. It was, oddly enough, very sad. It happened to be raining – pouring down – and the weather matched my mood. Even though I could not see the rain, I felt very grey and depressed. I hated the idea of having to leave the centre and all the friends I had made. Even more, I really did not want to go home, although I now had Emma, and kept trying to convince myself that things back in Nottingham were *bound* to be different. I was afraid that somehow I might be enveloped in the old ways again, despite Emma. I had not yet grasped to what an enormous extent she was about to change my life. I still had to learn to put my confidence in her.

Heavy with misgivings, I left Leamington with Emma on her harness beside me. The two of us arrived in Nottingham, were met and taken home. Once home, I let Emma off the lead and took off her harness: she went wild. Everyone was immediately taken with her. She bounded all over the place, through every room, round and round; I could hear her tearing about, sending rugs flying, stopping to sniff each chair and table leg. The air swished to the wagging of her tail, and resounded with her snortings and sniffings. This, she obviously realized, was where she was going to live. It was such a different Emma from the sober responsible animal on the harness, and for the first time I appreciated that there were two distinct sides to her character: one when she was working, and in charge of me, and the other when she was off the harness, totally joyous, full of fun and energy, and as far from any sense of responsibility as a clown. My misgivings began to evaporate.

That first night back, Emma slept at the bottom of the bed; she had decided that there was no other place good enough for her, and in the morning she woke me with her usual insistence. It struck me that this morning we were really starting a new life together. We would be going out into Nottingham on our own. I got out of bed and started dressing. This was not my usual form, because I'm normally a very slow, sleepy starter, but on this day of all days I could not wait to find out how Emma and I, put to the test, would get on together.

Over breakfast I decided we would go to visit some old friends, Norman and Yvonne, whom I hadn't seen recently and who live quite near. In the decision itself lay the prospect of freedom. With Emma, I would be able to go all over Nottingham!

I had the directions worked out in my mind after a telephone consultation. They presented no problems: all I had to do was to go out of our front gate, tell Emma to turn right to the top of the road, a main road, turn right again, go straight to the bottom, turn left, and ask Emma to find the first gate. So, off we went.

Twenty minutes after setting out, we were standing in the porch of Noman and Yvonne's house, and I was feeling for the bell. We had done it. To anyone walking down that Nottingham street of detached houses, lined with trees and built in the 1920s, there may have appeared nothing out of the ordinary about a girl and a dog standing in a doorway waiting for the bell to be answered. But inside me was a huge sense of triumph: it was a milestone. 'Good girl, Emma,' I kept saying. I was so proud of her.

Norman and Yvonne were naturally delighted to see me, and they were even more thrilled to meet Emma. They made a great fuss of her. Several hours later we set off home, and found our way back to the main road. Then came a terrible realization. In my excitement that everything was going so well with Emma, I had forgotten to count how many intersections we had crossed. There had been no need to count on the way there because we went as far as the road went, up to a T-junction. But I should have counted for getting back. And I hadn't. So there I was with no idea where I should tell Emma to turn left. After a whole month of training, I had straightaway forgotten one of the cardinal principles: always count the roads as you go.

What could I do? I thought: Here I am, and there's no trainer to save me. Emma, all unknowing, was taking me along at her furious pace, and I felt as if I were in an endless race to nowhere. Not only that, but I felt I had let Emma down. I seemed alienated from her through my own eagerness and thoughtlessness; I was sure, too, that she would never commit a mistake that would put us both in jeopardy. Emma wasn't in the least daunted, however, and, ignoring my commands, started taking me down a side road. I tried to stop her. 'No, Emma. No! Go back, go back!' But she paid no attention. In turn, I dared not let go of her, so I had to follow. At last she turned left again, and sat down. Instinctively I put my hand out. I felt leaded-lights and painted wood with one or two blisters. It was my back door. If I had forgotten to count the roads on the way out, Emma certainly hadn't!

Not long after we were home from Leamington I wrote to Paddy Wansborough, the marvellous woman who had puppy-walked Emma. By 'wrote' I mean, technically speaking, that I sent a tape-recorded cassette to tell her how much Emma had come to mean to me, and to thank her for giving Emma as a guide-dog after puppy-walking her. That was the beginning of a correspondence by cassette, and of a friendship that continues to this day.

Through this correspondence I learned all sorts of little details about Emma. Paddy had her from the age of eight weeks, and she sent me a photograph taken at this time. Although I had to rely on other people's descriptions of the photograph it was splendid to have a picture of Emma as she was when she was first picked out of the litter to be a guide-dog. She was already eighteen months old when I first met her, so of course I missed all her puppy ways, but to hear Paddy describe them on cassette was the best possible substitute. She said that Emma had always seemed a busy dog, was interested from the beginning in doing things constructively, and always gave the impression of having something on her mind. This confirmed what I knew of her.

On one cassette Paddy told me a story that I possibly found more amusing than she had at the time. One day Paddy planted some hundred and fifty bulbs in her garden. She had then gone indoors, leaving Emma still playing on the lawn. After about half an hour, Emma came in looking extremely pleased with herself. When Paddy happened to look out of the window a moment or so later, she was confronted with a huge pile of bulbs neatly stacked on the back doorstep. Emma had dug each one up with loving care and immense energy, and was thrilled to have been such a help in restoring them to their owner.

Before long, Paddy asked me to visit her in Yorkshire. They were having a small function to raise money for guide-dogs at a local fête and she rightly thought I would like to go with Emma. Through our cassette correspondence, I felt I already knew Paddy, but I wondered if Emma would remember her. As we got off the coach I heard Paddy's voice greeting us, 'Hello, Sheila. How are you?' And it was the signal for Emma to go wild. She leapt all over Paddy, but although she was delighted to see her again, she kept coming back to me as if to say, 'Well, I'm pleased to be here, but I haven't forgotten that I'm your dog.'

Emma and I started to go to work together as soon as we were settled again. At that time I lived in Carlton, on one side of Nottingham, and I worked right over the other side, the Bulwell side of the city. I had to catch two buses, with a walk across the Market Square in the middle of Nottingham in between. The terminus for the first bus was at the bottom of our road, so that part was easy. Emma trotted down the road with her tail in the air – I could feel it brushing my hand as we went along – and, at the same time, I began to learn how sensitive it was possible to be, via the harness, to what she was doing. Through it I could tell whether her ears were up or down, whether she was turning her head left or right, and all sorts of little movements.

We found the stop, and from that moment Emma loved going on buses. It was not just the bus itself, however. One important factor was the admiration she received that morning, and every time we got on a bus henceforth: 'Oh, what a lovely dog. Oh, what a beautiful colour.' And so on. I could sense Emma basking in the glory. She had picked the second seat on the right for me. For some reason, this was the place she always chose on this particular bus. I sat down, and Emma went under the seat. Strangely, this was the only bus on which she had such a preference: it always had to be the same one. After we had been going to work together for about three weeks, we were nearing the bus one morning when I began to pick up the sound of a great commotion going on inside it. As we came alongside I could hear a woman's muffled shout: 'You'll have to get up you know. You can't sit there, I tell you it's Emma's seat. Come on – they'll be here in a minute.'

On other buses, Emma simply went for any empty seat, preferably – in the winter at least – one near the heaters. But since we normally travelled in the rush-hour the buses, apart from our first one, were very often full, so she had to use a different technique. She would drag me along the aisle, nosing everyone else out of the way if there were standing passengers, decide on where she wanted us to sit, then stare at whoever was sitting there until they gave way. To be fair, they normally gave the seat up very quickly, and before the bus was in an uproar. This, of course, appealed to the exhibitionist in Emma. When she was sure she had got her audience, she would turn to me, lay her head across my knee, looking, I imagined, specially devoted and possibly a little pathetic. By this time the entire bus was hers.

But to get back to that first morning. When I walked into the office there was a reception committee waiting. While everyone said 'Hello' to me, they were clearly more interested in seeing what Emma was like. Emma once again responded with great delight, and when I had taken her harness off, took it round, her tail wagging, to show everyone in turn.

So she was a hit straight away, and when the others had gone she inspected her basket, played for a while with a rubber toy I had brought with me to occupy her, then settled down. The telephone had already started going, and soon it was like old times – with the tremendous difference of that reassuring sleeping form under my desk. The morning went on, and in a lull, thinking what a good quiet dog Emma was being, I put my hand down to pat her head. But, where her head should have been, there was nothing. I felt round in a wider circle. Emma had disappeared! I immediately got up and went to feel if my office door was open; sure enough, it was. I called her. No response. All sorts of anxieties began to crowd in on me. Had she got out? What if she had gone into the street? What if she were lost ... what ... then I heard the sound of paws coming down the corridor. Thank goodness. In came Emma. 'Emma,' I said, 'where *have* you been?' Her reply was to push something into my lap. I did not want to believe my fingers. It was a purse. I was horrified. 'Emma! Where did you get that from?' Her reply this time was to do her tattoo bit, bouncing up and down on her forelegs, and swishing me furiously with her tail. The message was clear: 'How about that for brilliance! I've brought you somebody's purse.' Fleetingly, the thought of a four-legged Artful Dodger came to mind. I took the purse from her, and hoped that someone would come to claim it, and accept my excuses.

The owner concerned eventually found out what had happened, and came to claim the purse. But no one would believe that I had not taught Emma to perform the trick, which did nothing to ease my mind about the prospect of the afternoon, or indeed of continuing to work for Industrial Pumps. It was a relief to take Emma out of the office for a run in the local park. This was something I decided I must do every day. Since she worked hard it was only fair that she should have a free run whenever possible.

I sat myself on a bench with my sandwiches, let her off the lead, and she went charging across the grass. I soon heard barking in the distance, and recognized Emma. But every so often she would come back to me, touch my hands with her nose, and then scamper off again. It was something that she never failed to do whenever we went to the park from then on. She was reassuring me: 'I'm here, and I haven't forgotten you.'

That afternoon I sat down at the switchboard, and, in between calls, waited uneasily for the sound of Emma bringing me another gift. But she settled down and slept, and after that did not bring any more presents – at least, not in the office. Perhaps it was her way of making a mark, and returning her welcome. Whatever it was, I was pleased it was over.

The first week went by very happily. Travelling to and from work, in fact, became easier every day. I did not have to give Emma all the lefts and rights in the Square because she soon began to take me straight to the right road and across to the forty-three bus stop. I started to appreciate, and this was something that established itself firmly as time went on, that Emma had only to take any route once and she knew it. I had no sooner discovered this than I found there was a drawback in having such an intelligent dog.

About the middle of the second week we set off for work as usual. I merely said to Emma that we were going to work, and, by now, knew she could do this without any corrections or promptings. We got our first bus, and reached the Market Square. Everything was fine. But when we got to the first road to cross in the Square, Emma sat down instead of going forward. I listened for traffic, and when I thought it was clear, told her to go forward. But she would not move. She simply continued to sit. I could not understand what was going on. I thought that perhaps I had misjudged the traffic, so when it was quiet I told her again. Still she would not go forward. Instead, she got up and turned right, and started taking me along the pavement. 'Emma,' I said, rather desperately, as I was being dragged along, 'where are you taking me? Where's the bus stop? Come on. Bus stop ...' But no, she would not listen, or if she did listen she certainly did not take any notice. We went on, across the road, made a sharp left turn, and crossed another road. Then she sat down again. I had no idea where we were. I had completely lost my sense of direction, and was utterly confused about the pattern I had to keep in my mind in order to reach the bus stop; this was the equivalent of the checks that sighted people, probably unconsciously, make when they are getting from A to B; right at St Mary's Church, past W. H. Smith's, left at the Royal Oak, and so on.

I was not only disappointed in Emma, but slightly upset and annoyed with her as well. 'Emma,' I said crossly, 'we shall be late for work.' How do you tell the boss that it was the dog who made you late? Thinking back, it must have looked a rather comic scene to anyone passing by. 'Excuse me,' I said as the next footsteps approached, 'can you tell me how to get to the forty-three bus stop, please?' There was a silence for a second or two, during which time I thought; they don't know, we really are lost. Then a man's voice, obviously puzzled, said, 'Forty-three bus stop? You're *at* the forty-three bus stop. Your dog's at the foot of the post.' I was relieved, astonished, and utterly baffled. We got on the bus when it came along, and I put the incident out of my mind. Until the following morning.

This time Emma went left instead of right, crossed another road, turned right, crossed a further road, walked along and sat down. We were at the forty-three bus stop again. I was unnerved, but by now getting used to the feeling. At work, I asked Carol, a friend, who I knew came to the office via the Market Square, if there were any roadworks on the route I had originally mapped out. She said no, and no new building either, or any kind of obstruction.

I was totally at a loss. I thought and thought, and then the only possible explanation came to me: Emma, having learnt a route, became bored with having to follow it every day. So she invented variations. From then on she found a series of routes round the Market Square quite independently of any guidance from me, and chose one of them every day. I soon became resigned to this and got up ten minutes earlier just to allow for Emma's possibly making a mistake. But, of course, she never did.

The Rabbit's Ghost Story

RICHARD ADAMS

THE RABBIT'S GHOST STORY

Hazel, (a male rabbit) leader of the rabbit settlement on Watership Down, has defeated a band of rabbits brought to attack him by General Woundwort, dictator of another warren. Some time before, Woundwort's warren, known as Efrafa, attacked another warren at a place called Nutley Copse, destroyed it and forced the survivors to join Efrafa. The General is now believed to be dead, but five of his defeated Efrafans, who surrendered to Hazel and Co., have been allowed to join the Watership Down warren. These five include Groundsel, Coltsfoot and Thistle.

Hazel's band of rabbits include Bigwig and Silver, tough but good-hearted fighters; Blackberry; Pipkin; Fiver, a clairvoyant, 'psychic' rabbit; Bluebell, a joker; Blackavar, an expert patroller in the wild; Dandelion, a story-teller, and Scabious and Threar, two youngsters.

The rabbits have a friend, Kehaar, a seagull, who visits Watership Down from time to time.

RABBIT WORDS

SILFLAY: Feeding above ground.

RAH: A term of respect. 'Hazel-rah' Lord Hazel.

THARN: Frightened silly. Hypnotised with fear.

FRITH: The sun. Also 'God' to rabbits.

MARKS: Different groups of rabbits (only in Efrafa.)

HRAIR: A thousand. An uncountable number.

OUTSKIRTER: A junior rabbit.

EL-AHRAIRAH: The rabbit folk-hero; something like King Arthur or Robin Hood.

HRAKA: Droppings.

HRUDUDU: A tractor.

'WHITE BLINDNESS': Myxomatosis.

OWSLA: A warren's group of senior rabbits.

Of the five Efrafans who surrendered to Fiver in the ravaged Honeycomb on the morning of Woundwort's defeat, four came in a short time to be liked well enough by Hazel and his friends.

Groundsel, indeed, who possessed a skill in patrolling even greater than Blackavar's was, despite his passionate devotion to the General's memory, a valuable addition to the warren, while young Thistle, freed from Efrafan discipline, soon developed a most attractive warmth and gaiety.

The exception was Coltsfoot. Nobody knew what to make of Coltsfoot. A dour, silent rabbit, civil enough to Hazel and Bigwig, but inclined to be distinctly brusque in his dealings with others, he had little enough to say even to his fellow Efrafans. On silflay he was nearly always to be seen grazing yards away from anybody else; and certainly no one would have dreamed of asking him to tell a story.

Hazel, when Bigwig complained to him one day about 'that pestilential fellow with a face as long as a rook's beak,' counselled letting him alone, since that seemed to be what he wanted, and waiting to see how he would go on as he came to feel more at home.

Bluebell, when asked to refrain from jokes at his expense, remarked that he was always mistaking his silent, mournful stare for that of a cow which had got shrunk in the rain.

The winter following that momentous summer turned out unusually mild. December was full of sunny days, bringing out the tiny, white flowers of chickweed and shepherd's purse and even, here and there below the Down, breaking the smooth black knobs of ash buds and disclosing the tiny, dark-red styles along the nut-bush branches.

Kehaar flew in one day amid great rejoicing, and brought with him a friend, one Lekkri, whose speech (as Silver remarked) set a new record for total incomprehensibility. Kehaar, of course, knew nothing of all that had happened since the morning after the great break-out from Efrafa. He heard the tale from Dandelion one windy, cloud-blown afternoon of flying beech leaves and rippling grass, and at the end remarked to the uncomprehending narrator that the Nuthanger cat was 'verser mean dan plenty cormorants': a view which Lekkri corroborated with a rasping croak that made a young rabbit near by jump a foot in the air and bolt for his hole.

Often, on fine mornings, the two could be seen from the north slope of the Down, shining white in the thin sunshine as they foraged together over the great ploughed field below, already green with next year's wheat.

One afternoon towards the end of the month, Blackavar had taken Scabious and young Threar (the son of Fiver) on a training raid to the garden of Ladle Hill House, about a mile away to the west. ('A soft touch,' as he called it). Hazel had felt some anxiety about the youngsters going so far, but had left the decision (which resembled Edward III's 'que l'enfant gagne ses épèrons' at Crecy) to Bigwig as captain of Owsla. They were not back by twilight and Hazel, after watching with Bigwig in the chilly December nightfall until it was almost completely dark, came down into the Honeycomb in some anxiety.

'Don't worry, Hazel-rah,' said Bigwig cheerfully. 'Likely as not Blackavar's keeping them out all night for the experience.'

'But he told you he wouldn't,' answered Hazel. 'Don't you remember he said –'

Just then there was a scuffling from up Kehaar's run, and after a few moments the three adventurers appeared, muddy and tired, but otherwise, to all appearances, none the worse.

Scabious, however, who seemed very much subdued, lay down at once on the floor where he was.

'What kept you?' asked Hazel rather sharply.

Blackavar said nothing. He had the air of a leader who is reluctant to speak ill of his subordinates.

'It was my fault, Hazel-rah,' said Scabious, rather jerkily. 'I had a – a nasty turn on the Down, coming back. I don't know what to make of it, I'm sure. Blackavar says –'

'Stupid young fellow, he's been listening to too many stories,' said Blackavar. 'Now look, Scabious, you're home and safe. Why not leave it there?'

'What was it?' persisted Hazel, in a more kindly tone.

'Oh, he thinks he saw the General, or the General's ghost, out on the down,' said Blackavar impatiently. 'I've told him –'

'I *did*,' said Scabious. 'Blackavar told me to go and look ahead, round some bushes, and I was out there by myself when I saw him, all black round the ears – a huge, great – just the way they tell you –'

'And *I've* told *you* that was a hare,' interrupted Blackavar with some annoyance. 'Frith on a cow, I saw it myself! Do you think I don't know what a hare looks like? Couldn't get him to move until I kicked him,' he added to Bigwig in an undertone. 'Talk about tharn –'

'It *was* a ghost,' said Scabious, but with less conviction. 'Perhaps it was a ghost-hare –'

'I don't know about ghost-hares,' said Bluebell, 'but I tell you, the other night I nearly met a ghost-flea. It must have been one, because I woke up bitten like a burnet, and I searched and searched and couldn't find it anywhere. Just think, all white and shining, this fearful phantom flea –'

Hazel had gone over to Scabious and was gently nuzzling his shoulder.
'Look,' he said, 'that wasn't a ghost – understand? I've never in my life
known a rabbit that's seen a ghost.'

'You have,' said a voice from the other side of the Honeycomb.
Everyone looked round in surprise. It was Coltsfoot who had spoken. He
was sitting by himself in a recess between two beech-roots: together with
his customary silence, the position seemed to set him apart and, as it
were, to confer upon him a kind of remoteness and authority, so that even
Hazel, bent as he was upon reassuring young Scabious, said no more,
waiting to hear what would follow.

'You mean *you've* seen a ghost?' asked Dandelion, quick to smell a
story. But Coltsfoot, so it seemed, needed no further stimulation, now
that he had found his tongue. Like the ancient mariner, he knew those
who must hear him; and he had a less reluctant audience, for under his
dark compulsion the whole Honeycomb fell silent and listened as he went
on.

'I don't know whether you all know that I'm not an Efrafan born. I was
born at Nutley Copse, the warren the General destroyed. I was in the
Owsla there and I would have fought as hard as the rest, but I happened
to be a long way out on silflay when the attack came and they took me
prisoner at once. I was put in the Neck Mark, as you can see, and then last
summer I was one of those picked for the attack on Watership Down.

'But none of that has to do with what I said to your chief rabbit just
now.' He fell silent. 'Well, what has?' asked Dandelion.

'There was a place across the fields, not very far from Nutley Copse,'
went on Coltsfoot. 'A kind of little, shallow dingle all overgrown with
brambles and thorn trees – so we were told – and full of old scrapes and
rabbit-holes. They were all empty and cold; and no Nutley Copse rabbit
would go near that place, not if there were hrair weasels after him.

'All we knew – and the story had been handed down for Frith knows
how long – was that something very bad had happened to rabbits there,
long, long ago – something to do with men, or boys – and that the place
was haunted and evil. The Owsla believed it, every one of them, so of
course the rest of the warren believed it too. As far as we knew, no rabbit
had flashed his tail there in living memory, or long before that. Only some
said that squealing had been heard, late in the evening dusk and on foggy
mornings. I can't say, though, that I ever thought about it much. I just
did what everyone else did – kept away.

'Now during my first year, when I was an outskirter at Nutley Copse, I
had a very thin time, and so did two or three of my friends. And the long
and short of it was that one day we decided we were going to move out and

find a better home. There were two other young bucks with me, my friend Burdock and a rather timid rabbit named Fescue. And there was a doe too – Mian, I think she was called. We set out about ni-Frith one rather cold day in April.'

Coltsfoot paused, chewed his pellets for a time, as though considering his words, and then continued.

'Everything went wrong with that expedition. Before evening it turned bitterly cold and the rain came down in sheets. We ran into a foraging cat and were lucky to get away. We were completely inexperienced. We had no idea where we meant to go and before long we lost all sense of direction. We couldn't see the sun, you understand, and when night fell there were no stars either. And then next morning a stoat found us – a big dog-stoat.

'I don't know what they do to you – I've never met one since, El-ahrairah be praised – but we all three just sat there helplessly while it killed Mian – she never made a sound. We got away somehow, but Fescue was in an awful state, crying and carrying on, poor little chap. And in the end, some time after ni-Frith on the second day, we decided to go back to the home warren.

'It was easier said than done. I believe now that we wandered in circles for a long time. But anyway, by evening we were as lost as ever and just wandering on in a kind of hopeless way, when all of a sudden I came down a slope and through a bramble bush and there was a rabbit – a stranger – quite close by. He was at silflay, browsing over the grass, and I could see his hole – several holes, in fact – beyond him, on the other side of the little dell we were in. I felt terribly relieved and glad and I was just going over to speak to him when all of a sudden something made me stop. And it was as I stopped and looked at him that it came over me where it was that we must have stumbled into.

'The wind – what there was – was blowing from him towards us, and as he browsed he stopped and passed hraka. I wasn't 10 lengths away, and he gave off no smell whatever – nothing – not the faintest trace. We'd come blundering through the brambles straight up in front of him and he hadn't looked up or given any sign of having noticed us. And then I saw something which frightens me even now – I can never get it out of my mind. A fly – a big bluebottle – flew down right on his eye. He didn't blink or even shake his head. He went on feeding and the fly – it – it disappeared; it vanished. A moment later he'd hopped his own length forward and I saw it on the grass where his head had been.

'Fescue was beside me and I heard him give a little, quick moan. And it was when I heard that that I realised there was no other sound in that dell where we were. It was a fine evening with a light breeze, but there wasn't a blackbird singing, not a leaf rustling – nothing. The earth round the rabbit holes was cold and hard – not a scratch or a mark anywhere. I knew then what I was seeing and all my senses clouded over – sight, smell – I felt a sort of surge of faintness pour up and through my body. The whole world seemed to topple away and leave me alone in some dreadful place of silence, where there were no smells. We were in nowhere. I caught a glimpse of Burdock beside me and he looked like a rabbit strangling in a snare.

'It was then that we saw the boy. He was crawling on his stomach through the bushes down a little to one side of us – down-wind of the rabbit on the grass. He was a big boy, and all I can say is that men may have looked like that once, but from what little I've seen of them they don't any more. There was a kind of dirty, far-away wildness about him, like the place itself. His clothes were foul and torn. He had old boots too big for him and a stupid, cruel face with bad teeth and great warts on one cheek. And he, too made no sound and had no smell.

'In one hand he was holding a forked stick with a sort of loop hanging from it, and as I watched he put a stone into it and pulled it back nearly to his eye. Then the stone flew out and hit the rabbit on the right hind-leg. I heard the bone break and the rabbit leapt up and screamed. Yes, I heard that all right – I still hear it, and dream about it too. Can you imagine what a breathless, a lungless scream might be like? It seemed to be in the air rather than to come from the rabbit kicking on the grass. It was as though the whole place had screamed.

'The boy stood up, cackling, and now the hollow seemed to be full of rabbits we couldn't see, all running for those cold, empty holes.

'You could see he was enjoying what he'd done – not just that he'd shot himself a rabbit, but that it was hurt and screaming. He went over to it, but he didn't kill it. He stood looking down at it and watching it kicking. The grass was bloody, but his boots left no mark, either on the grass or the mud.

'What had to happen next I don't know. Thank Frith I'll never know. I believe my heart would have stopped – I should have died. But suddenly, like a noise coming from a long way outside when you're underground, I heard men's voices approaching, smelt a white stick burning. And I was glad – yes, I was *glad* as a goldfinch on the tall grass – to hear those voices and smell that white stick. A moment later they came pushing through the flowering blackthorn, scattering the white petals all over the ground. There were two of them, big, flesh-smelling men, and they saw the boy – yes, they saw him and called out to him.

'How can I explain to you the difference between those men and the rest of that place? It was only when they came shoving in, rasping on the thorns, that I understood that the rabbit and the boy – and – everything there – they were like acorns falling from an oak tree. I saw a hrududu once roll down a slope by itself. Its man had left it on a slope and I suppose he'd done something wrong – it just went slowly rolling down into the brook and there it stopped.

'That's what they were like. They were doing what they had to do – they had no choice – they'd done it all before – they'd done it again and again – there was no light in their eyes – they weren't creatures that could see or feel –'

Coltsfoot stopped, choking. In dead silence Fiver left his place and lay down beside him, between the tree-roots, speaking in a very low voice which no one else could hear. After a long pause Coltsfoot sat up, shook his ears and went on.

'Those – those – sights – those things – the rabbit and the boy – they melted, even as the men spoke. They vanished, like frost on the grass when you breathe on it. And the men – they noticed nothing strange. I believe now that they saw the boy and spoke to him as part of a kind of dream, and that as he and his poor victim vanished so the dream vanished, and they remembered nothing of it. Well, be that as it may, they'd evidently come there because they'd heard the rabbit squeal, and you could see why at once.'

'One of them was carrying the body of a rabbit dead of the white blindness, I saw its poor eyes and I could see, too, that the body was still warm. I don't know whether you know how men go about this dirty work, but what they do is to put the still-warm body of a dead rabbit down a hole in a warren before the fleas have left the ears. Then as the body turns cold, the fleas go to other rabbits, who catch the white blindness from them. There's nothing you can do but run away – and only that if you realise in time what the danger is.

'The men stood looking round them and pointing at the deserted holes. Neither of them was the farmer – we all knew what he looked like. He must have asked them to come and bring the body of the rabbit and then been too lazy to go out with them; just told them where to go, and they weren't too sure about the exact place. You could see that from the way they looked about.

'After a little one of them trod out his white stick and started burning another, and then they went over to one of the holes and pushed the body right down it with a long pole. After that they went away.

'We went away, too – I can't remember how. Fescue was as good as mad – when we got back to Nutley Copse he just lay tharn in the first burrow he found and wouldn't come out next day or the day after. I don't know what happened to him in the end – I never saw him after that. Burdock and I managed to get hold of a burrow of our own later that summer and we shared it for a long time. We never spoke of what we'd seen, even when we were alone together. Burdock was killed later, when the Efrafans attacked the warren.

'I know you'll all think I'm unfriendly. Perhaps you've been thinking I don't like anyone here – that I'm against you. It isn't – now you know it isn't – oh, what haunts me always is that I keep thinking – does that poor rabbit have to go through it all again and again and again, for ever? The stone – the pain – and might we too –'

The big, burly Coltsfoot lay sobbing like a kitten. Pipkin, too, was crying and Hazel could feel Blackberry trembling against his side in the dark of the Honeycomb. Then Fiver spoke, with a quiet assurance that cut through the horror in the burrow like the calling of a plover across bare fields at night.

'No, Coltsfoot. That's not the way of it. It's true enough that there are many terrible and dangerous things in that land beyond, where you went with your friends that night; but in the end, however far away it may seem, Frith keeps his promise to El-ahrairah. I know this, and you can believe it. Those weren't real creatures that you saw. Only, in places where bad things have happened, sometimes a kind of strange force lingers on, like lonely pools of water after a storm; and now and then some of us fall into those pools. What you saw wasn't real – you said so yourself – it was an echo you heard, not a voice. And remember, it saved your warren that evening. Where else would that body have been put otherwise – and who can understand all that Frith knows and brings to pass?'

He was silent and, although Coltsfoot made no answer, himself said no more. Evidently he felt that Coltsfoot must take it from there on his own, without repetition or argument to convince him. After a little the others dispersed to their sleeping-burrows, leaving Coltsfoot and Fiver alone.

Coltsfoot did take it. For several days afterwards he was to be seen at silflay with Fiver, quietly browsing over the grass, talking and listening to his new friend.

As the winter passed his spirits gradually lightened and by the following spring he had become quite a talkative and cheerful rabbit, not infrequently to be found telling stories to kittens under the bank.

'Fiver,' said Bluebell one evening in early April, when the scent of the first violets was drifting under the new beech leaves, 'do you think you could order a nice, gentle, unfrightening sort of ghost for me? Only I've been thinking – they seem almost to do quite a bit of good in the long run.'

'The *very* long run,' answered Fiver, 'for those who can run without stopping.'

Tuppenny and The Travelling Circus

BEATRIX POTTER

Tuppenny was too depressed to argue

Illustration by Beatrix Potter

TUPPENNY AND THE TRAVELLING
CIRCUS

In the Land of Green Ginger there is a town called Marmalade, which is inhabited exclusively by guinea-pigs. They are of all colours, and of two sorts. The common, or garden, guinea-pigs are the most numerous. They have short hair, and they run errands and twitter. The guinea-pigs of the other variety are called Abyssinian Cavies. They have long hair and side whiskers, and they walk upon their toes.

The common guinea-pigs admire and envy the whiskers of the Abyssinian Cavies; they would give anything to be able to make their own short hair grow long. So there was excitement and twittering amongst the short-haired guinea-pigs when Messrs. Ratton and Scratch, Hair Specialists, sent out hundreds of advertisements by post, describing their new elixir.

The Abyssinian Cavies who required no hair stimulant were affronted by the advertisements. They found the twitterings tiresome.

During the night between March 31st and April 1st, Messrs. Ratton and Scratch arrived in Marmalade. They placarded the walls of the town with posters; and they set up a booth in the market place. Next morning quantities of elegantly stoppered bottles were displayed upon the booth. The rats stood in front of the booth, and distributed handbills describing the wonderful effects of their new quintessence. 'Come buy, come buy, come buy! Buy a bottleful and try it on a door-knob! We guarantee that it will grow a crop of onions!' shouted Messrs. Ratton and Scratch. Crowds of short-haired guinea-pigs swarmed around the booth.

The Abyssinian Cavies sniffed, and passed by upon their toes. They remarked that Mr. Ratton was slightly bald. The short-haired guinea-pigs continued to crowd around, twittering and asking questions; but they hesitated to buy. The price of a very small bottle holding only two thimblefuls was ten peppercorns.

And besides this high charge there was an uncomfortable doubt as to what the stuff was made of. The Abyssinian Cavies spread ill-natured reports that it was manufactured from slugs. Mr. Scratch emphatically contradicted this slander; he asserted that it was distilled from the purest Arabian moonshine; 'And Arabia is quite close to Abyssinia,' said Mr. Scratch with a wink, pointing to a particularly long-haired Abyssinian Cavy. 'Come buy a sample bottle can't you! Listen to these testimonials from our grateful customers,' said Mr. Ratton. He proceeded to read aloud a number of letters. But he did not specifically deny a rumour that got about; about a certain notorious nobleman, a much married nobleman, who had bought a large bottle of the quintessence by persuasion of the first of his eight wives. This nobleman – so the story ran – had used the hair stimulant with remarkable results. He had grown a magnificent beard. But the beard was blue. Which may be fashionable in Arabia; but the short-haired guinea-pigs were dubious. Messrs. Ratton and Scratch shouted themselves hoarse. 'Come buy a sample bottle half price, and try it for salad dressing! The cucumbers will grow of themselves while you are mixing the hair oil and vinegar! Buy a sample bottle, can't you?' shouted Messrs. Ratton and Scratch. The short-haired guinea-pigs determined to purchase one bottle of the smallest size, to be tried upon Tuppenny.

Tuppenny was a short-haired guinea-pig of dilapidated appearance. He suffered from toothache and chilblains; and he had never had much hair, not even of the shortest. It was thin and patchy. Whether this was the result of chilblains or of ill-treatment is uncertain. He was an object, whatever the cause. Obviously he was a suitable subject for experiment. 'His appearance can scarcely become worse, provided he does not turn blue,' said his friend Henry P.; 'let us subscribe for a small bottle, and apply it as directed.'

So Henry P. and nine other guinea-pigs bought a bottle and ran in a twittering crowd towards Tuppenny's house. On the way, they overtook Tuppenny going home. They explained to him that out of sympathy they had subscribed for a bottle of moonshine to cure his toothache and chilblains, and that they would rub it on for him as Mrs. Tuppenny was out.

Tuppenny was too depressed to argue; he allowed himself to be led away. Henry P. and the nine other guinea-pigs poured the whole bottleful over Tuppenny, and put him to bed. They wore gloves themselves while applying the quintessence. Tuppenny was quite willing to go to bed; he felt chilly and damp.

Presently Mrs. Tuppenny came in; she complained about the sheets. Henry P. and the other guinea-pigs went away. After tea they returned at 5.30. Mrs. Tuppenny said nothing had happened.

The short-haired guinea-pigs took a walk; they looked in again at 6. Mrs. Tuppenny was abusive. She said there was no change. At 6.30 they called again to inquire. Mrs. Tuppenny was still more abusive. She said Tuppenny was very hot. Next time they came she said the patient was in a fever, and felt as if he were growing a tail. She slammed the door in their faces and said she would not open it again for anybody.

Henry P. and the other guinea-pigs were perturbed. They betook themselves to the market place, where Messrs. Ratton and Scratch were still trying to sell bottles by lamplight, and they asked anxiously whether there were any risk of tails growing? Mr. Scratch burst into ribald laughter; and Mr. Ratton said – 'No sort of tail except pigtails on the head!'

During the night Messrs. Ratton and Scratch packed up their booth and departed from the town of Marmalade.

Next morning at daybreak a crowd of guinea-pigs collected on Tuppenny's doorstep. More and more arrived until Mrs. Tuppenny came out with a scrubbing brush and a pail of water. In reply to inquiries from a respectful distance, she said that Tuppenny had had a disturbed night. Further she would not say, except that he was unable to keep on his nightcap. No more could be ascertained, until, providentially, Mrs. Tuppenny discovered that she had nothing for breakfast. She went out to buy a carrot.

Henry P. and a crowd of other guinea-pigs swarmed into the house, as soon as she was round the corner of the street. They found Tuppenny out of bed, sitting on a chair, looking frightened. At least, presumably it was Tuppenny, but he looked different. His hair was over his ears and nose. And that was not all; for whilst they were talking to him, his hair grew down onto his empty plate. It grew something alarming. It was quite nice hair and the proper colour; but Tuppenny said he felt funny; sore all over, as if his hair were being brushed back to front; and prickly and hot, like needles and pins; and altogether uncomfortable.

And well he might! His hair – it grew, and it grew, and it grew; faster and faster and nobody knew how to stop it! Messrs. Ratton and Scratch had gone away and left no address. If they possessed an antidote there was no way of obtaining it. All day that day, and for several days – still the hair kept growing. Mrs. Tuppenny cut it, and cut it, and stuffed pincushions with it, and pillow cases and bolsters; but as fast as she cut it – it grew again. When Tuppenny went out he tumbled over it; and the rude little guinea-pig boys ran after him, shouting 'Old Whiskers!' His life became a burden.

Then Mrs. Tuppenny began to pull it out. The effect of the quintessence was beginning to wear off, if only she would have exercised a little patience; but she was tired of cutting; so she pulled. She pulled so painfully and shamelessly that Tuppenny could not stand it. He determined to run away – away from the hair pulling and the chilblains and the long-haired and the short-haired guinea-pigs, away and away, so far away that he would never come back.

So that is how it happened that Tuppenny left his home in the town of Marmalade, and wandered into the world alone.

In after years Tuppenny never had any clear recollection of his adventures while he was running away. It was like a bad mixed up dream that changes into morning sunshine and is forgotten. A long, long journey: noisy, jolting, terrifying; too frightened and helpless to understand anything that happened before the journey's end. The first thing that he remembered was a country lane, a steep winding lane always climbing up hill. Tuppenny ran and ran, splashing through the puddles with little bare feet. The wind blew cold against him; he wrapped his hands in his mop of hair, glad to feel its pleasant warmth over his ears and nose. It had stopped growing, and his chilblains had disappeared. Tuppenny felt like a new guinea-pig. For the first time he smelt the air of the hills. What matter if the wind were chilly; it blew from the mountains. The lane led to a wide common, with hillocks and hollows and clumps of bushes. The short cropped turf would soon be gay with wild flowers; even in early April it was sweet. Tuppenny felt as though he could run for miles. But night was coming. The sun was going down in a frosty orange sunset behind purple clouds – was it clouds, or was it the hills? He looked for shelter, and saw smoke rising behind some tall savin bushes.

Tuppenny advanced cautiously, and discovered a curious little encampment. There were two vehicles, unharnessed; a small shaggy pony was grazing nearby. One was a two-wheeled cart, with a tilt, or hood, made of canvas stretched over hoops. The other was a tiny four-wheeled caravan. It was painted yellow picked out with red. Upon the sides were these words in capital letters – 'ALEXANDER AND WILLIAM'S CIRCUS.' Upon another board was printed – The Pigmy Elephant! The Learned Pig! The Fat Dormouse of Salisbury! Live Polecats and Weasels!

The caravan had windows with muslin curtains, just like a house. There were outside steps up to the back door, and a chimney on the roof. A canvas screen fastened to light posts sheltered the encampment from the wind. The smoke which Tuppenny had seen did not come from the chimney; there was a cheerful fire of sticks burning on the ground in the midst of the camp.

Several animals sat beside it, or busied themselves with cooking. One of them was a white West Highland terrier. When he noticed Tuppenny he commenced to bark. The pony stopped grazing, and looked round. A bird, who had been running up and down on the grass, flew up to the roof of the caravan.

The little dog came forward barking. Tuppenny turned and fled. He heard yap! yap! yap! and grunt, grunt, grunt! and pattering feet behind him. He tripped over his hair, and fell in a twittering heap.

A cold nose and a warm tongue examined Tuppenny and turned him over. He gazed up in terror at the little dog and a small black pig, who were sniffing all over him. 'What? what? what? Whatever sort of animal is it, Sandy?' 'Never saw the like! it seems to be all hair! What do you call yourself, fuzzy wig?' 'P-p-please sir, I'm not a fuzzy wig, a fuzzy pig, a please sir I'm a guinea-pig.' 'What, what? a pig? Where's your tail?' said the little black pig. 'Please Sir, no tail, I never had – no guinea-pig – no tail – no guinea-pigs have tails,' twittered Tuppenny in great alarm. 'What? what? no tails? I had an uncle with no tail, but that was accidental. Carry him to the fire, Sandy; he is cold and wet.'

Sandy lifted Tuppenny delicately by the scruff of the neck; he held his own head high and curled his tail over his back, to avoid treading on Tuppenny's hair. Paddy Pig scampered in front; 'What! what! we've found a new long-haired animal! Put more sticks on the fire Jenny Ferret! Set him down beside the dormouse, Sandy; let him warm his toes.'

The person addressed as Jane Ferret was an oldish person, about twelve inches high when she stood upright. She wore a cap, a brown stuff dress, and always a small crochet cross-over. She filled up the tea-pot from a kettle on the fire, and gave Tuppenny a mug of hot balm tea and a baked apple. He was much comforted by the warmth of the fire, and by their kindness. In reply to questions he said his name was 'Tuppenny'; but he seemed to have forgotten where he came from. Only he remembered vaguely that his hair had been a grievance.

The circus company admired it prodigiously. 'It is truly mar-veel-ious,' said the Dormouse stretching out a small pink hand, and touching a damp draggled tress. 'Do you use hairpins?' 'I'm afraid, I'm sorry, I haven't any,' twittered Tuppenny apologetically. 'Let hairpins be provided – hair – pins,' said the Dormouse, falling fast asleep. 'I will go fetch some in the morning if you will lend me your purse,' said Iky Shepster the starling, who was pecking a hole in the turf to hide something. 'You will do nothing of the sort. Bring me my teaspoon, please,' said Jenny Ferret. The starling chittered and laughed, and flew to the top of the caravan where he roosted at night.

The sun had set. The red fire-light danced and flickered round the camp circle. The pony dozed beside the caravan, lazily whisking his long tail. Sandy was lying stretched before the fire and panting with the heat. He watched Tuppenny with bright brown eyes, through his shaggy white eyebrows. 'Tuppenny, where are you going to?' 'I have forgotten.' 'What do you intend to do with yourself?' 'I don't know.' 'Let him ride in the tilt-cart,' said Pony Billy; they were the first words that he had spoken. 'Tuppenny, will you come with us? You shall have your share of the fun, and peppercorns, and sugar candy. Come with us and join the circus, Tuppenny!' cried all the little animals. 'I think I would like to, yes please, thank you,' twittered Tuppenny shyly. 'Quite right, quite right! what! what!' said the small black pig, 'Lucky you found us today; we will be over the hills and far away tomorrow.'

'Wake up, wake up! Xarifa Dormouse! get into your sleeping box. And you, Tuppenny, shall go to bed in this hamper. Good night!'

Mary

JOHN COLLIER

MARY

There was in those days – I hope it is there still – a village called Ufferleigh, lying all among the hills and downs of North Hampshire. In every cottage garden there was a giant apple tree, and when these trees were hung red with fruit, and the newly lifted potatoes lay gleaming between bean-row and cabbage-patch, a young man walked into the village who had never been there before.

He stopped in the lane just under Mrs. Hedges's gate, and looked up into her garden. Rosie, who was picking the beans, heard his tentative cough, and turned and leaned over the hedge to hear what he wanted. 'I was wondering,' said he, 'if there was anybody in the village who had a lodging to let.'

He looked at Rosie, whose cheeks were redder than the apples, and whose hair was the softest yellow imaginable. 'I was wondering,' said he in amendment, 'if *you* had.'

Rosie looked back at him. He wore a blue jersey such as seafaring men wear, but he seemed hardly like a seafaring man. His face was brown and plain and pleasant, and his hair was black. He was shabby and he was shy, but there was something about him that made it very certain he was not just a tramp. 'I'll ask,' said Rosie.

With that she ran for her mother, and Mrs. Hedges came out to interview the young man. 'I've got to be near Andover for a week,' said he, 'but somehow I didn't fancy staying right in the town.'

'There's a bed,' said Mrs. Hedges. 'If you don't mind having your meals with us –'

'Why, surely, ma'am,' said he. 'There's nothing I'd like better.'

Everything was speedily arranged; Rosie picked another handful of beans, and in an hour he was seated with them at supper. He told them his name was Fred Baker, but apart from that, he was so polite that he could hardly speak, and in the end Mrs. Hedges had to ask him outright what his business was. 'Why, ma'am,' said he, looking her straight in the face, 'I've done one thing and another ever since I was so high, but I heard an old proverb once, how to get on in the world. 'Feed 'em or amuse 'em,' it said. So that's what I do, ma'am. I travel with a pig.'

Mrs. Hedges said she had never heard of such a thing.

'You surprise me,' said he. 'Why, there are some in London, they tell me, making fortunes on the halls. Spell, count, add up, answer questions, anything. But let them wait,' said he, smiling, 'till they see Mary.'

'Is that the name of your pig?' asked Rosie.

'Well,' said Fred, shyly, 'it's what I call her just between ourselves like. To her public, she's Zola. Sort of Frenchified, I thought. Spicy, if you'll excuse the mention of it. But in the caravan I call her Mary.'

'You live in a caravan?' cried Rosie, delighted by the doll's house idea.

'We do,' said he. 'She has her bunk, and I have mine.'

'I don't think I should like that,' said Mrs. Hedges. 'Not a pig. No.'

'She's as clean,' said he, 'as a new-born babe. And as for company, well, you'd say she's human. All the same, it's a bit of a wandering life for her – up hill and down dale, as the saying goes. Between you and me I shan't be satisfied till I get her into one of these big London theatres. You can see us in the West End!'

'I should like the caravan best,' said Rosie, who seemed to have a great deal to say for herself, all of a sudden.

'It's pretty,' said Fred. 'Curtains, you know. Pot of flowers. Little stove. Somehow I'm used to it. Can't hardly think of myself staying at one of them big hotels. Still, Mary's got her career to think of. I can't stand in the way of her talent, so that's that.'

'Is she big,' asked Rosie.

'It's not her size,' said he. 'No more than Shirley Temple. It's her brains and personality. Clever as a wagon-load of monkeys! You'd like her. She'd like you, I reckon. Yes, I reckon she would. Sometimes I'm afraid I'm a bit slow by way of company for her, never having had much to do with the ladies.'

'Don't tell me,' said Mrs. Hedges archly, as convention required.

''Tis so, ma'am,' said he. 'Always on the move, you see, ever since I was a nipper. Baskets and brooms, pots and pans, then some acrobat stuff, then Mary. Never two days in the same place. It don't give you the time to get acquainted.'

'You're going to be here a whole week, though,' said Rosie artlessly, but at once her red cheeks blushed a hundred times redder than before, for Mrs. Hedges gave her a sharp look, which made her see that her words might have been taken the wrong way.

Fred, however, had noticed nothing. 'Yes,' said he. 'I shall be here a week. And why? Mary ran a nail in her foot in the marketplace, Andover. Finished her act – and collapsed. Now she's at the vet's, poor creature.'

'Oh, poor thing!' cried Rosie.

'I was half afraid,' said he, 'it was going wrong on her. But it seems she'll pull round all right, and I took the opportunity to have the van repaired a bit, and soon we'll be on the road again. I shall go in and see her. Maybe I can find some blackberries, to take her by way of a relish.'

'Colley Bottom,' said Rosie. 'That's the place where they grow big and juicy.'

'Ah! If I knew where it was –' said Fred tentatively.

'Perhaps, in the morning, if she's got time, she'll show you,' said Mrs. Hedges, who began to feel kindly disposed towards the young man.

In the morning, surely enough, Rosie did have time, and she showed Fred the place; and helped him pick the berries. Returning from Andover, later in the day, Fred reported that Mary had tucked into them a fair treat, and he had little doubt that, if she could have spoken; she would have sent her special thanks. Nothing is more affecting than the gratitude of a dumb animal, and Rosie was impelled to go every morning with Fred to pick a few more berries for the invalid pig.

On these excursions Fred told her a great deal more about Mary, a bit about the caravan, and a little about himself. She saw that he was very bold and knowing in some ways, but incredibly simple and shy in others. This, she felt, showed he had a good heart.

The end of the week seemed to come very soon, and all at once they were coming back from Colley Bottom for the last time. Fred said he would never forget Ufferleigh, nor the nice time he had had there.

'You ought to send us a postcard when you're on your travels,' said Rosie.

'Yes,' he said. 'That's an idea. I will.'

'Yes, do,' said Rosie.

'Yes,' said he again. 'I will. Do you know, I was altogether down-hearted at going away, but now I'm half wishing I was on the road again already. So I could be sending that card right away,' said he.

'At that rate,' said Rosie, looking the other way, 'you might as well make it a letter.'

'Ah!' said he. 'And do you know what I should feel like putting at the bottom of that letter? If you was my young lady, that is. Which, of course, you're not. Me never having had one.

'What?' said Rosie.

'A young lady,' said he.

'But what would you put?' said she.

'Ah!' said he. 'What I'd put. Do you know what I'd put? If – *if*, mind you – if you was my young lady?'

'No,' said she, 'what?'

'I don't hardly like to tell you,' said he.

'Go on,' she said. 'You don't want to be afraid.'

'All right,' said he. 'Only mind you, it's *if*.' And with his stick he traced three crosses in the dust.

'If I was anybody's young lady,' said Rosie, 'I shouldn't see anything wrong in that. After all, you've got to move with the times.'

Neither of them said another word, for two of the best reasons in the world. First, they were unable to; second, it was not necessary. They walked on with their faces as red as fire, in an agony of happiness.

Fred had a word with Mrs. Hedges, who had taken a fancy to him from the start. Not that she had not always looked down upon caravan people, and could have been knocked over with a feather, had anyone suggested, at any earlier date, that she would allow a daughter of hers to marry into such company. But right was right: this Fred Baker was different, as anyone with half an eye could see. He had kept himself to himself, almost to a fault, for his conversation showed that he was as innocent as a new-born babe. Moreover, several knowledgeable people in the village had agreed that his ambitions for Mary, his pig, were in no way unjustified. Everyone had heard of such talented creatures, reclining on snow-white sheets in the best hotels of the metropolis, drinking champagne like milk, and earning for their fortunate owners ten pounds, or ever twenty pounds, a week.

So Mrs. Hedges smilingly gave her consent, and Rosie became Fred's real, genuine, proper young lady. He was to save all he could during the winter, and she to stitch and sing. In the spring, he would come back and they were to get married.

'At Easter,' said he.

'No,' said Mrs. Hedges, counting on her fingers. 'In May. Then tongues can't wag, caravan or no caravan.'

Fred had not the faintest idea what she was driving at, for he had lived so much alone that no one had told him certain things that every young man should know. However, he well realized that this was an unusually short engagement for Ufferleigh, and represented a great concession to the speed and dash of the entertainment industry, so he respectfully agreed, and set off on his travels.

'*My Darling Rosie,*

Well here we are in Painswick having had a good night Saturday at Evesham. Mary cleverer than ever that goes without saying now spells four new words thirty-six in all and when I say now Mary how do you like Painswick or Evesham or wherever it is she picks F I N E it goes down very well. She is in the best of health and hope you are the same. Seems to understand every word I say more like a human being every day. Well I suppose I must be getting our bit of supper ready she always sets up her cry for that specially when I am writing to you.

With true love FRED XXX'

Mary

In May the apple trees were all in bloom, so it was an apple-blossom wedding, which in those parts is held to be an assurance of flowery days. Afterwards they took the bus to the market town, to pick up the caravan, which stood in a stable yard. On the way Fred asked Rosie to wait a moment, and dived into the confectioner's shop. He came out with a huge box of chocolates. Rosie smiled all over her face with joy. 'For me?' she said.

'Yes,' said he. 'To give to her as soon as she claps eyes on you. They're her weakness. I want you two to be real pals.'

'All right,' said Rosie, who was the best-hearted girl in the world.

The next moment they turned into the yard: there was the caravan.

'Oh, it's lovely!' cried Rosie.

'Now you'll see her,' said Fred.

At the sound of his voice a falsetto squeal rose from within.

'Here we are, old lady,' said Fred, opening the door. 'Here's a friend of mine come to help look after you. Look, she's brought you something you'll fancy.'

Rosie saw a middle-sized pig, flesh-coloured, neat, and with a smart collar. It had a small and rather calculating eye. Rosie offered the chocolates: they were accepted without any very effusive acknowledgement.

Fred put the old horse in, and soon they were off, jogging up the long hills to the west. Rosie sat beside Fred on the driving seat; Mary took her afternoon nap. Soon the sky began to redden where the road divided the woods on the far hill-top. Fred turned into a green lane, and they made their camp.

He lit the stove, and Rosie put on the potatoes. They took a lot of peeling, for it seemed that Mary ate with gusto. Rosie put a gigantic rice pudding into the oven, and soon had the rest of the meal prepared.

Fred set the table. He laid three places.

'I say,' said Rosie.

'What?' said Fred.

'Does she eat along with us?' said Rosie. 'A pig?'

Fred turned quite pale. He beckoned her outside the caravan. 'Don't say a thing like that,' said he. 'She won't never take to you if you say a thing like that. Didn't you see her give you a look?'

'Yes, I did,' said Rosie. 'All the same – Well, never mind, Fred. I don't care, really. I just thought I did.'

'You wait,' said Fred. 'You're thinking of ordinary pigs. Mary's different.'

Certainly Mary seemed a comparatively tidy eater. All the same, she gave Rosie one or two very odd glances from under her silky straw-coloured lashes. She seemed to hock her rice pudding about a bit with the end of her nose.

'What's up, old girl?' said Fred. 'Didn't she put enough sugar in the pudden? Never mind – can't get everything right first time.'

Mary, with a rather cross hiccup, settled herself on her bunk. 'Let's go out,' said Rosie, 'and have a look at the moon.'

'I suppose we might,' said Fred. 'Shan't be long, Mary. Just going about as far as that gate down the lane.' Mary grunted morosely and turned her face to the wall.

Rosie and Fred went out and leaned over the gate. The moon, at least, was all that it should be.

'Seems funny, being married and all,' said Rosie softly.

'Seems all right to me,' said Fred.

'Remember them crosses you drew in the dirt in the road that day?' said Rosie.

'That I do,' said Fred.

'And all them you put in the letters?' said Rosie.

'All of 'em,' said Fred.

'Kisses, that's what they're supposed to stand for,' said Rosie.

'So they say,' said Fred.

'You haven't given me one, not since we was married,' said Rosie. 'Don't you like it?'

'That I do,' said Fred. 'Only, I don't know –'

'What?' said Rosie.

'It makes me feel all queer,' said Fred, 'when I kiss you. As if I wanted –'

'What?' said Rosie.

'I dunno,' said Fred. 'I don't know if it's I want to eat you all up, or what.'

'Try and find out, they say,' said Rosie.

A delicious moment followed. In the very middle of it a piercing squeal rose from the caravan. Fred jumped as if he were shot.

'Oh dear,' he cried. 'She's wondering what's up. Here I come, old girl! Here I come! It's her bed-time, you see. Here I come to tuck you in!'

Mary, with an air of some petulance, permitted this process. Rosie stood by. 'I suppose we'd better make it lights out,' said Fred. 'She likes a lot of sleep, you see, being a brain worker.'

'Where do *we* sleep?' said Rosie.

'I made the bunk all nice for you this morning,' said Fred. 'Me, I'm going to doss below. A sack full of straw, I've got.'

'But —' said Rosie. 'But —'

'But what?' said he.

'Nothing,' said she. 'Nothing.'

They turned in. Rosie lay for an hour or two, thinking what thoughts I don't know. Perhaps she thought how charming it was that Fred should have lived so simple and shy and secluded all these years, and yet be so knowing about so many things, and yet be so innocent, and never have been mixed up in bad company – It is impossible to say what she thought.

In the end she dozed off, only to be wakened by a sound like the bagpipes of the devil himself. She sat up, terrified. It was Mary.

'What's up? What's up?' Fred's voice came like the ghost's in *Hamlet* from under the floor. 'Give her some milk,' he said.

Rosie poured out a bowl of milk. Mary ceased her fiendish racket while she drank, but the moment Rosie had blown out the light, and got into bed again, she began a hundred times worse than before.

There were rumblings under the caravan. Fred appeared in the doorway, half dressed and with straw in his hair.

'She *will* have me,' he said, in great distress.

'Can't you – Can't you lie down here?' said Rosie.

'What? And you sleep below?' said Fred, astounded.

'Yes,' said Rosie, after a rather long pause. 'And me sleep below.'

Fred was overwhelmed with gratitude and remorse. Rosie couldn't help feeling sorry for him. She even managed to give him a smile before she went down to get what rest she could on the sack of straw.

In the morning, she woke feeling rather dejected. There was a mighty breakfast to be prepared for Mary; afterwards Fred drew her aside.

'Look here,' he said. 'This won't do. I can't have you sleeping on the ground, worse than a gippo. I'll tell you what I'm going to do. I'm going to get up to my acrobat stuff again. I used to make a lot that way, and I liked it fine. Hand springs, double somersaults, bit of conjuring: it went down well. Only I didn't have time to keep in practice with Mary to look after. But if you'd do the looking after her, we'd make it a double turn, and soon we'd have a good bit of cash. And then –'

'Yes?' said Rosie.

'Then,' said Fred, 'I could buy you a trailer.'

'All right,' said Rosie, and turned away. Suddenly she turned back with her face flaming. "You may know a lot about pigs,' she said bitterly. 'And about somersaults, and conjuring and baskets and brooms and I don't know what-all. But there's *one* thing you *don't* know.' And with that she went off and cried behind a hedge.

After a while she got the upper hand of it, and came back to the caravan. Fred showed her how to give Mary her morning bath, then the depilatory – that was very hard on the hands – then the rubbing with Cleopatra Face Cream – and not on her face merely – then the powdering, then the manicuring and polishing of her trotters.

Rosie, resolved to make the best of it, conquered her repugnance, and soon mastered these handmaidenly duties. She was relieved at first that the spoiled pig accepted her ministrations without protest. Then she noticed the gloating look in its eye.

However, there was no time to brood about that. No sooner was the toilet finished than it was time to prepare the enormous lunch. After lunch Mary had her little walk, except on Saturdays when there was an afternoon show, then she took her rest. Fred explained that during this period she liked to be talked to, and have her back scratched a bit. Mary had quite clearly decided that in future she was going to have it scratched a lot. Then she had her massage. Then tea, then another little walk, or the evening show, according to where they were, and then it was time to prepare dinner. At the end of the day Rosie was thankful to curl up on her poor sack of straw.

When she thought of the bunk above, and Fred, and his simplicity, her heart was fit to break. The only thing was, she loved him dearly, and she felt that if they could soon snatch an hour alone together, they might kiss a little more, and a ray of light might dispel the darkness of excessive innocence.

Each new day she watched for that hour, but it didn't come. Mary saw to that. Once or twice Rosie suggested a little stroll, but at once the hateful pig grumbled some demand or other that kept her hard at work till it was too late. Fred, on his side, was busy enough with his practising. He meant it so well, and worked so hard – but what did it lead to? A trailer!

As the days went by, she found herself more and more the slave of this arrogant grunter. Her back ached, her hands got chapped and red, she never had a moment to make herself look nice, and never a moment alone with her beloved. Her dress was spotted and spoiled, her smile was gone, her temper was going. Her pretty hair fell in elf locks and tangles, and she had neither time nor heart to comb it.

She tried to come to an explanation with Fred, but it was nothing but cross purposes and then cross words. He tried in a score of ways to show that he loved her: these seemed to her a mere mockery, and she gave him short answers. Then he stopped, and she thought he loved her no longer. Even worse, she felt she no longer loved him.

So the whole summer went by, and things got worse and worse, and you would have taken her for a gipsy indeed.

The blackberries were ripe again; she found a whole brake of them. When she tasted one, all sorts of memories flooded into her heart: she went and found Fred. 'Fred,' she said, 'the blackberries are ripe again. I've brought you one or two.' She held out some in her grubby hand. Fred took them and tasted them; she watched to see what the result would be.

'Yes,' said he, 'they're ripe. They won't gripe her. Take her and pick her some this afternoon.'

Rosie turned away without a word, and in the afternoon she took Mary across the stubbles to where the ripe berries grew. Mary, when she saw them, dispensed for once with dainty service, and began to help herself very liberally. Rosie, finding she had nothing more urgent to attend to, sat down on a bank and sobbed bitterly.

In the middle of it all she heard a voice asking what was the matter. She looked up and there was a fat, shrewd, jolly-looking farmer. 'What is it, my girl?' said he. 'Are you hungry?'

'No,' said she, 'I'm fed up.'

'What with?' said he.

'A pig!' said she, with a gulp.

'You've got no call to bawl and cry,' said he. 'There's nothing like a bit of pork. I'd have indigestion for that any day.'

'It's not pork,' she said. 'It's a pig. A live pig.'

'Have you lost it?' said he.

'I wish I had,' said she. 'I'm that miserable I don't know what to do.'

'Tell me your troubles,' said he. 'There's no harm in a bit of sympathy.'

So Rosie told him about Fred, and about Mary, and what hopes she'd had and what they'd all come to, and how she was the slave of this insolent, spoiled, jealous pig, and in fact she told him everything except one little matter which she could hardly bring herself to repeat, even to the most sympathetic of fat farmers.

The farmer, pushing his hat over his eyes, scratched his head very thoughtfully. 'Really,' said he. 'I can't hardly believe it.'

'It's true,' said Rosie, 'every word.'

'I mean,' said the farmer. 'A young man – a young gal – the young gal sleeping down on a sack of straw – a pretty young gal like you. Properly married and all. Not to put too fine a point on it, young missus, aren't the bunks wide enough, or what?'

'He doesn't know,' sobbed Rosie. 'He just doesn't know no more'n a baby. And she won't let us ever be alone a minute. So he'd find out.'

The farmer scratched his head more furiously than ever. Looking at her tear-stained face, he found it hard to doubt her. On the other hand it seemed impossible that a pig should know so much and a young man should know so little. But at that moment Mary came trotting through the bushes, with an egoistical look on her face, which was well besmeared with the juice of ripe berries.

'Is this your pig?' said the farmer.

'Well,' said Rosie, 'I'm just taking her for a walk.'

The shrewd farmer was quick to notice the look that Rosie got from the haughty grunter when it heard the expression "your pig." This, and Rosie's hurried, nervous disclaimer, convinced the worthy man that the story he had heard was well founded.

'You're taking her for a walk?' said the farmer musingly. 'Well! Well! Well! I'll tell you what. If you'd ha' been here this time tomorrow you'd have met *me* taking a walk, with a number of very dear young friends of mine, all very much like her. You might have come along. Two young sows, beautiful creatures, though maybe not so beautiful as that one. Three young boars, in the prime of their health and handsomeness. Though I say it as shouldn't, him that's unattached – he's a prince. Oh, what a beautiful young boar that young boar really is!'

'You don't say?' said Rosie.

'For looks and pedigree both,' said the farmer, 'he's a prince. The fact is, it's their birthday, and I'm taking 'em over to the village for a little bit of a celebration. I suppose this young lady has some other engagement tomorrow.'

'She has to have her sleep just about this time,' said Rosie, ignoring Mary's angry grunt.

'Pity!' said the farmer. 'She'd have just made up the party. Such fun they'll have! Such refreshments! Sweet apples, cakes, biscuits, a bushel of chocolate creams. Everything most refined, of course, but plenty. You know what I mean – plenty. And that young boar – you know what I mean. If she *should* be walking by –'

'I'm afraid not,' said Rosie.

'Pity!' said the farmer. 'Ah, well. I must be moving along.'

With that, he bade them good afternoon, raising his hat very politely to Mary, who looked after him for a long time, and then walked sulkily home, gobbling to herself all the way.

The next afternoon Mary seemed eager to stretch out on her bunk, and, for once, instead of requiring the usual number of little attentions from Rosie, she closed her eyes in sleep. Rosie took the opportunity to pick up a pail and go off to buy the evening ration of fresh milk. When she got back Fred was still at his practice by the wayside, and Rosie went round to the back of the caravan, and the door was swinging open, and the bunk was empty.

She called Fred. They sought high and low. They went along the roads, fearing she might have been knocked over by a motor car. They went calling through the woods, hoping she had fallen asleep under a tree. They looked in ponds and ditches, behind haystacks, under bridges, everywhere. Rosie thought of the farmer's joking talk, but she hardly liked to say anything about it to Fred.

They called and called all night, scarcely stopping to rest. They sought all the next day. It grew dark, and Fred gave up hope. They plodded silently back to the caravan.

He sat on a bunk, with his head in his hand.

'I shall never see her again,' he said. 'Been pinched, that's what she's been.

'When I think,' he said, 'of all the hopes I had for that pig –

'When I think,' he said, 'of all you've done for her! And what it's meant to you –

'I know she had some faults in her nature,' he said. 'But that was artistic. Temperament, it was. When you got a talent like that –

'And now she's gone!' he said. With that he burst into tears.

'Oh, Fred!' cried Rosie. 'Don't!'

Suddenly she found she loved him just as much as ever, more than ever. She sat down beside him and put her arms round his neck. 'Darling Fred, don't cry!' she said again.

'It's been rough on you, I know,' said Fred. 'I didn't ever mean it to be.'

'There! There,' said Rosie. She gave him a kiss, and then she gave him another. It was a long time since they had been as close as this. There was nothing but the two of them and the caravan; the tiny lamp, and darkness all round; their kisses, and grief all round. 'Don't let go,' said Fred. 'It makes it better.'

'I'm not letting go,' she said.

'Rosie,' said Fred. 'I feel – Do you know how I feel?'

'I know,' she said. 'Don't talk.'

'Rosie,' said Fred, but this was some time later. 'Who'd have thought it?'

'Ah! Who would, indeed?' said Rosie.

'Why didn't you tell me?' said Fred.

'How could I tell you?' said she.

'You know,' said he. 'We might never have found out – never! – if she hadn't been pinched.'

'Don't talk about her,' said Rosie.

'I can't help it,' said Fred. 'Wicked or not, I can't help it – I'm glad she's gone. It's worth it. I'll make enough on the acrobat stuff. I'll make brooms as well. Pots and pans, too.'

'Yes,' said Rosie. 'But look! It's morning. I reckon you're tired, Fred – running up hill and down dale all day yesterday. You lie abed now, and I'll go down to the village and get you something good for breakfast.'

'All right,' said Fred. 'And tomorrow I'll get yours.'

So Rosie went down to the village, and bought the milk and the bread and so forth. As she passed the butcher's shop she saw some new-made pork sausages of a singularly fresh, plump, and appetizing appearance. So she bought some, and very good they smelled too while they were cooking.

'That's another thing we couldn't have while she was here,' said Fred, as he finished his plateful. 'Never no pork sausages, on account of her feelings. I never thought to see the day I'd be glad she was pinched. I only hope she's gone to someone who appreciates her.'

'I'm sure she has,' said Rosie. 'Have some more.'

'I will,' said he. 'I don't know if it's the novelty; or the way you cooked 'em, or what. I never ate a better sausage in my life. If we'd gone up to London, with her, best hotels and all, I doubt if ever we'd have had as sweet a sausage as these here.'

Hijacking a television studio is not easy

DESMOND MORRIS

HIJACKING A TELEVISION STUDIO
IS NOT EASY

When we decided to present a whole edition of *Zootime* from behind the scenes of the Reptile House, I went to the length of opening the programme by announcing what we were about to do and suggesting that the scenes we were about to transmit were in my opinion, unsuitable for adult viewing. The younger viewers, naturally enough, were delighted by this and several wrote to me to suggest that in addition to the usual 'X' certificate, for adults only, there should be a 'Z' certificate for children only.

As it turned out, the mouse problem was to be the least of our worries in the Reptile House presentation. There were other, more dangerous, hazards ahead. The show started badly, when a giant tortoise escaped. You may imagine that an escaped tortoise is about as troublesome as a legless bag-snatcher and as easy to catch, but it is not that simple. A fully grown giant tortoise can weigh anything up to a quarter of a ton, and if he decides to vacate the scene it is more than one man can do to stop him. Captive giants usually lack the necessary determination to take off in this way, however, and we had prepared a low, wooden pen to enclose a few of them behind my speaking position, which we thought would be sufficient to keep them in place until we were ready to display them to the waiting millions.

There was one fact we had overlooked: television lighting appreciably increases the temperature, even in a hot Reptile House at the zoo. Reptiles, especially tortoises, respond quickly to a temperature increase by becoming more active than usual. So it was for one of our penned-in giants. Gearing himself into unaccustomed mobility, he lunged forward at his wooden barrier at the very moment I was saying : 'Hallo, and welcome once again to *Zootime*, coming to you from the heart of London Zoo. Today we are inside the Urggh ...' I broke off suddenly as I felt something huge and massively heavy pressing against the back of my legs. Looking down I saw the vast bulk of the giant tortoise lumbering over the defeated and flattened wooden barrier which had been torn loose, nails and all, from its companion planks.

Trying to smile, I continued my introduction, knowing that all that could be seen at the moment was my face, in close-up. What was invisible was my legs, slowly doing the splits to let through the broadest shell in the animal world. Stumping steadfastly onwards, the giant met the distraught figure of the 'floor manager', the man who gave me all the vital timing signals from the director in the control van outside the building. The floor manager firmly placed the heel of one shoe against the front edge of the giant's carapace and tried to force him to a halt. All that happened was that the struggling man slowly slid backwards and disappeared between the two cameras that were facing me. The giant plunged sedately on and jammed tight between two camera supports.

Now, neither camera could move and this was the point at which I had to walk across to my left to introduce a charmingly professional python – about the only animal that day which did not cause us havoc. I started to move across hopefully, but caught sight of the TV monitor which was showing me what the viewers could see at home. Its screen was a blank except for an unusually boring wall. I was trapped. Moving back to the only spot where I could be seen, I suggested that we take a look at the crocodiles outside. While talking about them, I signalled wildly for the python to be brought across to me, where it could be seen. While this was being done, the floor manager somehow contrived to get the giant tortoise past the cameras and, opening the door to the outside area of the Reptile House, shooed the giant through it. We breathed again, but now the TV monitor had been knocked out of my line of vision and I could no longer see the crocodiles about which I was supposed to be giving a running commentary. Covering the microphone as best I could I hissed at the floor manager: 'The monitor, the monitor!'

That led to the next unhappy incident. It so happens that the word 'monitor' is not only used by TV technicians to denote what the rest of us would call a 'television set', but is also the popular name given to a type of giant lizard. One of these monitor lizards was due to appear later in the programme and was being held, with some difficulty, by another keeper, over to my left. Hearing me call for the monitor, he naturally assumed that, in the chaos of the moment, I had decided to bring his item forward in the programme sequence. He responded helpfully by closing in on my left flank with his monitor just as the python keeper closed in from the right. As the director cut back to me from the crocodile scene, the two huge reptiles came face to face and both disliked intensely what they saw. Struggling between their writhing forms I suggested that perhaps we might take just one more peep at the crocodiles. The director, thoroughly confused by now, took me at my word and switched again to the crocodile pool, or what should have been the crocodile pool. What none of us knew was that, outside the escaped giant tortoise had by now clumped its way round to where the camera was positioned and was thrusting it backwards to a point where all it could show us was yet another blank wall.

Had I been more experienced I would have explained the whole sorry story to the viewers, who would no doubt have enjoyed the situation immensely. But I was still at the stage where I did not like to admit that things were going awry. So I soldiered bravely on by suggesting that we look at something a little smaller – a charming frog from South America. This would give the monitor lizard keeper and the python keeper time to calm their charges down. The frog keeper came forward and placed the exotic-looking frog on a little platform I had moved hurriedly into position. The frog, which I noticed had an exceptionally large mouth, eyed the scene for a second and then made the leap of the century, vanishing instantly from view. Beautifully fielded by the frog keeper he was caught in mid-air, but objected so strongly to this cricket-ball treatment, that he promptly clamped his remarkably strong jaws on to the man's thumb. Luckily we were still in the days of black-and-white television because in the next close-up, blood was clearly oozing from the seized thumb and the keeper was in considerable pain. I had no idea that a frog could inflict such a bite, but I had to take attention away from the keeper's plight and suppress my interest in his thumb, so I snatched up a salamander from a nearby container and began talking rapidly about that instead. The keeper, imagining like me, that we were now in close-up on the salamander started to try and shake the frog free, flicking his hand vigorously, as if trying to remove from it a piece of sticky paper. Unfortunately his actions were all too visible to the viewing millions, and the next day we received angry complaints about the brutal way we had treated that 'charming little frog'. Not a word, of course, about the poor man's brutalized thumb. I wished then that we did have colour television, so that they could have seen the blood properly and understood.

We were not yet out of trouble. The climax to the Reptile House programme was to be a demonstration involving a cobra. This was the one truly dangerous item we were going to attempt. Most snake-charmers who work with live cobras render them harmless before showing them in public. This is done in a number of ways. Some of them cut out the fangs, others block the fangs with wax, or stitch the mouth of the wretched snake tightly shut. But the London Zoo would never dream of harming a cobra in any of these ways. So we were going to be dealing with a live and fully venomous snake – one of the deadliest in the world. If you are struck by one, you take half an hour to die and it is one of the most painful deaths known. We had prepared everything with great care. Nothing could go wrong. Reg Lanworn, the Overseer of Reptiles at the zoo was one of the most experienced snake handlers alive. So it was almost in jest that I had given the camera crew a short lecture before we went on the air, asking them to keep well away if they saw a hooded snake approaching them unexpectedly.

Everyone knows the classic image of an Eastern snake-charmer in turban and loin-cloth, squatting on the ground, playing a flute to his cobra as it rears up out of a small wicker basket. As the snake-charmer swings from side to side playing his instrument the great snake sways back and forth in time with him, its sinister, spectacled hood widely spread. This was the scene we wished to re-create, though without the fancy costume.

The scientific object of the exercise was to demonstrate, once and for all, that, despite the flute-playing performance and the cobra's apparent musical interest, snakes are in reality totally deaf. It is not the music to which they respond, but the swaying movement of the flute. To prove this, we were planning to show the full flute ritual first, using a snake-charmer's flute I had managed to acquire from an Indian shop in the West End, and then to repeat the performance, but without the music. If all went well, the cobra would sway just as much to the silent flute as to the played one.

You may perhaps have wondered why cobras rearing up from wicker baskets do not simply slither away and disappear. The answer is that their tail-ends are tightly bound with tape to the bottom of the baskets. This does not hurt them, but secures them and prevents their escape. Reg Lanworn had prepared his cobra in this manner and placed the round lid on top of the basket. All was ready. When we came to the cobra climax of the programme, I briefly explained the danger involved, to impress the viewers, and Reg carefully lifted the lid. The cobra responded magnificently, rearing up and facing us with it glassy stare, its long, forked tongue flickering. I began playing my flute and swaying from side to side in the approved manner. The snake followed suit. Then I repeated the movements in total silence and, to our great relief, the snake obligingly swayed once more. We had proved our point. At least something in the programme had gone as planned, I thought. But I was premature – the snake still had to be calmed back into the basket and the lid replaced.

As Reg Lanworn reached forward with a snake-rod, to encourage the cobra to withdraw, the lid poised in his other hand, the serpent slowly turned away from us and lowered itself on to the table top. Then, to our utter dismay, it slowly began to slither out of the basket, across the table and down towards the floor of the Reptile House. Reaching ground level it made off with unseemly haste, heading straight for camera number two. The cameraman, thank heaven, had taken my little lecture seriously and instead of helpfully trying to field the snake, began to shin up his camera pedestal until he was more or less on top of his machine. It is the only time I have ever seen a television camera operated from above.

The cobra slithered gracefully across the base of the camera and disappeared into the darkness of the Reptile House, with two assistant keepers in hot pursuit. Trying to keep as calm as possible, I thanked Reg for a fascinating display and covered our confusion by suggesting that as a farewell to the Reptile House, we might perhaps have a last look at the giant tortoises. While I was saying this, another keeper rushed across to remove the front of the wooden pen in which all but the escapee were still sitting, quietly munching large lettuces. With the front of the pen in place, we could see nothing, and I knew it had been only lightly nailed down before the programme had started. That was why it was possible for the liveliest of the giants to knock the front panel down and take off on its disastrous stroll. What I did not know was that, following the escape, the panel had been replaced much more firmly than before. Now, the tortoise keeper was lying behind me on the floor, hiding from view, and sweating to prise it loose. It refused to budge. I sensed something was wrong and filled in with a few well-chosen words about the conservation of giant tortoises in the wild state. Eventually I was given a frantic wind-up for the end of the show, just as I heard a terrifying creaking and a crash, as the panel finally gave up the struggle. Unfortunately the keeper had no time to get out of the way, as the camera moved in on him for the final scene. All he could do was to fling himself flat on the ground behind the group of tortoises and hope that they would hide him. But big as they were, his buttocks still showed clearly in amongst their shelly humps. As the credit titles rolled slowly up over the humps and buttocks, I wondered what exactly people would make of this bizarre combination of reptilian and human protrusions. But I was even more intrigued by the mystery of the cobra's escape.

When we gratefully at last came off the air, I looked at Reg Lanworn and he shook his head. He was as mystified as I was. As soon as we had made sure that the cobra had been safely recaptured, we went to look at the wicker basket. There, neatly bound inside it was the shed tail-skin of the snake. The one detail we had overlooked was that the cobra was about to shed its skin, and the tightness of the binding had been just enough to start the process off prematurely. It was a freak chance; but then it had been a day of freak chances and one more at this stage hardly surprised us.

Curiously, we never received any complaints about the many mishaps that occurred during our *Zootime* programmes, so long as we were the ones who suffered. Providing the animals were unharmed, it seemed to add spice to the series. Meeting some *Zootime* viewers in the grounds one day, I asked whether they noticed how often things went wrong and whether they minded. On the contrary, they explained, it was the chance that I would be eaten, or at least bitten, before the half-hour was over, which gave the programmes their special charm. They knew they were watching a live programme, rather than some carefully edited, canned film.

The Celebrated Jumping Frog of Calaveras County

MARK TWAIN

THE CELEBRATED JUMPING FROG
OF CALAVERAS COUNTY

In compliance with the request of a friend of mine, who wrote me from the East, I called on good-natured, garrulous old Simon Wheeler, and inquired after my friend's friend, Leonidas W. Smiley, as requested to do, and I hereunto append the result. I have a lurking suspicion that *Leonidas W.* Smiley is a myth; that my friend never knew such a personage; and that he only conjectured that if I asked old Wheeler about him, it would remind him of his infamous *Jim* Smiley, and he would go to work and bore me to death with some exasperating reminiscence of him as long and tedious as it should be useless to me. If that was the design, it succeeded.

I found Simon Wheeler dozing comfortably by the bar room stove of the dilapidated tavern in the decayed mining camp of Angel's, and I noticed that he was fat and bald-headed, and had an expression of winning gentleness and simplicity upon his tranquil countenance. He roused up, and gave me good-day. I told him a friend of mine had commissioned me to make some inquiries about a cherished companion of his boyhood *Leonidas W.* Smiley – *Rev. Leonidas W.* Smiley, a young minister of the Gospel, who he had heard was at one time a resident of Angel's Camp. I added that if Mr. Wheeler could tell me anything about this Rev. Leonidas W. Smiley, I would feel under many obligations to him.

Simon Wheeler backed me into a corner and blockaded me there with his chair, and then sat down and reeled off the monotonous narrative which follows this paragraph. He never smiled, he never frowned, he never changed his voice from the gentle-flowing key to which he turned his initial sentence, he never betrayed the slightest suspicion of enthusiasm; but all through the interminable narrative there ran a vein of impressive earnestness and sincerity, which showed me plainly that, so far from his imagining that there was anything ridiculous or funny about his story, he regarded it as a really important matter, and admired its two heroes as men of transcendent genius in *finesse*. I let him go on in his own way, and never interrupted him once.

'Rev. Leonidas W. H'm, Reverend Le – well, there was a feller here once by the name of *Jim* Smiley, in the winter of '49 – or may be it was the spring of '50 – I don't recollect exactly, somehow, though what makes me think it was one or the other is because I remember the big flume warn't finished when he first come to the camp; but any way, he was the curiosest man about always betting on anything that turned up you ever see, if he could get anybody to bet on the other side; and if he couldn't he'd change sides. Any way that suited the other man would suit *him* – any way just so's he got a bet, *he* was satisfied. But still he was lucky, uncommon lucky; he most always come out winner. He was always ready and laying for a chance; there couldn't be no solit'ry thing mentioned but that feller'd offer to bet on it, and take any side you please, as I was just telling you. If there was a horse-race, you'd find him flush or you'd find him busted at the end of it; if there was a dog-fight, he'd bet on it; if there was a cat-fight, he'd bet on it; if there was a chicken-fight, he'd bet on it; why if there was two birds setting on a fence, he would bet you which one would fly first; or if there was a camp-meeting, he would be there reg'lar to bet on Parson Walker, which he judged to be the best exhorter about here, and so he was too, and a good man. If he even see a straddle-bug start to go anywhere, he would bet you how long it would take him to get to – to wherever he was going to, and if you took him up, he would foller that straddle-bug to Mexico but what he would find out where he was bound for and how long he was on the road. Lots of the boys here has seen that Smiley, and can tell you about him. Why, it never made no difference to *him* – he'd bet on *any* thing – the dangdest feller. Parson Walker's wife laid very sick once, for a good while, and it seemed as if they warn't going to save her; but one morning he come in, and Smiley up and asked him how she was, and he said she was considable better – thank the Lord for his inf'nite mercy – and coming on so smart that with the blessing of Prov'dence she'd get well yet; and Smiley, before he thought, says, 'Well, I'll resk two-and-a-half she don't anyway.'

Thish-yer Smiley had a mare – the boys called her the fifteen-minute nag, but that was only in fun, you know, because of course she was faster than that – and he used to win money on that horse, for all she was so slow and always had the asthma, or the distemper, or the consumption, or something of that kind. They used to give her two or three hundred yards start, and then pass her under way; but always at the fag end of the race she'd get excited and desperate like, and come cavorting and straddling up, and scattering her legs around limber, sometimes in the air, and sometimes out to one side among the fences, and kicking up m-o-r-e dust and raising m-o-r-e racket with her coughing and sneezing and blowing her nose – and *always* fetch up at the stand just about a neck ahead, as near as you could cipher it down.

And he had a little small bull-pup, that to look at him you'd think he warn't worth a cent but to set around and look ornery and lay for a chance to steal something. But as soon as money was up on him he was a different dog; his under-jaw'd begin to stick out like the fo'castle of a steamboat, and his teeth would uncover and shine like the furnaces. And a dog might tackle him and bully-rag him, and bite him, and throw him over his shoulder two or three times, and Andrew Jackson – which was the name of the pup – Andrew Jackson would never let on but what *he* was satisfied, and hadn't expected nothing else – and the bets being doubled and doubled on the other side all the time, till the money was all up; and then all of a sudden he would grab the other dog jest by the j'int of his hind leg and freeze to it – not chaw, you understand, but only just grip and hang on till they throwed up the sponge, if it was a year. Smiley always come out winner on that pup, till he harnessed a dog once that didn't have no hind legs, because they'd been sawed off in a circular saw, and when the thing had gone along far enough, and the money was all up, and he come to make a snatch for his pet holt, he see in a minute how he'd been imposed on, and how the other dog had him in the door, so to speak, and he 'peared surprised, and then he looked sorter discouraged-like, and didn't try no more to win the fight, and so he got shucked out bad. He give Smiley a look, as much as to say his heart was broke, and it was *his* fault for putting up a dog that hadn't no hind legs for him to take holt of, which was his main dependence in a fight, and then he limped off a piece and laid down and died. It was a good pup, was that Andrew Jackson, and would have made a name for hisself if he'd lived, for the stuff was in him and he had genius – I know it, because he hadn't no opportunities to speak of, and it don't stand to reason that a dog could make such a fight as he could under them circumstances if he hadn't no talent. It always makes me feel sorry when I think of that last fight of his'n, and the way it turned out.

Well, thish-yer Smiley had rat-tarriers, and chicken cocks, and tomcats and all them kind of things, till you couldn't rest, and you couldn't fetch nothing for him to bet on but he'd match you. He ketched a frog one day, and took him home, and said he cal'lated to educate him; and so he never done nothing for three months but set in his back yard and learn that frog to jump. And you bet you he *did* learn him, too. He'd give him a little punch behind, and the next minute you'd see that frog whirling in the air like a doughnut – see him turn one summerset, or may be a couple, if he got a good start, and come down flat-footed and all right, like a cat. He got him up so in the matter of ketching flies, and kep' him in practice so constant, that he'd nail a fly every time as fur as he could see him. Smiley said all a frog wanted was education, and he could do 'most anything – and I believe him. Why, I've seen him set Dan'l Webster down here on this floor – Dan'l. Webster was the name of the frog – and

sing out, 'Flies, Dan'l, flies!' and quicker'n you can wink he'd spring
straight up and snake a fly off'n the counter there, and flop down on the
floor ag'in as solid as a gob of mud, and fall to scratching the side of his
head with his hind foot as indifferent as if he hadn't no idea he'd been
doin' any more'n any frog might do. You never see a frog so modest and
straightfor'ard as he was, for all he was so gifted. And when it come to fair
and square jumping on a dead level, he could get over more ground at one
straddle than any animal of his breed you ever see. Jumping on a dead
level was his strong suit, you understand; and when it come to that,
Smiley would ante up money on him as long as he had a red. Smiley was
monstrous proud of his frog, and well he might be, for fellers that had
travelled and been everywheres all said he laid over any frog that ever *they*
see.

Well, Smiley kep' the beast in a little lattice box, and he used to fetch
him down town sometimes and lay for a bet. One day a feller – a stranger
in the camp, he was – come acrost him with his box, and says:

'What might it be that you've got in the box?'

And Smiley says, sorter indifferent like, 'It might be a parrot, or it
might be a canary, maybe, but it ain't – it's only just a frog.'

And the feller took it, and looked at it careful, and turned it round this
way and that, and says, 'H'm – so 'tis. Well, what's *he* good for?'

'Well,' Smiley says, easy and careless, 'he's good enough for *one* thing,
I should judge – he can outjump any frog in Calaveras county.'

The feller took the box again, and took another long, particular look,
and give it back to Smiley, and says, very deliberate, 'Well,' he says, 'I
don't see no p'ints about that frog that's any better'n any other frog.'

'Maybe you don't,' Smiley says. 'Maybe you understand frogs and
maybe you don't understand 'em; maybe you've had experience, and
maybe you ain't only a amature, as it were. Anyways, I've got *my* opinion,
and I'll resk forty dollars that he can outjump any frog in Calaveras
county.'

And the feller studied a minute, and then says, kinder sad like, 'Well,
I'm only a stranger here, and I ain't got no frog; but if I had a frog, I'd bet
you.'

And then Smiley says, 'That's all right – that's all right – if you'll hold
my box a minute, I'll go and get you a frog.' And so the feller took the box,
and put up his forty dollars along with Smiley's and set down to wait.

So he set there a good while thinking and thinking to hisself, and then
he got the frog out and prized his mouth open and took a teaspoon and
filled him full of quail shot – filled him pretty near up to his chin – and set
him on the floor. Smiley he went to the swamp and slopped around in the

mud for a long time, and finally he ketched a frog, and fetched him in, and give him to this feller, and says:

'Now, if you're ready, set him alongside of Dan'l, with his forepaws just even with Dan'l's, and I'll give the word.' Then he says, 'One – two – three – *git!*' and him and the feller touched up the frogs from behind, and the new frog hopped off lively, but Dan'l give a heave, and hysted up his shoulders – so – like a Frenchman, but it warn't no use – he couldn't budge: he was planted as solid as a church, and he couldn't no more stir than if he was anchored out. Smiley was a good deal surprised, and he was disgusted too, but he didn't have no idea what the matter was, of course.

The feller took the money and started away; and when he was going out the door, he sorter jerked his thumb over his shoulder – so – at Dan'l, and says again, very deliberate, 'Well,' he says, '*I* don't see no p'ints about that frog that's any better'n any other frog.'

Smiley he stood scratching his head and looking down at Dan'l a long time, and at last he says, 'I do wonder what in the nation that frog throw'd off for – I wonder if there ain't something the matter with him – he 'pears to look mighty baggy, somehow.' And he ketched Dan'l by the nap of the neck, and hefted him, and says, 'Why blame my cats if he don't weigh five pound!' and turned him upside down and he belched out a double handful of shot. And then he see how it was, and he was the maddest man – he set the frog down and took out after that feller, but he never ketched him. And –'

[Here Simon Wheeler heard his name called from the front yard, and got up to see what was wanted.] And turning to me as he moved away, he said: 'Just set where you are, stranger, and rest easy – I ain't going to be gone a second.'

But, by you're leave, I did not think that a continuation of the history of the enterprising vagabond *Jim* Smiley would be likely to afford me much information concerning the Rev. *Leonidas W.* Smiley, and so I started away.

At the door I met the sociable Wheeler returning, and he button-holed me and re-commenced:

'Well, thish-yer Smiler had a yaller one-eyed cow that didn't have no tail, only just a short stump like a bannanner, and –'

However, lacking both time and inclination, I did not wait to hear about the afflicted cow, but took my leave.

The Sounding of
the Call

JACK LONDON

THE SOUNDING OF THE CALL

Thrown into the hard life of the frozen north of America, Buck has learnt to fight for his survival. Rough treatment by the men who drive the sleighs and the savagery of the other dogs has almost turned him into a wild animal. Now, only the love of John Thornton, his master, keeps him from joining a wolf pack.

Spring came on once more, and at the end of all their wandering they found, not the Lost Cabin, but a shallow place in a broad valley where the gold showed like yellow butter across the bottom of the washing-pan. They sought no farther. Each day they worked earned them thousands of dollars in clean dust and nuggets, and they worked every day. The gold was sacked in moose-hide bags, fifty pounds to the bag, and piled like so much firewood outside the spruce-bough lodge. Like giants they toiled, days flashing on the heels of days like dreams as they heaped the treasure up.

There was nothing for the dogs to do, save the hauling in of meat now and again that Thornton killed, and Buck spent long hours musing by the fire. The vision of the short-legged hairy man came to him more frequently, now that there was little work to be done; and often, blinking by the fire, Buck wandered with him in that other world which he remembered.

The salient thing of this other world seemed fear. When he watched the hairy man sleeping by the fire, head between his knees and hands clasped above, Buck saw that he slept restlessly, with many starts and awakenings, at which times he would peer fearfully into the darkness and fling more wood upon the fire. Did they walk by the beach of a sea, where the hairy man gathered shell-fish and ate them as he gathered, it was with eyes that roved everywhere for hidden danger and with legs prepared to run like the wind at its first appearance. Through the forest they crept noiselessly, Buck at the hairy man's heels; and they were alert and vigilant, the pair of them, ears twitching and moving and nostrils quivering, for the man heard and smelled as keenly as Buck. The hairy man could spring up into the trees and travel ahead as fast as on the ground, swinging by the arms from limb to limb, sometimes a dozen feet apart, letting go and catching, never falling, never missing his grip. In fact, he seemed as much at home among the trees as on the ground; and Buck had memories of nights of vigil spent beneath trees wherein the hairy man roosted, holding on tightly as he slept.

And closely akin to the visions of the hairy man was the call still sounding in the depths of the forest. It filled him with a great unrest and strange desires. It caused him to feel a vague, sweet gladness, and he was aware of wild yearnings and stirrings for he knew not what. Sometimes he pursued the call into the forest, looking for it as though it were a tangible thing, barking softly or defiantly, as the mood might dictate. He would thrust his nose into the cool wood moss, or into the black soil where long grasses grew, and snort with joy at the fat earth smells; or he would crouch for hours, as if in concealment, behind fungus-covered trunks of fallen trees, wide-eyed and wide-eared to all that moved and sounded about him. It might be, lying thus, that he hoped to surprise this call he could not understand. But he did not know why he did these various things. He was impelled to do them, and did not reason about them at all.

Irresistible impulses seized him. He would by lying in camp, dozing lazily in the heat of the day, when suddenly his head would lift and his ears cock up, intent and listening, and he would spring to his feet and dash away, and on and on, for hours, through the forest aisles and across the open spaces where the niggerheads bunched. He loved to run down dry watercourses, and to creep up and spy upon the bird life in the woods. For a day at a time he would lie in the underbrush where he could watch the partridges drumming and strutting up and down. But especially he loved to run in the dim twilight of the summer midnights, listening to the subdued and sleepy murmurs of the forest, reading signs and sounds as man may read a book, and seeking for the mysterious something that called – called, waking or sleeping, at all times, for him to come.

One night he sprang from sleep with a start, eager-eyed, nostrils quivering and scenting, his mane bristling in recurrent waves. From the forest came the call (or one note of it, for the call was many noted), distinct and definite as never before – a long-drawn howl, like, yet unlike, any noise made by husky dog. And he knew it, in the old familiar way, as a sound heard before. He sprang through the sleeping camp and in swift silence dashed through the woods. As he drew closer to the cry he went more slowly, with caution every moment, till he came to an open place among the trees, and looking out saw, erect on haunches, with nose pointed to the sky, a long, lean, timber wolf.

He had made no noise, yet it ceased from its howling and tried to sense his presence. Buck stalked into the open, half crouching, body gathered compactly together, tail straight and stiff, feet falling with unwonted care. Every movement advertised commingled threatening and overture of friendliness. It was the menacing truce that marks the meeting of wild beasts that prey. But the wolf fled at sight of him. He followed, with wild leapings, in a frenzy to overtake. He ran him into a blind channel, in the bed of the creek, where a timber jam barred the way. The wolf whirled about, pivoting on his hind legs after the fashion of Joe and of all cornered husky dogs, snarling and bristling, clipping his teeth together in a continuous and rapid succession of snaps.

Buck did not attack, but circled him about and hedged him in with friendly advances. The wolf was suspicious and afraid; for Buck made three of him in weight, while his head barely reached Buck's shoulder. Watching his chance, he darted away, and the chase was resumed. Time and again he was cornered, and the thing repeated, though he was in poor condition or Buck could not so easily have overtaken him. He would run till Buck's head was even with his flank, when he would whirl around at bay, only to dash away again at the first opportunity.

But in the end Buck's pertinacity was rewarded; for the wolf, finding that no harm was intended, finally sniffed noses with him. Then they became friendly, and played about in the nervous, half-coy way with which fierce beasts belie their fierceness. After some time of this the wolf started off at an easy lope in a manner that plainly showed he was going somewhere. He made it clear to Buck that he was to come, and they ran side by side through the sombre twilight, straight up the creek bed, into the gorge from which it issued, and across the bleak divide where it took its rise.

On the opposite slope of the watershed they came down into a level country where were great stretches of forest and many streams, and through these great stretches they ran steadily, hour after hour, the sun rising higher and the day growing warmer. Buck was wildly glad. He knew he was at last answering the call, running by the side of his wood brother towards the place from where they surely came. Old memories were coming upon him fast, and he was stirring to them as of old he stirred to the realities of which they were the shadows. He had done this thing before, somewhere in that other and dimly remembered world, and he was doing it again, now, running free in the open, the unpacked earth underfoot, the wide sky overhead.

They stopped by a running stream to drink, and, stopping, Buck remembered John Thornton. He sat down. The wolf started on towards the place from where the call surely came, then returned to him, sniffing noses and making actions as though to encourage him. But Buck turned about and started slowly on the back track. For the better part of an hour the wild brother ran by his side, whining softly. Then he sat down, pointed his nose upward, and howled. It was a mournful howl, and as

Buck held steadily on his way he heard it grow faint and fainter until it was lost in the distance.

John Thornton was eating his dinner when Buck dashed into camp and sprang upon him in a frenzy of affection, overturning him, scrambling upon him, licking his face, biting his hand – 'playing the general tom-fool,' as John Thornton characterized it, the while he shook Buck back and forth and cursed him lovingly.

For two days and nights Buck never left camp, never let Thornton out of his sight. He followed him about at his work, watched him while he ate, saw him into his blankets at night and out of them in the morning. But after two days the call of the forest began to sound more imperiously than ever. Buck's restlessness came back on him, and he was haunted by recollections of the wild brother, and of the smiling land beyond the divide and the run side by side through the wide forest stretches. Once again he took to wandering in the woods, but the wild brother came no more; and though he listened through long vigils, the mournful howl was never raised.

He began to sleep out at night, staying away from camp for days at a time; and once he crossed the divide at the head of the creek and went down into the land of timber and streams. There he wandered for a week, seeking vainly for fresh sign of the wild brother, killing his meat as he travelled and travelling with the long easy lope that seems never to tire. He fished for salmon in a broad stream that emptied somewhere into the sea, and by this stream he killed a large black bear, blinded by the mosquitoes while likewise fishing, and raging through the forest helpless and terrible. Even so, it was a hard fight, and it aroused the last latent remnants of Buck's ferocity. And two days later, when he returned to his kill and found a dozen wolverenes quarrelling over the spoil, he scattered them like chaff; and those that fled left two behind who would quarrel no more.

The blood-longing became stronger than ever before. He was a killer, a thing that preyed, living on the things that lived, unaided, alone, by virtue of his own strength and prowess, surviving triumphantly in a hostile environment where only the strong survived. Because of all this he became possessed of a great pride in himself, which communicated itself like a contagion to his physical being. It advertised itself in all his movements, was apparent in the play of every muscle, spoke plainly as speech in the way he carried himself, and made his glorious furry coat if anything more glorious. But for the stray brown of his muzzle and above his eyes, and for the splash of white hair that ran midmost down his chest, he might well have been mistaken for a gigantic wolf, larger than the largest of the breed. From his St. Bernard father he had inherited size and weight, but it was his shepherd mother who had given shape to that size and weight. His muzzle was the long wolf muzzle, save that it was larger than the muzzle of any wolf; and his head, somewhat broader, was the wolf head on a massive scale.

His cunning was wolf cunning, and wild cunning; his intelligence, shepherd intelligence and St. Bernard intelligence; and all this, plus an experience gained in the fiercest of schools, made him as formidable a creature as any that roamed the wild. A carnivorous animal, living on a straight meat diet, he was in full flower, at the high tide of his life, overspilling with vigour and virility. When Thornton passed a caressing hand along his back, a snapping and crackling followed the hand, each hair discharging its pent magnetism at the contact. Every part, brain and body, nerve tissue and fibre, was keyed to the most exquisite pitch; and between all the parts there was a perfect equilibrium or adjustment. To sights and sounds and events which required action, he responded with lightning-like rapidity. Quickly as a husky dog could leap to defend from attack or to attack, he could leap twice as quickly. He saw the movement, or heard sound, and responded in less time than another dog required to compass the mere seeing or hearing. He perceived and determined and responded in the same instant. In point of fact the three actions of perceiving, determining, and responding were sequential; but so infinitesimal were the intervals of time between them that they appeared simultaneous. His muscles were surcharged with vitality, and snapped into play sharply, like steel springs. Life streamed through him in splendid flood, glad and rampant, until it seemed that it would burst him asunder in sheer ecstacy and pour forth generously over the world.

'Never was there such a dog,' said John Thornton one day, as the partners watched Buck marching out of camp.

'When he was made, the mould was broke,' said Pete.

'Py jingo! I t'ink so mineself,' Hans affirmed.

They saw him marching out of camp, but they did not see the instant and terrible transformation which took place as soon as he was within the secrecy of the forest. He no longer marched. At once he became a thing of the wild, stealing along softly, cat-footed, a passing shadow that appeared and disappeared among the shadows. He knew how to take advantage of every cover, to crawl on his belly like a snake, and like a snake to leap and strike. He could take a ptarmigan from its nest, kill a rabbit as it slept, and snap in mid-air the little chipmunks fleeing a second too late for the trees. Fish, in open pools, were not too quick for him; nor were beaver, mending their dams, too wary. He killed to eat, not from wantonness; but he preferred to eat what he killed himself. So a lurking humour ran through his deeds, and it was his delight to steal upon the squirrels, and, when he had all but had them, to let them go, chattering in mortal fear to the tree-tops.

As the fall of the year came on, the moose appeared in greater abundance, moving slowly down to meet the winter in the lower and less rigorous valleys. Buck had already dragged down a stray part-grown calf; but he wished strongly for larger and more formidable quarry, and he came upon it one day on the divide at the head of the creek. A band of twenty moose had crossed over from the land of streams and timber, and chief among them was a great bull. He was in a savage temper, and, standing over six feet from the ground, was as formidable an antagonist as even Buck could desire. Back and forth the bull tossed his great palmated antlers, branching to fourteen points and embracing seven feet within the tips. His small eyes burned with a vicious and bitter light, while he roared with fury at sight of Buck.

From the bull's side, just forward of the flank, protruded a feathered arrow-end, which accounted for his savageness. Guided by that instinct which came from the old hunting days of the primordial world, Buck proceeded to cut the bull out from the herd. It was no slight task. He would bark and dance about in front of the bull, just out of reach of the great antlers and of the terrible splay hoofs which could have stamped his life out with a single blow. Unable to turn his back on the fanged danger and go on, the bull would be driven into paroxysms of rage. At such moments he charged Buck, who retreated craftily, luring him on by a simulated inability to escape. But when he was thus separated from his fellows two or three of the younger bulls would charge back upon Buck and enable the wounded bull to rejoin the herd.

There is a patience of the wild – dogged, tireless, persistent as life itself – that holds motionless for endless hours the spider in its web, the snake in its coils, the panther in its ambuscade; this patience belongs peculiarly to life when it hunts its living food; and it belonged to Buck as he clung to the flank of the herd, retarding its march, irritating the young bulls, worrying the cows with their half-grown calves, and driving the wounded bull mad with helpless rage. For half a day this continued. Buck multiplied himself, attacking from all sides, enveloping the herd in a whirlwind of menace, cutting out his victim as fast as it could rejoin its mates, wearing out the patience of creatures preyed upon, which is a lesser patience than that of creatures preying.

As the day wore along and the sun dropped to its bed in the north-west (the darkness had come back and the fall nights were six hours long), the young bulls retraced their steps more and more reluctantly to the aid of their beset leader. The down-coming winter was harrying them on to the lower levels, and it seemed they could never shake off this tireless creature that held them back. Besides, it was not the life of the herd, or of the young bulls that was threatened. The life of only one member was demanded, which was a remoter interest than their lives, and in the end they were content to pay the toll.

As twilight fell the old bull stood with lowered head, watching his mates – the cows he had known, the calves he had fathered, the bulls he had mastered – as they shambled on at a rapid pace through the fading night. He could not follow, for before his nose leaped the merciless fanged terror that would not let him go. Three hundredweight more than half a ton he weighed; he had lived a long, strong life, full of fight and struggle, and at the end he faced death at the teeth of a creature whose head did not reach beyond his great knuckled knees.

From then on, night and day, Buck never left his prey, never gave it a moment's rest, never permitted it to browse the leaves of trees or the shoots of young birch and willow. Nor did he give the wounded bull opportunity to slake his burning thirst in the slender trickling streams they crossed. Often, in desperation, he burst into long stretches of flight. At such times Buck did not attempt to stay him, but loped easily at his heels, satisfied with the way the game was played, lying down when the moose stood still, attacking him fiercely when he strove to eat or drink.

The great head drooped more and more under its tree of horns, and the shambling trot grew weak and weaker. He took to standing for long periods, with nose to the ground and dejected ears dropped limply; and Buck found more time in which to get water for himself and in which to rest. At such moments, panting with red lolling tongue and with eyes fixed upon the big bull, it appeared to Buck that a change was coming over the face of things. He could feel a new stir in the land. As the moose were coming into the land, other kinds of life were coming in. Forest and stream and air seemed palpitant with their presence. The news of it was borne in upon him, not by sight, or sound, or smell, but by some other and subtler sense. He heard nothing, saw nothing, yet knew that the land was somehow different; that through it strange things were afoot and ranging; and he resolved to investigate after he had finished the business in hand.

At last, at the end of the fourth day, he pulled the great moose down. For a day and a night he remained by the kill, eating and sleeping, turn and turn about. Then, rested, refreshed and strong, he turned his face towards camp and John Thornton. He broke into the long easy lope, and went on, hour after hour, never at loss for the tangled way, heading straight home through strange country with a certitude of direction that put man and his magnetic needle to shame.

As he held on he became more and more conscious of the new stir in the land. There was life abroad in it different from the life which had been there throughout the summer. No longer was this fact borne upon him in some subtle, mysterious way. The birds talked of it, the squirrels chattered about it, the very breeze whispered of it. Several times he stopped and drew in the fresh morning air in great sniffs, reading a message which made him leap on with greater speed. He was oppressed with a sense of calamity happening, if it were not calamity already happened; and as he crossed the last watershed and dropped down into the valley towards camp, he proceeded with greater caution.

Three miles away he came upon a fresh trail that sent his neck hair rippling and bristling. It led straight towards camp and John Thornton. Buck hurried on, swiftly and stealthily, every nerve straining and tense, alert to the multitudinous details which told a story – all but the end. His nose gave him a varying description of the passage of life on the heels of which he was travelling. He remarked the pregnant silence of the forest. The bird life had flitted. The squirrels were in hiding. One only he saw – a sleek grey fellow, flattened against a grey dead limb so that he seemed a part of it, a woody excrescence upon the wood itself.

As Buck slid along with the obscureness of a gliding shadow, his nose was jerked suddenly to the side as though a positive force had gripped and pulled it. He followed the new scent into a thicket and found Nig. He was lying on his side, dead where he had dragged himself, an arrow protruding, head and feathers, from either side of his body.

A hundred yards farther on, Buck came upon one of the sled-dogs Thornton had bought in Dawson. This dog was thrashing about in a death-struggle, directly on the trail, and Buck passed around him without stopping. From the camp came the faint sound of many voices, rising and falling in a sing-song chant. Bellying forward to the edge of the clearing, he found Hans, lying on his face, feathered with arrows like a porcupine. At the same instant Buck peered out where the spruce-bough lodge had been and saw what made his hair leap straight up on his neck and shoulders. A gust of overpowering rage swept over him. He did not know that he growled, but he growled aloud with a terrible ferocity. For the last time in his life he allowed passion to usurp cunning and reason, and it was because of his great love for John Thornton that he lost his head.

The Yeehats were dancing about the wreckage of the spruce-bough when they heard a fearful roaring and saw rushing upon them an animal the like of which they had never seen before. It was Buck, a live hurricane of fury, hurling himself upon them in a frenzy to destroy. He sprang at the foremost man (it was the chief of the Yeehats), ripping the throat wide open till the rent jugular spouted a fountain of blood. He did not pause to worry the victim, but ripped in passing, with the next bound tearing wide the throat of a second man. There was no withstanding him. He plunged about in their very midst, tearing, rending, destroying, in constant and terrific motion which defied the arrows they discharged at him. In fact, so inconceivably rapid were his movements, and so closely were the Indians tangled together, that they shot one another with the arrows; and one young hunter, hurling a spear at Buck in mid-air, drove it through the chest of another hunter with such force that the point broke through the skin of the back and stood out beyond. Then a panic seized the Yeehats, and they fled in terror to the woods, proclaiming as they fled the advent of the Evil Spirit.

And truly Buck was the Fiend incarnate, raging at their heels and dragging them down like deer as they raced through the trees. It was a fateful day for the Yeehats. They scattered far and wide over the country, and it was not till a week later that the last of the survivors gathered together in a lower valley and counted their losses. As for Buck, wearying of the pursuit, he returned to the desolated camp. He found Pete where he had been killed in his blankets in the first moment of surprise. Thornton's desperate struggle was fresh-written on the earth, and Buck scented every detail of it down to the edge of a deep pool. By the edge, head and fore feet in the water, lay Skeet, faithful to the last. The pool itself, muddy and discoloured from the sluice boxes, effectually hid what it contained, and it contained John Thornton; for Buck followed his trace into the water, from which no trace led away.

All day Buck brooded by the pool or roamed restlessly about the camp. Death, as a cessation of movement, as a passing out and away from the lives of the living, he knew, and he knew John Thornton was dead. It left a great void in him, somewhat akin to hunger, but a void which ached and ached, and which food could not fill. At times, when he paused to contemplate the carcasses of the Yeehats, he forgot the pain of it; and at such times he was aware of a great pride in himself – a pride greater than any he had yet experienced. He had killed man, the noblest game of all, and he had killed in the face of the law of club and fang. He sniffed the bodies curiously. They had died so easily. It was harder to kill a husky dog than them. They were no match at all, were it not for their arrows and spears and clubs. Thenceforward he would be unafraid of them except when they bore in their hands, arrows, spears, and clubs.

Night came on, and a full moon rose high over the trees into the sky, lighting the land till it lay bathed in ghostly day. And with the coming of the night, brooding and mourning by the pool, Buck became alive to a stirring of the new life in the forest other than that which the Yeehats had made. He stood up, listening and scenting. From far away drifted a faint, sharp yelp, followed by a chorus of similar sharp yelps. As the moments passed the yelps grew closer and louder. Again Buck knew them as things heard in that other world which persisted in his memory. He walked to the centre of the open space and listened. It was the call, the many-noted call, sounding more luringly and compellingly than ever before. And as never before, he was ready to obey. John Thornton was dead. The last tie was broken. Man and the claims of man no longer bound him.

Hunting their living meat, as the Yeehats were hunting it, on the flanks of the migrating moose, the wolf pack had at last crossed over from the land of streams and timber and invaded Buck's valley. Into the clearing where the moonlight streamed, they poured in a silvery flood; and in the centre of the clearing stood Buck, motionless as a statue, waiting their coming. They were awed, so still and large he stood, and a moment's pause fell, till the boldest one leaped straight for him. Like a flash Buck struck, breaking the neck. Then he stood, without movement, as before, the stricken wolf rolling in agony behind him. Three others tried it in sharp succession; and one after the other they drew back, streaming blood from slashed throats or shoulders.

This was sufficient to fling the whole pack forward pell-mell, crowded together, blocked and confused by its eagerness to pull down the prey. Buck's marvellous quickness and agility stood him in good stead. Pivoting on his hind legs, and snapping and gashing, he was everywhere at once, presenting a front which was apparently unbroken so swiftly did he whirl and guard from side to side. But to prevent them from getting behind him, he was forced back, down past the pool and into the creek bed, till he brought up against a high gravel bank. He worked along to a right angle in the bank which the men had made in the course of mining, and in this angle he came to bay, protected on three sides and with nothing to do but face the front.

And so well did he face it, that at the end of half an hour the wolves drew back discomfited. The tongues of all were out and lolling, the white fangs showing cruelly white in the moonlight. Some were lying down with heads raised and ears pricked forward; others stood on their feet, watching him; and still others were lapping water from the pool. One wolf, long and lean and grey, advanced cautiously, in a friendly manner, and Buck recognized the wild brother with whom he had run for a night and a day. He was whining softly, and, as Buck whined, they touched noses.

Then an old wolf, gaunt and battle-scarred, came forward. Buck writhed his lips into the preliminary of a snarl, but sniffed noses with him. Whereupon the old wolf sat down, pointed nose at the moon, and broke out the long wolf howl. The others sat down and howled. And now the call came to Buck in unmistakable accents. He, too, sat down and howled. This over, he came out of his angle and the pack crowded around him, sniffing in half-friendly, half-savage manner. The leaders lifted the yelp of the pack and sprang away into the woods. The wolves swung in behind, yelping in chorus. And Buck ran with them, side by side with the wild brother, yelping as he ran.

And here may well end the story of Buck. The years were not many when the Yeehats noted a change in the breed of timber wolves; for some were seen with splashes of brown on head and muzzle, and with a rift of white centring down the chest. But more remarkable than this, the Yeehats tell of a Ghost Dog that runs at the head of the pack. They are afraid of this Ghost Dog, for it has cunning greater than they, stealing from their camps in fierce winters, robbing their traps, slaying their dogs, and defying their bravest hunters.

Nay, the tale grows worse. Hunters there are who fail to return to the camp, and hunters there have been whom their tribesmen found with their throats slashed cruelly open and with wolf prints about them in the snow greater than the prints of any wolf. Each fall, when the Yeehats follow the movement of the moose, there is a certain valley which they never enter. And women there are who become sad when the word goes over the fire of how the Evil Spirit came to select that valley for an abiding-place.

In the summers there is one visitor, however, to that valley, of which the Yeehats do not know. It is a great, gloriously coated wolf, like, and yet unlike, all other wolves. He crosses alone from the smiling timber land and comes down into an open space among the trees. Here a yellow stream flows from rotted moose-hide sacks and sinks into the ground, with long grasses growing through it and vegetable mould overrunning it and hiding its yellow from the sun; and here he muses for a time, howling once, long and mournfully, ere he departs.

But he is not always alone. When the long winter nights come on and the wolves follow their meat into the lower valleys, he may be seen running at the head of the pack through the pale moonlight or glimmering borealis, leaping gigantic above his fellows, his great throat a-bellow as he sings a song of the young world, which is the song of the pack.

Monty the Bull

JAMES HERRIOT

MONTY THE BULL

Ben Ashby the cattle dealer looked over the gate with his habitual deadpan expression. It always seemed to me that after a lifetime of buying cows from farmers he had developed a terror of showing any emotion which might be construed as enthusiasm. When he looked at a beast his face registered nothing beyond, occasionally, a gentle sorrow.

This was how it was this morning as he leaned on the top spar and directed a gloomy stare at Harry Sumner's heifer. After a few moments he turned to the farmer.

'I wish you'd had her in for me, Harry. She's too far away. I'm going to have to get over the top.' He began to climb stiffly upwards and it was then that he spotted Monty. The bull hadn't been so easy to see before as he cropped the grass among the group of heifers but suddenly the great head rose high above the others, the nose ring gleamed, and an ominous, strangled bellow sounded across the grass. And as he gazed at us he pulled absently at the turf with a fore foot.

Ben Ashby stopped climbing, hesitated for a second then returned to ground level.

'Aye well,' he muttered, still without changing expression. 'It's not that far away. I reckon I can see all right from here.'

Monty had changed a lot since the first day I saw him about two years ago. He had been a fortnight old then, a skinny, knock-kneed little creature, his head deep in a calf bucket.

'Well, what do you think of me new bull?' Harry Sumner had asked, laughing. 'Not much for a hundred quid is he?'

I whistled. 'As much as that?'

'Aye, it's a lot for a new-dropped calf, isn't it? But I can't think of any other way of getting into the Newton strain. I haven't the brass to buy a big 'un.'

Not all the farmers of those days were as far-seeing as Harry and some of them would use any type of male bovine to get their cows in calf.

One such man produced a gaunt animal for Siegfried's inspection and asked him what he thought of his bull. Siegfried's reply of 'All horns and balls' didn't please the owner but I still treasure it as the most graphic description of the typical scrub bull of that period.

Harry was a bright boy. He had inherited a little place of about a hundred acres on his father's death and with his young wife had set about making it go. He was in his early twenties and when I first saw him I had been deceived by his almost delicate appearance into thinking that he wouldn't be up to the job; the pallid face, the large, sensitive eyes and slender frame didn't seem fitted for the seven days a week milking, feeding, mucking-out slog that was dairy farming. But I had been wrong.

The fearless way he plunged in and grabbed at the hind feet of kicking cows for me to examine and his clenched-teeth determination as he hung on to the noses of the big loose beasts at testing time made me change my mind in a hurry. He worked endlessly and tirelessly and it was natural that his drive should have taken him to the south of Scotland to find a bull.

Harry's was an Ayrshire herd – unusual among the almost universal shorthorns in the Dales – and there was no doubt an injection of the famous Newton blood would be a sure way of improving his stock.

'He's got prize winners on both his sire and dam's side,' the young farmer said. 'And a grand pedigree name, too. Newton Montmorency the Sixth – Monty for short.'

As though recognising his name, the calf raised his head from the bucket and looked at us. It was a comic little face – wet muzzled, milk slobbered half way up his cheeks and dribbling freely from his mouth. I bent over into the pen and scratched the top of the hard little head, feeling the tiny horn buds no bigger than peas under my fingers. Limpid-eyed and unafraid, Monty submitted calmly to the caress for a few moments then sank his head again in the bucket.

I saw quite a lot of Harry Sumner over the next few weeks and usually had a look at his expensive purchase. And as the calf grew you could see why he had cost £100. He was in a pen with three of Harry's own calves and his superiority was evident at a glance; the broad forehead and wide-set eyes; the deep chest and short straight legs; the beautifully even line of the back from shoulder to tail head. Monty had class; and small as he was he was all bull.

He was about three months old when Harry rang to say he thought the calf had pneumonia. I was surprised because the weather was fine and warm and I knew Monty was in a draught-free building. But when I saw him I thought immediately that his owner's diagnosis was right. The heaving of the rib cage, the temperature of 105 degrees – it looked fairly straightforward. But when I got my stethoscope on his chest and listened for the pneumonic sounds I heard nothing. His lungs were perfectly clear. I went over him several times but there was not a squeak, not a râle, not the slightest sign of consolidation.

This was a facer. I turned to the farmer. 'It's a funny one, Harry. He's sick, all right, but his symptoms don't add up to anything recognisable.'

I was going against my early training because the first vet I ever saw practice with in my student days told me once: 'If you don't know what's wrong with an animal for God's sake don't admit it. Give it a name – call it McLuskie's Disease or Galloping Dandruff – anything you like, but give it a name.' But no inspiration came to me. I looked at the panting, anxious-eyed little creature.

Treat the symptoms. That was the thing to do. He had a temperature so I'd try to get that down for a start. I brought out my pathetic armoury of febrifuges; the injection of non-specific antiserum, the 'fever drink' of sweet spirit of nitre; but over the next two days it was obvious that the time-honoured remedies were having no effect.

On the fourth morning, Harry Sumner met me as I got out of my car. 'He's walking funny, this morning, Mr Herriot – and he seems to be blind.'

'Blind!' An unusual form of lead-poisoning – could that be it? I hurried into the calf pen and began looking round the walls, but there wasn't a scrap of paint anywhere and Monty had spent his entire life in there.

And anyway, as I looked at him I realised that he wasn't really blind; his eyes were staring and slightly upturned as he blundered unseeingly around the pen, but he blinked as I passed my hand in front of his face. To complete my bewilderment he walked with a wooden, stiff-legged gait almost like a mechanical toy and my mind began to scratch at diagnostic straws – tetanus, no – meningitis – no, no; I always tried to maintain the calm, professional exterior but I had to fight an impulse to scratch my head and stand gaping.

I got off the place as quickly as possible and settled down to serious thought as I drove away. My lack of experience didn't help, but I did have a knowledge of pathology and physiology and when stumped for a diagnosis I could usually work something out on rational grounds. But this thing didn't make sense.

That night I got out my books, notes from college, back numbers of the Veterinary Record and anything else I could find on the subject of calf diseases. Somewhere here there would surely be a clue. But the volumes on medicine and surgery were barren of inspiration and I had about given up hope when I came upon the passage in a little pamphlet on calf diseases. 'Peculiar, stilted gait, staring eyes with a tendency to gaze upwards, occasionally respiratory symptoms with high temperature.' The words seemed to leap out at me from the printed page and it was as though the unknown author was patting me on the shoulder and murmuring reassuringly: 'This is it, you see. It's all perfectly clear.'

I grabbed the phone and rang Harry Sumner. 'Harry, have you ever noticed Monty and those other calves in the pen licking each other?'

'Aye, they're allus at it, the little beggars. It's like a hobby with them. Why?'

'Well I know what's wrong with your bull. He's got a hair ball.'

'A hair ball? Where?'

'In the abomasum – the fourth stomach. That's what setting up all those strange symptoms.'

'Well I'll go to hell. What do we do about it, then?'

'It'll probably mean an operation, but I'd like to try dosing him with liquid paraffin first. I'll put a pint bottle on the step for you if you'll come and collect it. Give him half a pint now and the same first thing in the morning. It might just grease the thing through. I'll see you tomorrow.'

I hadn't a lot of faith in the liquid paraffin. I suppose I suggested it for the sake of doing something while I played nervously with the idea of operating. And next morning the picture was as I expected; Monty was still rigid-limbed, still staring sightlessly ahead of him, and an oiliness round his rectum and down his tail showed that the paraffin had by-passed the obstruction.

'He hasn't had a bite now for three days,' Harry said. 'I doubt he won't stick it much longer.'

I looked from his worried face to the little animal trembling in the pen. 'You're right. We'll have to open him up straight away to have any hope of saving him. Are you willing to let me have a go?'

'Oh aye, let's be at t'job – sooner the better.' He smiled at me. It was a confident smile and my stomach gave a lurch. His confidence could be badly misplaced because in those days abdominal surgery in the bovine was in a primitive state. There were a few jobs we had begun to tackle fairly regularly but removal of a hair ball wasn't one of them and my knowledge of the procedure was confined to some rather small-print reading in the text books.

But this young farmer had faith in me. He thought I could do the job so it was no good letting him see my doubts. It was at times like this that I envied our colleagues in human medicine. When a surgical case came up they packed their patient off to the hospital but the vet just had to get his jacket off on the spot and make an operating theatre out of the farm buildings.

Harry and I busied ourselves in boiling up the instruments, setting out buckets of hot water and laying a clean bed of straw in an empty pen. Despite his weakness the calf took nearly sixty c.c.'s of Nembutal into his vein before he was fully anaesthetised but finally he was asleep, propped on his back between two straw bales, his little hooves dangling above him. I was ready to start.

164

It's never the same as it is in the books. The pictures and diagrams look so simple and straightforward but it is a different thing when you are cutting into a living, breathing creature with the abdomen rising and falling gently and the blood oozing beneath your knife. The abomasum, I knew, was just down there, slightly to the right of the sternum but as I cut through the peritoneum there was this slippery mass of fat-streaked omentum obscuring everything; and as I pushed it aside one of the bales moved and Monty tilted to the left causing a sudden gush of intestines into the wound. I put the flat of my hand against the shining pink loops – it would be just great if my patient's insides started spilling out on to the straw before I had started.

'Pull him upright, Harry, and shove that bale back into place,' I gasped. The farmer quickly complied but the intestines weren't at all anxious to return to their place and kept intruding coyly as I groped for the abomasum. Frankly I was beginning to feel just a bit lost and my heart was thudding when I came upon something hard. It was sliding about – beyond the wall of one of the stomachs – at the moment I wasn't sure which, I gripped it and lifted it into the wound. I had hold of the abomasum and that hard thing inside must be the hair ball.

Repelling the intestines which had made another determined attempt to push their way into the act, I incised the stomach and had my first look at the cause of the trouble. It wasn't a ball at all, rather a flat plaque of densely matted hair mixed freely with strands of hay, sour curd and a shining covering of my liquid paraffin. The whole thing was jammed against the pyloric opening.

Gingerly I drew out through the incision and dropped it in the straw. It wasn't till I had closed the stomach wound with the gut, stitched up the muscle layer and had started on the skin that I realised that the sweat was running down my face. As I blew away a droplet from my nose end Harry broke the silence.

'It's a hell of a tricky job, isn't it?' he said. Then he laughed and thumped my shoulder. 'I bet you felt a bit queer the first time you did one of these!'

I pulled another strand of suture silk through and knotted it. 'You're right, Harry.' I said. 'How right you are.'

When I had finished we covered Monty with a horse rug and piled straw on top of that, leaving only his head sticking out. I bent over and touched the corner of the eye. Not a vestige of a corneal reflex. God, he was deep – had I given him to much anaesthetic? And of course there'd be surgical shock, too. As I left I glanced back at the motionless little animal. He looked smaller than ever and very vulnerable under the bare walls of the pen.

I was busy for the rest of the day but that evening my thoughts kept coming back to Monty. Had he come out of it yet? Maybe he was dead. I hadn't the experience of previous cases to guide me and I simply had no idea of how a calf reacted to an operation like that. And I couldn't rid myself of the nagging consciousness of how much it all meant to Harry Sumner. The bull is half the herd, they say, and half of Harry's future herd was lying there under the straw – he wouldn't be able to find that much money again.

The following morning came, it was no good, I had to find out what was happening. Part of me rebelled at the idea of looking amateurish and unsure of myself by going fussing back, but, I thought, I could always say I had returned to look for an instrument.

The farm was in darkness as I crept into the pen. I shone my torch on the mound of straw and saw with a quick bump of the heart that the calf had not moved. I dropped to my knees and pushed a hand under the rug; he was breathing anyway. But there was still no eye reflex – either he was dying or he was taking a hell of a time to come out.

In the shadows of the yard I looked across at the soft glow from the farmhouse kitchen. Nobody had heard me. I slunk over to the car and drove off with the sick knowledge that I was no further forward. I still didn't know how the job was going to turn out.

Next morning I had to go through the same thing again and as I walked stiffly across to the calf pen I knew for sure I'd see something this time. Either he'd be dead or better. I opened the outer door and almost ran down the passage. It was the third pen along and I stared hungrily into it.

Monty was sitting up on his chest. He was still under the rug and straw and he looked sorry for himself but when a bovine animal is on its chest I always feel hopeful. The tensions flowed from me in a great wave. He had survived the operation – the first stage was over; and as I knelt rubbing the top of his head I had the feeling that we were going to win.

And, in fact, he did get better, though I have always found it difficult to explain to myself scientifically why the removal of that pad of tangled fibres could cause such a dramatic improvement in so many directions. But there it was. His temperature did drop and his breathing returned to normal, his eyes did stop staring and the weird stiffness disappeared from his limbs.

But though I couldn't understand it, I was none the less delighted. Like a teacher with his favourite pupil I developed a warm proprietary affection for the calf and when I happened to be on the farm I found my feet straying unbidden to his pen. He always walked up to me and regarded me with friendly interest; it was as if he had a fellow feeling for me, too.

He was rather more than a year old when I noticed the change. The friendly interest gradually disappeared from his eyes and was replaced by a thoughtful, speculative look; and he developed a habit of shaking his head at me at the same time.

'I'd stop going in there, Mr Herriot, if I were you,' Harry said one day. 'He's getting big and I reckon he's going to be a cheeky bugger before he's finished.'

But cheeky was the wrong word. Harry had a long, trouble-free spell and Monty was nearly two years old when I saw him again. It wasn't a case of illness this time. One or two of Harry's cows had been calving before their time and it was typical of him that he should ask me to blood test his entire herd for Brucellosis.

We worked our way easily through the cows and I had a long row of glass tubes filled with blood in just over an hour.

'Well, that's the lot in here,' the farmer said. 'We only have bull to do and we're finished.' He led the way across the yard through the door into the calf pens and along a passage to the bull box at the end. He opened the half door and as I looked inside I felt a sudden sense of shock.

Monty was enormous. The neck with its jutting humps of muscle supported a head so huge that the eyes looked tiny. And there was nothing friendly in those eyes now; no expression at all, in fact, only a cold black glitter. He was standing sideways to me, facing the wall, but I knew he was watching me as he pushed his head against the stones, his great horns scoring the whitewash with slow, menacing deliberation. Occasionally he snorted from deep in his chest but apart from that he remained ominously still. Monty wasn't just a bull – he was a vast, brooding presence.

Harry grinned as he saw me staring over the door. 'Well, do you fancy popping inside to scratch his head? That's what you allus used to do.'

'No thanks.' I dragged my eyes away from the animal. 'But I wonder what my expectation of life would be if I did go in.'

'I reckon you'd last about a minute,' Harry said thoughtfully. 'He's a grand bull – all I ever expected – but by God he's a mean 'un. I never trust him an inch.'

'And how,' I asked without enthusiasm, 'am I supposed to get a sample of blood from him?'

'Oh I'll trap his head in yon corner.' Harry pointed to a metal yoke above a trough in an opening into the yard at the far side of the box. 'I'll give him some meal to 'tice him in.' He went back down the passage and

167

soon I could see him out in the yard scooping meal into the trough.

The bull at first took no notice and continued to prod at the wall with his horns, then he turned with awesome slowness, took a few unhurried steps across the box and put his nose down to the trough. Harry, out of sight in the yard, pulled the lever and the yoke crashed shut on the great neck.

'All right,' the farmer cried, hanging on to the lever, 'I have 'im. You can go in now.'

I opened the door and entered the box and though the bull was held fast by the head there was still the uneasy awareness that he and I were alone in that small space together. And as I passed along the massive body and put my hand on the neck I sensed a quivering emanation of pent up power and rage. Digging my fingers into the jugular furrow I watched the vein rise up and poised my needle. It would take a good hard thrust to pierce that leathery skin.

The bull stiffened but did not move as I plunged the needle in and with relief I saw the blood flowing darkly into the syringe. Thank God I had hit the vein first time and didn't have to start poking around. I was withdrawing the needle and thinking that the job had been so simple after all when everything started to happen. The bull gave a tremendous bellow and whipped round at me with no trace of his former lethargy. I saw that he had got one horn out of the yoke and though he couldn't reach me with his head his shoulder knocked me on my back with a terrifying revelation of unbelievable strength. I heard Harry shouting from outside and as I scrambled up and headed for the box door I saw that the madly plunging creature had almost got his second horn clear and when I reached the passage I heard the clang of the yoke as he finally freed himself.

Anybody who has travelled a narrow passage a few feet ahead of about a ton of snorting, pounding death will appreciate that I didn't dawdle. I was spurred on by the certain knowledge that if Monty caught me he would plaster me against the wall as effortlessly as I would squash a ripe plum, and though I was clad in a long oilskin coat and wellingtons I doubt whether an olympic sprinter in full running kit would have bettered my time.

I made the door at the end with a foot to spare, dived through and crashed it shut. The first thing I saw was Harry Sumner running round from the outside of the box. He was very pale. I couldn't see my face but it felt pale; even my lips were cold and numb.

'God, I'm sorry!' Harry said hoarsely. 'The yoke couldn't have closed properly – that bloody great neck of his. The lever just jerked out of my hand. Damn, I'm glad to see you – I thought you were a goner!'

I looked down at my hand. The blood-filled syringe was still tightly clutched there. 'Well I've got my sample anyway, Harry. And it's just as well, because it would take some fast talking to get me in there to try for another. I'm afraid you've just seen the end of a beautiful friendship.'

'Aye, the big sod!' Harry listened for a few moments to the thudding of Monty's horns against the door. 'And after all you did for him. That's gratitude for you.'

The Wonderful Tar Baby Story

JOEL CHANDLER HARRIS

Illustration by A. B. Frost

THE WONDERFUL TAR BABY STORY

Uncle Remus is an old black slave (freed after the American war between the States) on a plantation in Georgia, about a hundred and ten years ago. He has become a trusted and respected servant of the white family owning the estate on which he has spent his life. In the evenings he tells bedtime stories to a little white boy, the son of his beloved employer 'Miss Sally' and her husband (formerly a Federal officer in the war.)

One evening recently, the lady whom Uncle Remus calls 'Miss Sally' missed her little seven-year-old boy. Making search for him through the house and through the yard, she heard the sound of voices in the old man's cabin, and, looking through the window, saw the child sitting by Uncle Remus. His head rested against the old man's arm, and he was gazing with an expression of the most intense interest into the rough, weather-beaten face, that beamed so kindly upon him. This is what 'Miss Sally' heard:

'Bimeby, one day, arter Brer Fox bin doin' all dat he could fer ter ketch Brer Rabbit, en Brer Rabbit bin doin' all he could fer to keep 'im fum it, Brer Fox say to hisse'f dat he'd put up a game on Brer Rabbit, en he ain't mo'n got de wuds out'n his mouf twel Brer Rabbit come a lopin' up de big road, lookin' des ez plump, en ez fat, en ez sassy ez a Moggin hoss in a barley-patch.

'"Hol' on dar, Brer Rabbit," sez Brer Fox, sezee.

'"I ain't got time, Brer Fox," sez Brer Rabbit, sezee, sorter mendin' his licks.

'"I wanter have some confab wid you, Brer Rabbit," sez Brer Fox, sezee.

'"All right, Brer Fox, but you better holler fum whar you stan'. I'm monstrus full er fleas dis mawnin'," sez Brer Rabbit, sezee.

'"I seed Brer B'ar yistiddy," sez Brer Fox, sezee, "en he sorter rake me over de coals kaze you en me ain't make frens en live naberly, en I told 'im dat I'd see you."

'Den Brer Rabbit scratch one year wid his off hinefoot sorter jub'usly, en den he ups en sez, sezee:

'"All a settin', Brer Fox. Spose'n you drap roun' ter-morrer en take dinner wid me. We ain't got no great doin's at our house, but I speck de old 'oman en de chilluns kin sorter scramble roun' en git up sump'n fer ter stay yo' stummuck.'

'"I'm 'gree'ble, Brer Rabbit," sez Brer Fox, sezee.

'"Den I'll 'pen' on you," sez Brer Rabbit, sezee.

'Nex' day, Mr. Rabbit an' Miss Rabbit got up soon, 'fo' day, en raided on a gyarden like Miss Sally's out dar, en got some cabbiges, en some roas'n years, en some sparrer grass, en dey fix up a smashin' dinner. Bimeby one er de little Rabbits, playin' out in de back-yard, come runnin' in hollerin', "Oh, ma! oh, ma! I seed Mr. Fox a comin'!" En den Brer Rabbit he tuck de chilluns by der years en make um set down, en den him and Miss Rabbit sorter dally roun' waitin' for Brer Fox. En dey keep on waitin', but no Brer Fox ain't come. Atter 'while Brer Rabbit goes to de do', easy like, en peep out, en dar, stickin' fum behime de cornder, wuz de tip-een' er Brer Fox tail. Den Brer Rabbit shot de do'en sot down, en put his paws behime his years en begin fer ter sing:

'De place wharbouts you spill de grease,
    Right dar youer boun' ter slide,
An' whar you fine a bunch er ha'r,
    You'll sholy fine de hide.'

'Nex' day, Brer Fox sont word by Mr. Mink, en skuze hisse'f kaze he wuz too sick fer ter come, en he ax Brer Rabbit fer to come en take dinner wid him, en Brer Rabbit say he wuz 'gree'ble.

'Bimeby, w'en de shadders wuz at der shortes', Brer Rabbit he sorter brush up en santer down ter Brer Fox's house, en w'en he got dar, he hear somebody groanin', en he look in de do' en dar he see Brer Fox settin' up in a rockin' cheer all wrop up wid flannil, en he look mighty weak. Brer Rabbit look all 'roun', he did, but he ain't see no dinner. De dish-pan wuz settin' on de table, en close by wuz a kyarvin' knife.

'"Look like you gwineter have chicken fer dinner, Brer Fox," sez Brer Rabbit, sezee.

'Yes, Brer Rabbit, deyer nice, en fresh, en tender,' sez Brer Fox, sezee.

'Den Brer Rabbit sorter pull his mustarsh, en say: 'You ain't got no calamus root, is you, Brer Fox? I done got so now dat I can't eat no chicken 'ceppin she's seasoned up wid calamus root.' En wid dat Brer Rabbit lipt out er de do' and dodge 'mong de bushes, en sot dar watchin' fer Brer Fox; en he ain't watch long, nudder, kaze Brer Fox flung off de flannil en crope out er de house en got whar he could cloze in on Brer Rabbit, en bimeby Brer Rabbit holler out: 'Oh, Brer Fox! I'll des put yo' calamus root out yer on dish yer stump. Better come git it while hit's fresh,' and wid dat Brer Rabbit gallop off home. En Brer Fox ain't never kotch 'im yit, en w'at's mo', honey, he ain't gwineter.'

The
Volcano Rat

HUGH LOFTING

'We would squat on the edge'

Illustration by Hugh Lofting

THE VOLCANO RAT

Doctor Dolittle can speak animal languages. In his private zoo he has founded a number of clubs for different kinds of animal. One of these is the Rat and Mouse Club. The doctor, with his boy assistant Tommy Stubbins, visits the club one evening and hears the Volcano Rat tell his story.

The adventure related by the Hotel Rat reminded various members of things of interest in their own lives – as is the case with stories told to a large audience. And as soon as it was ended a buzz of general conversation and comment began.

'You know,' said the Doctor to the white mouse, 'you rats and mice really lead much more thrilling and exciting lives than we humans do.'

'Yes, I suppose that's true,' said the white mouse. 'Almost every one of the members here has had adventures of his own. The Volcano Rat, for instance, has a very unusual story which he told me a week or so ago.'

'I'd like to hear some more of these anecdotes of rat and mouse life,' said the Doctor. 'But I suppose we ought to be getting home now. It's pretty late.'

'Why don't you drop in again some other night soon?' said the white mouse. 'There's always quite a crowd here in the evenings. I've been thinking it would be nice if you or Tommy would write out a few of these life stories of the members and make them into a book for us, a collection. We'd call it, say, "Tales of the Rat and Mouse Club."'

At this suggestion quite a number of rats and mice who had been listening to our conversation joined in with remarks. They were all anxious for the honour of having their own stories included in the club's book of adventures. And before we left that night it was agreed that we should return the following evening to hear the tale of the Volcano Rat. I knew it would be no easy matter for me to take down the stories word for word. But the white mouse said he would see that they were told slowly and distinctly; and with the Doctor's assistance (his knowledge of rat and mouse language was of course greatly superior to mine) I thought I might be able to manage it. I was most anxious to, for we both realized that by this means we would add a book of great distinction to Animal Literature.

Considerable excitement and rejoicing were shown when it became known that we had consented to the plan. It was at once arranged that a notice should be put up on the club bulletin-board, in the room called the

Lounge, showing which member was chosen to tell his story for each night in the week. And as we carefully rose from our seats and made our difficult way down the tunnel into the open air, we heard rats and mice all round us assuring one another they would be certain to come to-morrow night.

When he arose amid a storm of applause the following evening to address the large audience gathered to hear his story, the Volcano Rat struck me at once by his distinctly foreign appearance. He was the same colour as most rats, neither larger nor smaller; but there was something Continental about him – almost Italian, one might say. He had sparkling eyes and very smooth movements, yet clearly he was no longer young. His manner was a rather curious mixture of gaiety and extreme worldliness.

'Our president,' he began with a graceful bow towards the white mouse, 'was speaking last night of the high state of civilization to which, through Doctor John Dolittle and our club, this community has reached. To-night I would like to tell you of another occasion – perhaps the only other occasion in history – when our race rose to great heights of culture and refinement.

'Many years ago I lived on the side of a volcano. For all we knew, it was a dead volcano. On its slopes there were two or three villages and one town. I knew every inch of the whole mountain well. Once or twice I had explored the crater at the top – a great mysterious basin of sponge-like rock, with enormous cracks in it running way down into the heart of the earth. In these, if you listened carefully, you could hear strange rumbling noises deep, deep down.

'The third occasion when I went up to the crater I was trying to get away from some farm dogs who had been following my scent through the vineyards and olive groves of the lower slopes. I stayed up there a whole night. The funny noises sort of worried me; they sounded so exactly like people groaning and crying. But in the morning I met an old, old rat who, it seemed, lived there regularly. He was a nice old chap and we got to chatting. He took me all round the crater and showed me the sights – grottoes, steaming underground lakes and lots of queer things. He lived in these cracks in the mountain.

'"How do you manage for food?" I asked.

'"Acorns," he replied. "There are oak trees a little way down the slope. And I lay in a good big store each autumn. And then for water there's a brook or two. I manage all right."

'"Why, you live like a squirrel!" I said – "storing up your nuts for the winter. What made you choose this place for a home?"

'"Well, you see," said he, "truth is, I'm getting old and feeble, Can't run like I used to. Any cat or dog could catch me in the towns. But they never come up here to the crater. Superstitious! They're afraid of the rumbling voices. They believe there are demons here."

'Well, I lived with the old Hermit Rat for two days. It was a nice change after the noisy bustling life of the town. It was a great place just to sit and think, that crater. In the evenings we would squat on the edge of it, looking down at the twinkling lights of the town far, far below – and the sea, a misty horizon in blue-black, far out beyond.

'I asked the old rat if he didn't often get lonely, living up there all alone.

'"Oh, sometimes," said he. "But to make up for the loneliness, I have peace. I could never get that down there."

'Every once in a while, when the rumbling voices coming out of the heart of the mountain got louder, he'd go down a crack and listen. And I asked him what it was he expected to hear. At first he wouldn't tell me and seemed afraid that I might laugh at him or something. But at last he told me.

'"I'm listening for an eruption," says he.

'"What on earth is that?" I asked.

'"That's when a volcano blows up," says he. "This one has been quiet a long time, many years. But I've listened to those voices so long that I can understand 'em – Yes, you needn't laugh," he added, noticing I was beginning to grin. "I tell you I've an idea that I shall know – for certain – when this mountain is going to blow up. The voices will tell me."

'Well, of course I thought he was crazy. And after I had grown tired of the lonely life myself, I bade him good-bye and came back to live in the town.

'It was not long after that that the citizens imported a whole lot of cats of a new kind. Us rats had got too plentiful and the townsfolk had made up their minds to drive us out. Well, they did. These cats were awful hunters. They never stopped; went after us day and night. And as there were thousands of them, life for us became pretty nearly impossible.

'After a good many of our people had been killed some of the leaders of the colonies got together in an old cellar one night to discuss what we should do about it. And after several had made suggestions which weren't worth much, I started thinking of my old friend the hermit and the peaceful life of his crater-home. And I suggested to the meeting that I should lead them all up there, where we could live undisturbed by cats or dogs. Some didn't like the idea much. But beggars can't be choosers. And it was finally decided that word should be passed round to all the rats in the town that at dawn the next day I would lead them forth beyond the walls and guide them to a new home.'

'So,' the Volcano Rat continued, 'the following day a great departure of rats took place from that town. And the old hermit of the mountain-top had the surprise of his life when from his crow's-nest look-out he saw several thousand of us trailing up the slope to share his loneliness.

'Fortunately the autumn was not yet over and there were still great quantities of acorns lying beneath the oak trees. These we harvested into the many funny little underground chambers with which the walls of the crater were riddled.

'Because I had led them out of danger into this land of safety I came to be looked upon as a sort of leader. Of course after the first excitement of the migration was over a good deal of grumbling began. It seems people always have to grumble. Many young fellows who thought themselves clever made speeches to those willing to listen. They told the crowd that I had led them into as bad a plight as they were in before. Rat and mouse civilization had gone backward, they said, instead of forward. Now they were no better than squirrels living on stored-up acorns. Whereas in the towns, though they may have had the constant dangers that always had to be faced in cities, life at least had some colour and variety; they hadn't got to eat the same food *every* day; and if they wanted to line their nests with silk or felt they knew where to find it, etc., etc., etc., and a whole lot more.

'These discontented orators got the common people so worked up against me that for a time my life was actually in danger from the mob. Finally – though I am a rat of few words – I had to make a speech on my own account in self-defence. I pointed out to the people that the life we were now leading was nothing more nor less than the original life of our forefathers. "After the Flood," I told them, "this was how you lived, the simple outdoor life of the fields. Then when the cities of Men arose with their abominable crowding you were tempted by the gay life of cellars and larders. We rats," I said proudly, "were at first a hardy race of agriculturists, living by corn and the fruits of the earth. Lured by idleness and ease, we became a miserable lot of crumb-snatchers and cheese-stealers. I gave you the chance to return to your healthy, independent, outdoor life. Now, after you have listened to these wretched cellar-loungers, you long to go back to the sneaking servitude of the dwellings of Men. Go then, you fleas, you parasites!" (I was dreadfully cross.) "But never," I said, "never ask me to lead you again!"

'And yet Fate seemed to plot and conspire to make me a leader of rats. I didn't want to be. I never had any taste or ambition for politics. But no sooner had I ended my speech, even while the cheers and yells of the audience were still ringing in my ears (for I had completely won them over to my side), the old hermit came up behind me and croaked into my ear. "The eruption! – the voices in the earth have spoken. Beware! We must fly!"

'Something prompted me to believe him – though even to this day I don't see how he could have known, and I thought I had better act, and act quickly, while I had the crowd on my side.

'"Hark!" I shouted, springing to my feet once more. "This mountain is no longer safe. Its inner fires are about to burst forth. All must leave. Do not wait to take your acorns with you. For there is no time to lose."

'Then like one rat they rose up and shouted, "Lead us and we will follow. We believe in you. You are the leader whom we trust!"

'After that came a scene of the wildest kind. In a few minutes I had to organize a train of thousands of rats and mice and get it down that mountain-side the quickest possible way. Somehow or other I managed it – even though darkness came on before I started them off and the route was precipitous and dangerous. In addition to everything else, I had to make arrangements for six rats to carry the old hermit, who couldn't walk fast enough to keep up with the rest.

'So, through the night, past the walls of the town – the town which had turned us out – we hurried on and on and on, down, down into the valley. Even there, tired though we all were, I would not let them halt for long, but hurried the train on after a few moments' rest across the valley, over the wide river by a stone bridge and up the slopes of another range of hills twenty miles away from the spot we had started from. And even as I wearily shouted the command to halt, the volcano-top opened with a roar and sent a funnel of red fire and flying rocks hurtling into the black night sky.

'Never have I seen anything so terrifying as the anger of that death-spitting mountain. A sea of red-hot stones and molten mud flowed down the slopes, destroying all in its path. Even where we stood and watched, twenty miles away across the valley, a light shower of ashes and dust fell around us.

'The next day the fire had ceased and only a feather of smoke rising from the summit remained. But the villages were no more; the town, the town that had turned us out, could not be seen.

'Well, we settled down to country life and for some years lived in peace. My position as leader, whether I willed it or no, seemed more than ever confirmed now that I had led the people out of further dangers.

'And so time passed and the Second Migration was declared a great success. But presently, as always seemed to be the way, I foresaw that before long we would have to move again. Our trouble this time was weasels. Suddenly in great numbers they cropped up all over the countryside and made war on rats, mice, rabbits, and every living thing. I began to wonder where I could lead the people this time. Often I had looked across the valley at our old mountain, our old home. The hermit had told me that he was sure that the volcano would not speak again for fifty years. He had been right once: he probably would be again. One day I made up my mind to go back across the valley and take a look around. Alone I set off.

'Dear me, how desolate! The beautiful slopes that had been covered with vineyards, olive groves and fig trees were now grey wastes of ashes, shadeless and hot in the glaring sun. Wearily I walked up the mountain till I came to about the place where I reckoned the town had stood. I began wondering what the buildings looked like underneath. I hunted around and finally found a hole in the lava; through it I made my way downward. Everything of course, after all these years, was quite cold; and to get out of the sun into the shade beneath the surface of the ground was in itself a pleasure. I started off to do some subterranean exploring.

'Down and down I burrowed. In some places it was easy and in some places it was hard. But finally I got through all that covering of ashes and lava crust and came into the town beneath.

'I almost wept as I ran all over it. I knew every inch of the streets, every stone in the buildings. Nothing had changed. The dead city stood beneath the ground, silent and at peace, but in all else just as it had been when the rain of fire had blotted it out from the living world.

'"So!" I said aloud, "here I will bring the people – back to the town that turned us out. At last we have a city of our own!"'

The white mouse, seeing that the Volcano Rat seemed a little hoarse, motioned to a club waiter to fetch water – which was promptly done.

With a nod of thanks to the chairman the Volcano Rat took a sip from the acorn-cup and then proceeded.

'On my return I called the people together and told them that the time had come for our Third Migration. Many, when they found out whither I meant to lead them, grumbled as usual – this time that I was taking them back to the place from which we had already once taken flight.

'"Wait!" I said. "You complained years ago that I had set your civilization back, that I had reduced you to the level of squirrels. Well, now I'm going to give you a chance to advance your civilization to a point it never dreamed of before. Have patience."

'So, once more under the protection of darkness, I led the people across the valley and up the slopes of the sleeping mountain. When I had shown them where to dig, holes were made by the hundred, and through them we entered into possession of our subterranean town.

'It took us about a month to get the place in working order. Tons of ashes had to be removed from doorways, a great deal of cleaning up was needed, and many other things required attention. But it would take me more than a month to tell you in detail of the wonderful Rat City we made of it in the end. All the things which Men had used were now ours. We slept in feather beds. We had a marble swimming pool, built originally by the Romans, to bathe in. We had barbers' shops furnished with every imaginable perfume, pomade and hair-oil. Fashionable rat ladies went to the manicure establishments and beauty-parlours at least twice a week. And well-groomed dandies promenaded of an evening up and down the main street. We had athletic clubs where wrestling, swimming, boxing and jumping contests were held. All the best homes were filled with costly works of art. And an atmosphere of education and culture was everywhere noticeable.

'Of course much of the food which was in the town when the catastrophe happened had since decayed and become worthless. But there were great quantities of things that were not perishable, like corn, raisins, dried beans, and what not. These at the beginning were taken over by me and the Town Council as city property; and for the first month every rat who wanted an ounce of corn had to work for it. In that way we got a tremendous lot of things done for the public good, such as cleaning up the streets, repairing the houses, carrying away rotting refuse, etc.

'But perhaps the most interesting part of our new city life was the development of professions and government. In our snug town beneath the earth we were never disturbed by enemies of any kind, except occasional sickness; and we grew and flourished. At the end of our first year of occupation a census was taken, and it showed our population as ten and three-quarter millions. So you see we were one of the largest cities in history. For such an enormous colony a proper system of government became very necessary. Quite early we decided to give up the municipal plan and formed ourselves into a city republic with departments and a Chamber of Deputies. Still later, when we outgrew that arrangement, we reorganized and called ourselves The United Rat States Republic. I had the honour of being elected the first Premier of the Union Parliament.

'After a while of course rats from outside colonies got to hear of our wonderful city, and tourists were to be seen on our streets almost any day in the week looking at the sights. But we were very particular about whom we took in as citizens. If you wanted citizenship you had to pass quite serious examinations both for education and for health. We were especially exacting on health. Our Medical College – which turned out exceptionally good rat doctors – had decided that most of our catching diseases had been brought in first by foreigners. So after a while a law was passed that not even tourists and sight-seers could be admitted to the town without going through a careful medical examination. This, with the exceptionally good feeding conditions, the freedom of the life and the popular interest in sports and athletics, made the standard of physical development very high. I don't suppose that at any time in the whole history of our race have there been bigger or finer rats than the stalwart sons of the United Rat States Republic. Why, I've seen young fellows in our high-school athletic teams as big as rabbits and twice as strong.

'Building and architecture were brought to a very fine level, too. In order to keep the lava and ashes from falling in on us we constructed in many places regular roofs over the streets and squares. Some rats will always love a hole, even if you give them a palace to live in. And many of us clung to this form of dwelling still.

'One morning I was being measured for a new hole by a well-known digging contractor when my second valet rushed in excitedly waving the curling-irons with which he used to curl my whiskers.

'"Sir," he cried, "the Chief of the Street Cleaning Department is downstairs and wants to be admitted at once. Some Men have come. They are digging into the mountain-side above our heads. The roof over the Market Square is falling in and the people are in a panic!"

'I hurried at once with the Chief of the Street Cleaning Department to the Market Square. There I found all in the greatest confusion. Men with pick-axes and shovels were knocking in the roof of lava and ashes which hid our city from the world. The moment I saw them I knew it was the end. Man had returned to reclaim the lost town and restore it to its former glory.

'Some of our people thought at first that the newcomers might only dig for a little while and then go away again. But not I. And sure enough, the following day still more Men came and put up temporary houses and tents and went on digging and digging. Many of our hot-headed young fellows were for declaring war. A volunteer army, calling itself *The Sons of Rat Freedom*, three million strong, raised itself at the street-corners overnight. A committee of officers from this army came to me the third day and pointed out that with such vast numbers they could easily drive these few Men off. But I said to them:

'"No. The town, before it was ours, belonged to Man. You might drive them off for a while; but they would come back stronger than ever, with cats and dogs and ferrets and poison; and in the end we would be vanquished and destroyed. No. Once more we must migrate, my people, and find ourselves new homes."

'I felt terribly sad, as you can easily imagine. While I was making my way back through the wrecked streets to my home, I saw some of the Men preparing to take away a statue of myself carved by one of our most famous rat sculptors. It had been set up over a fountain by the grateful townsfolk to commemorate what I had done for them. On the base was written, *The Saviour of His People – The Greatest of All Leaders.*' The men were peering at the writing trying to decipher it. I suppose that later they put the statue into one of their museums as a Roman relic or something. It was a good work of art – even if the rat sculptor did make my stomach too large. Anyhow, as I watched them I determined that I would be a leader of rats no more. I had, as it were, reached the top rung of the ladder; I had brought the people to a higher pitch of civilization than they had ever seen before. And now I would let some one else lead them. The Fourth Migration would be made without me.

'Sneaking quietly into my home I gathered a few things together in a cambric handkerchief. Then I slipped out and by unfrequented back streets made my way down the mountain-side – suddenly transformed from a Prime Minister of the biggest government, the greatest empire our race had ever seen, into a tramp-rat, a lonely vagabond.'

The Wolves of Cernogratz

"SAKI"

THE WOLVES OF CERNOGRATZ

'Are there any old legends attached to the castle?' asked Conrad of his sister. Conrad was a prosperous Hamburg merchant, but he was the one poetically-dispositioned member of an eminently practical family.

The Baroness Gruebel shrugged her plump shoulders.

'There are always legends hanging about these old places. They are not difficult to invent and they cost nothing. In this case there is a story that when any one dies in the castle all the dogs in the village and the wild beasts in the forest howl the night long. It would not be pleasant to listen to, would it?'

'It would be weird and romantic,' said the Hamburg merchant.

'Anyhow, it isn't true,' said the Baroness complacently; 'since we bought the place we have had proof that nothing of the sort happens. When the old mother-in-law died last springtime we all listened, but there was no howling. It is just a story that lends dignity to the place without costing anything.'

'The story is not as you have told it,' said Amalie, the grey old governess. Every one turned and looked at her in astonishment. She was wont to sit silent and prim and faded in her place at table, never speaking unless some one spoke to her, and there were few who troubled themselves to make conversation with her. To-day a sudden volubility had descended on her; she continued to talk, rapidly and nervously, looking straight in front of her and seeming to address no one in particular.

'It is not when *any one* dies in the castle that the howling is heard. It was when one of the Cernogratz family died here that the wolves came from far and near and howled at the edge of the forest just before the death hour. There were only a few couple of wolves that had their lairs in this part of the forest, but at such a time, the keepers say, there would be scores of them, gliding about in the shadows and howling in chorus, and the dogs of the castle and the village and all the farms round would bay and howl in fear and anger at the wolf chorus, and as the soul of the dying one left its body a tree would crash down in the park. That is what happened when a Cernogratz died in his family castle. But for a stranger dying here, of course no wolf would howl and no tree would fall. Oh, no.'

There was a note of defiance, almost of contempt, in her voice as she said the last words. The well-fed, much-too-well dressed Baroness stared angrily at the dowdy old woman who had come forth from her usual and seemly position of effacement to speak so disrespectfully.

'You seem to know quite a lot about the von Cernogratz legends, Fräulein Schmidt,' she said sharply; 'I did not know that family histories were among the subjects you are supposed to be proficient in.'

The answer to her taunt was even more unexpected and astonishing than the conversational outbreak which had provoked it.

'I am a von Cernogratz myself,' said the old woman, 'that is why I know the family history.'

'You a von Cernogratz? You!' came in an incredulous chorus.

'When we became very poor,' she explained, 'and I had to go out and give teaching lessons, I took another name; I thought it would be more in keeping. But my grandfather spent much of his time as a boy in this castle, and my father used to tell me many stories about it, and, of course, I knew all the family legends and stories. When one has nothing left to one but memories, one guards and dusts them with especial care. I little thought when I took service with you that I should one day come with you to the old home of my family. I could wish it had been anywhere else.'

There was a silence when she finished speaking, and then the Baroness turned the conversation to a less embarrassing topic than family histories. But afterwards, when the old governess had slipped away quietly to her duties, there arose a clamour of derision and disbelief.

'It was impertinence,' snapped out the Baron, his protruding eyes taking on a scandalised expression; 'fancy the woman talking like that at our table. She almost told us we were nobodies, and I don't believe a word of it. She is just Schmidt and nothing more. She has been talking to some of the peasants about the old Cernogratz family, and raked up their history and their stories.'

'She wants to make herself out of some consequence,' said the Baroness; 'she knows she will soon be past work and she wants to appeal to our sympathies. Her grandfather, indeed!'

The Baroness had the usual number of grandfathers, but she never, never boasted about them.

'I dare say her grandfather was a pantry boy or something of the sort in the castle,' sniggered the Baron; 'that part of the story may be true.'

The merchant from Hamburg said nothing; he had seen tears in the old woman's eyes when she spoke of guarding her memories – or, being of an imaginative disposition, he thought he had.

'I shall give her notice to go as soon as the New Year festivities are over,' said the Baroness; 'till then I shall be too busy to manage without her.'

But she had to manage without her all the same, for in the cold biting weather after Christmas, the old governess fell ill and kept to her room.

'It is most provoking,' said the Baroness, as her guests sat round the fire on one of the last evenings of the dying year; 'all the time that she has been with us I cannot remember that she was ever seriously ill, too ill to go about and do her work, I mean. And now, when I have the house full, and she could be useful in so many ways, she goes and breaks down. One is sorry for her, of course, she looks so withered and shrunken, but it is intensely annoying all the same.'

'Most annoying,' agreed the banker's wife, sympathetically; 'it is the intense cold, I expect, it breaks the old people up. It has been unusually cold this year.'

'The frost is the sharpest that has been known in December for many years,' said the Baron.

'And, of course, she is quite old,' said the Baroness; 'I wish I had given her notice some weeks ago, then she would have left before this happened to her. Why, Wappi, what is the matter with you?'

The small, woolly lapdog had leapt suddenly down from its cushion and crept shivering under the sofa. At the same moment an outburst of angry barking came from the dogs in the castle-yard, and other dogs could be heard yapping and barking in the distance.

'What is disturbing the animals?' asked the Baron.

And then the humans, listening intently, heard the sound that had roused the dogs to their demonstrations of fear and rage; heard a long-drawn whining howl, rising and falling, seeming at one moment leagues away, at others sweeping across the snow until it appeared to come from the foot of the castle walls. All the starved, cold misery of a frozen world, all the relentless hunger-fury of the wild, blended with other forlorn and haunting melodies to which one could give no name, seemed concentrated in that wailing cry.

'Wolves!' cried the Baron.

Their music broke forth in one raging burst, seeming to come from everywhere.

'Hundreds of wolves,' said the Hamburg merchant, who was a man of strong imagination.

Moved by some impulse which she could not have explained, the Baroness left her guests and made her way to the narrow cheerless room where the old governess lay watching the hours of the dying year slip by. In spite of the biting cold of the winter night, the window stood open. With a scandalised exclamation on her lips, the Baroness rushed forward to close it.

'Leave it open,' said the old woman in a voice that for all its weakness carried an air of command such as the Baroness had never heard before from her lips.

'But you will die of cold!' she expostulated.

'I am dying in any case,' said the voice, 'and I want to hear their music. They have come from far and wide to sing the death-music of my family. It is beautiful that they have come; I am the last von Cernogratz that will die in our old castle, and they have come to sing to me. Hark, how loud they are calling!'

The cry of the wolves rose on the still winter air and floated round the castle walls in long-drawn piercing wails; the old woman lay back on her couch with a look of long-delayed happiness on her face.

'Go away,' she said to the Baroness; 'I am not lonely any more. I am one of a great old family. ...'

'I think she is dying,' said the Baroness when she had rejoined her guests; 'I suppose we must send for a doctor. And that terrible howling! Not for much money would I have such death-music.'

'That music is not to be bought for any amount of money,' said Conrad.

'Hark! What is that other sound?' asked the Baron, as a noise of splitting and crashing was heard.

It was a tree falling in the park.

There was a moment of constrained silence, and then the banker's wife spoke.

'It is the intense cold that is splitting the trees. It is also the cold that brought the wolves out in such numbers. It is many years since we have had such a cold winter.'

The Baroness eagerly agreed that the cold was responsible for these things. It was the cold of the open window, too, which caused the heart failure that made the doctor's ministrations unnecessary for the old Fräulein. But the notice in the newspapers looked very well –

'On December 29th, at Schloss Cernogratz, Amalie von Cernogratz, for many years the valued friend of Baron and Baroness Gruebel.'

Jumble

RICHMAL CROMPTON

It stopped in front of William with a glad bark of welcome.

Illustration by Henry Thomas

JUMBLE

William's father carefully placed the bow and arrow at the back of the library cupboard, then closed the cupboard door and locked it in grim silence. William's eyes, large, reproachful, and gloomy, followed every movement.

'Three windows and Mrs. Clive's cat all in one morning,' began Mr. Brown sternly.

'I didn't *mean* to hit the cat,' said William earnestly. 'I didn't – honest. I wouldn't go round teasin' cats. They get so mad at you, cats do. It jus' got in the way. I couldn't stop shootin' in time. An' I didn't *mean* to break those windows. I wasn't *tryin'* to hit them. I've not hit anything I was trying to hit yet,' wistfully. 'I've not got into it. It's jus' a knack. It jus' wants practice.'

Mr. Brown pocketed the key.

'It's a knack you aren't likely to acquire by practice on this instrument,' he said drily.

William wandered out into the garden and looked sadly up at the garden wall. But The Little Girl Next Door was away and could offer no sympathy, even if he climbed up to his precarious seat on the top. Fate was against him in every way. With a deep sigh he went out of the garden gate and strolled down the road disconsolately, hands in pockets.

Life stretched empty and uninviting before him without his bow and arrow. And Ginger would have his bow and arrow, Henry would have his bow and arrow, Douglas would have his bow and arrow. He, William, alone would be a thing apart, a social outcast, a boy without a bow and arrow; for bows and arrows were the fashion. If only one of the others would break a window or hit a silly old cat that hadn't the sense to keep out of the way.

He came to a stile leading into a field and took his seat upon it dejectedly, his elbows on his knees, his chin in his hands. Life was simply not worth living.

'A rotten old cat!' he said aloud, 'a rotten old cat! – and didn't even hurt it. It – it made a fuss – jus' out of spite, screamin' and carryin' on! And windows! – as if glass wasn't cheap enough – and easy to put in. I could – I could mend 'em myself – if I'd got the stuff to do it. I –' He stopped. Something was coming down the road. It came jauntily with a light, dancing step, fox-terrier ears cocked, retriever nose raised, collie tail wagging, slightly dachshund body a-quiver with the joy of life.

It stopped in front of William with a glad bark of welcome, then stood eager, alert, friendly, a mongrel unashamed.

'Rats! Fetch 'em out!' said William idly.

It gave a little spring and waited, front paws apart and crouching, a waggish eye upraised to William. William broke off a stick from the hedge and threw it. His visitor darted after it with a shrill bark, took it up, worried it, threw it into the air, caught it, growled at it, finally brought it back to William and waited, panting, eager, unmistakably grinning, begging for more.

William's drooping spirits revived. He descended from his perch and examined its collar. It bore the one word 'Jumble.'

'Hey! Jumble!' he called, setting off down the road.

Jumble jumped up around him, dashed off, dashed back, worried his boots, jumped up at him again in wild, eager friendship, dashed off again, begged for another stick, caught it, rolled over with it, growled at it, then chewed it up and laid the remains at William's feet.

'Good ole chap!' said William encouragingly. 'Good ole Jumble! Come on, then.'

Jumble came on. William walked through the village with a self-conscious air of proud yet careless ownership, while Jumble gambolled round his heels.

Every now and then he would turn his head and whistle imperiously, to recall his straying *protégé* from the investigation of ditches and roadside. It was a whistle, commanding, controlling, yet withal careless, that William had sometimes practised privately in readiness for the blissful day when Fate should present him with a real live dog of his own. So far Fate, in the persons of his father and mother, had been proof against all his pleading.

William passed a blissful morning. Jumble swam in the pond, he fetched sticks out of it, he shook himself violently all over William, he ran after a hen, he was chased by a cat, he barked at a herd of cows, he pulled down a curtain that was hanging out in a cottage garden to dry – he was mischievous, affectionate, humorous, utterly irresistible – and he completely adopted William. William would turn a corner with a careless swagger and then watch breathlessly to see if the rollicking, frisky little figure would follow after him, and always it came tearing after him.

William was rather late to lunch. His father and mother and elder brother and sister were just beginning the meal. He slipped quietly and unostentatiously into his seat. His father was reading a newspaper. Mr. Brown always took two daily papers, one of which he perused at breakfast and the other at lunch.

'William,' said Mrs. Brown, 'I do wish you'd be in time, and I do wish you'd brush your hair before you come to table.'

William raised a hand to perform the operation, but catching sight of its colour, hastily lowered it.

'No, Ethel dear, I didn't know anyone had taken Lavender Cottage. An artist? How nice! William dear, *do* sit still. Have they moved in yet?'

'Yes,' said Ethel, 'they've taken it furnished for two months, I think. Oh, my goodness, just *look* at William's hands!'

William put his hands under the table and glared at her.

'Go and wash you hands, dear,' said Mrs. Brown patiently.

For eleven years she had filled the trying position of William's mother. It had taught her patience.

William rose reluctantly.

'They're not dirty,' he said in a tone of righteous indignation. 'Well, anyway, they've been dirtier other times and you've said nothin'. I can't be *always* washin' them, can I? Some sorts of hands get dirty quicker than others an' if you keep on washin' it only makes them worse an' –'

Ethel groaned and William's father lowered his paper. William withdrew quickly but with an air of dignity.

'And just *look* at his boots!' said Ethel as he went. 'Simply caked; and his stockings are soaking wet – you can see from here. He's been right *in* the pond by the look of him and –'

William heard no more. There were moments when he actively disliked Ethel.

He returned a few minutes later, shining with cleanliness, his hair brushed back fiercely off his face.

'His *nails*,' murmured Ethel as he sat down.

'Well,' said Mrs. Brown, 'go on telling us about the new people. William, do hold your knife properly, dear. Yes, Ethel?'

William finished his meal in silence, then brought forth his momentous announcement.

'I've gotter dog,' he said with an air of importance.

'What sort of dog?' and 'Who gave it to you?' said Robert and Ethel simultaneously.

'No one gave it me,' he said. 'I jus' got it. It began following me this morning an' I couldn't get rid of it. It wouldn't go, anyway. It followed me all round the village an' it came home with me. I couldn't get rid of it, anyhow.'

'Where is it now?' said Mr. Brown anxiously.

'In the back garden.'

Mr. Brown folded up his paper.

'Digging up my flower-beds, I suppose,' he said with despairing resignation.

'He's tied up all right,' William reassured him. 'I tied him to the tree in the middle of the rose-bed.'

'The rose-bed!' groaned his father. 'Good Lord!'

'Has he had anything to eat?' demanded Robert sternly.

'Yes,' said William, avoiding his mother's eye. 'I found a few bits of old things for him in the larder.'

William's father took out his watch and rose from the table.

'Well, you'd better take it to the Police Station this afternoon,' he said shortly.

'The Police Station!' repeated William hoarsely. 'It's not a *lost* dog. It – it jus' doesn't belong to anyone, at least it didn't. Poor thing,' feelingly. 'It – it doesn't want *much* to make it happy. It can sleep in my room an' jus' eat scraps.'

'You'll have to take it, you know, William,' said Mrs. Brown, 'so be quick. You know where the Police Station is, don't you? Shall I come with you?'

'No, thank you,' said William hastily.

A few minutes later he was walking down to the Police Station followed by the still eager Jumble, who trotted along, unconscious of his doom.

Upon William's face was a set, stern expression which cleared slightly as he neared the Police Station. He stood at the gate and looked at Jumble. Jumble placed his front paws ready for a game and wagged his tail.

'Well,' said William, 'here you are. Here's the Police Station.'

Jumble gave a shrill bark. 'Hurry up with that stick or that race, whichever you like,' he seemed to say.

'Well, go in,' said William, nodding his head in the direction of the door.

Jumble began to worry a big stone in the road. He rolled it along with his paws, then ran after it with fierce growls.

'Well, it's the Police Station,' said William. 'Go in if you want.'

With that he turned on his heel and walked home, without one backward glance. But he walked slowly, with many encouraging 'Hey! Jumbles' and many short commanding whistles. And Jumble trotted happily at his heels. There was no one in the garden, there was no one in the hall, there was no one on the stairs. Fate was for once on William's side.

William appeared at the tea-table well washed and brushed, wearing that air of ostentatious virtue that those who knew him best connected with his most daring coups.

'Did you take that dog to the Police Station, William?' said William's father.

William coughed.

'Yes, father,' he said meekly with his eyes upon his plate.

'What did they say about it?'

'Nothing, father.'

'I suppose I'd better spend the evening re-planting those rose-trees,' went on his father bitterly.

'And William gave him a *whole* steak and kidney pie,' murmured Mrs. Brown. 'Cook will have to make another for to-morrow.'

William coughed again politely, but did not raise his eyes from his plate.

'What is that noise?' said Ethel. 'Listen!'

They sat, listening intently. There was a dull grating sound as of the scratching of wood.

'It's upstairs,' said Robert with the air of a Sherlock Holmes.

Then came a shrill, impatient bark.

'It's a *dog!*' said the four of them simultaneously. 'It's William's dog.'

They all turned horrified eyes upon William, who coloured slightly but continued to eat a piece of cake with an unconvincing air of abstraction.

'I thought you said you'd taken that dog to the Police Station, William,' said Mr. Brown sternly.

'I did,' said William with decision. 'I did take it to the Police Station an' I came home. I s'pose it must of got out an' come home an' gone up into my bedroom.'

'Where did you leave it? In the Police Station?'

'No – at it – jus' at the gate.'

Mr. Brown rose with an air of weariness.

'Robert,' he said, 'will you please see that that animal goes to the Police Station this evening?'

'Yes, father,' said Robert, with a vindictive glare at William.

William followed him upstairs.

'Beastly nuisance!' muttered Robert.

Jumble, who was chewing William's door, greeted them ecstatically.

'Look!' said William bitterly. 'Look at how it knows one! Nice thing to send a dog that knows one like that to the Police Station! Mean sort of trick!'

Robert surveyed it coldly.

'Rotten little mongrel!' he said from the heights of superior knowledge.

'Mongrel!' said William indignantly. 'There jus' isn't no mongrel about *him*. Look at him! An' he can learn tricks easy as easy. Look at him sit up and beg. I only taught him this afternoon.'

He took a biscuit out of his pocket and held it up. Jumble rose unsteadily on to his hind legs and tumbled over backwards. He wagged his tail and grinned, intensely amused. Robert's expression of superiority relaxed.

'Do it again,' he said. 'Not so far back. Here! Give it me. Come on, come on, old chap! That's it! Now stay there! Stay there! Good dog! Got any more? Let's try him again.'

During the next twenty minutes they taught him to sit up and almost taught him 'Trust' and 'Paid for.' There was certainly a charm about Jumble. Even Robert felt it. Then Ethel's voice came up the stairs.

'Robert! Sydney Bellew's come for you.'

'Blow the wretched dog!' said the fickle Robert rising, red and dishevelled from stooping over Jumble. 'We were going to walk to Fairfields and the beastly Police Station's right out of our way.'

'I'll take it Robert,' said William kindly. 'I will really.'

Robert eyed him suspiciously.

'Yes, you took it this afternoon, didn't you?'

'I will honest, to-night, Robert. Well, I couldn't, could I?'

'I don't know,' said Robert darkly. 'No one ever knows what *you* are going to do!'

Sydney's voice came up.

'Hurry up, old chap! We shall never have time to do it before dark, if you aren't quick.'

'I'll take him, honest, Robert.'

Robert hesitated and was lost.

'Well,' he said, 'just mind you do, that's all, or I'll jolly well hear about it. I'll see *you* do too.

So William started off once more towards the Police Station with Jumble, still blissfully happy, at his heels. William walked slowly, eyes fixed on the ground, brows knit in deep thought. It was very rarely that William admitted himself beaten.

'Hello, William!'

Ginger stood before him holding his bow and arrows ostentatiously.

'You've had your bow and arrow took off you!' he jeered.

William fixed his eye moodily upon him for a minute, then very gradually his eye brightened and his face cleared. William had an idea.

'If I give you a dog half time,' he said slowly, 'will you give me your bow and arrows half time?'

'Where's your dog?' said Ginger suspiciously.

William did not turn his head.

'There's one behind me, isn't there,' he said anxiously. 'Hey Jumble!'

'Oh, yes, he's just come out of the ditch.'

'Well,' continued William, 'I'm taking him to the Police Station and I'm just goin' on an' he's following me and if you take him off me I won't see you 'cause I won't turn round and jus' take hold of his collar an' he's called Jumble an' take him up to the old barn and we'll keep him there an' join at him and feed him days and days about and you let me practise on your bow and arrow. That's fair, isn't it?'

Ginger considered thoughtfully.

'All right,' he said laconically.

William walked on to the Police Station without turning round.

'Well?' whispered Robert sternly that evening.

'I took him, Robert – least – I started off with him, but when I'd got there he'd gone. I looked round and he'd jus' gone. I couldn't see him anywhere, so I came home.'

'Well, if he comes to this house again,' said Robert, 'I'll wring his neck, so just you look out.'

Two days later William sat in the barn on an upturned box, chin in hands, gazing down at Jumble. A paper bag containing Jumble's ration for the day lay beside him. It was his day of ownership. The collecting of Jumble's 'scraps' was a matter of infinite care and trouble. They consisted of – a piece of bread that William had managed to slip into his pocket during breakfast, a piece of meat he had managed to slip into his pocket during dinner, a jam puff stolen from the larder and a bone removed from the dustbin. Ginger roamed the fields with his bow and arrow while William revelled in the ownership of Jumble. To-morrow William would roam the fields with bow and arrow and Ginger would assume ownership of Jumble.

William spent the morning teaching Jumble several complicated tricks, and adoring him more and more completely each moment. He grudged him bitterly to Ginger, but – the charm of the bow and arrow was strong. He wished to terminate the partnership, to resign Ginger's bow and arrow and take the irresistible Jumble wholly to himself. He thought of the bow and arrow in the library cupboard; he thought, planned, plotted, but could find no way out. He did not see a man come to the door of the barn and stand there leaning against the door-post watching him. He was a tall man with a thin, lean face and a loose-fitting tweed suit. As his eyes lit upon William and Jumble they narrowed suddenly and his mobile lips curved into a slight unconscious smile.

Jumble saw him first and went towards him wagging his tail. William looked up and scowled ungraciously. The stranger raised his hat.

'Good afternoon,' he said politely. 'Do you remember what you were thinking about just then?'

William looked at him with a certain interest, speculating upon his probable insanity. He imagined lunatics were amusing people.

'Yes.'

'Well, if you'll think of it again and look just like that, I'll give you anything you like. It's a rash promise, but I will.'

William promptly complied. He quite forgot the presence of the strange man, who took a little block out of his pocket and began to sketch William's inscrutable, brooding face.

'Daddy!'

The man sighed and put away his block.

'You'll do it again for me one day, won't you, and I'll keep my promise. Hello!'

A little girl appeared now at the barn door, dainty, dark-eyed and exquisitely dressed. She threw a lightning flash at the occupants of the barn.

'Daddy!' she screamed. 'It's Jumble! It *is* Jumble! Oh, you horrid dog-stealing boy!'

Jumble ran to her with shrill barks of welcome, then ran back to William to reassure him of his undying loyalty.

'It *is* Jumble,' said the man. 'He's called Jumble,' he explained to William, 'because he is a jumble. He's all sorts of dog, you know. This is Ninette, my daughter, and my name is Jarrow, and we've taken Lavender Cottage for two months. We're roving vagabonds. We never stay anywhere longer than two months. So now you know all about us. Jumble seems to have adopted you. Ninette, my dear, you are completely ousted from Jumble's heart. This gentleman reigns supreme.'

'I *didn't* steal him,' said William indignantly. 'He just came. He began following me. I didn't want him to – not jus' at first anyway, not much anyway. I suppose,' a dreadful fear came to his heart, 'I suppose you want him back?'

'You can keep him for a bit if you want him, can't he Daddy? Daddy's going to buy me a Pom – a dear little white Pom. When we lost Jumble, I thought I'd rather have a Pom. Jumble's so rough and he's not really a *good* dog. I mean he's no pedigree.'

'Then can I keep him jus' for a bit?' said William, his voice husky with eagerness.

'Oh, yes. I'd much rather have a quieter sort of dog. Would you like to come and see our cottage? It's just over here.'

William, slightly bewildered but greatly relieved, set off with her. Mr. Jarrow followed slowly behind. It appeared that Miss Ninette Jarrow was rather a wonderful person. She was eleven years old. She had visited every capital in Europe, seen the best art and heard the best music in each. She had been to every play then on in London. She knew all the newest dances.

'Do you like Paris?' she asked William as they went towards Lavender Cottage.

'Never been there,' said William stolidly, glancing round surreptitiously to see that Jumble was following.

She shook her dark curly head from side to side – a little trick she had. 'You funny boy. *Mais vous parlez Francais, n'est ce pas?*'

William disdained to answer. He whistled to Jumble, who was chasing an imaginary rabbit in a ditch.

'Can you jazz?' she asked.

'I don't know,' he said guardedly. 'I've not tried. I expect I could.'

She took a few flying graceful steps with slim black silk-encased legs.

'That's it. I'll teach you at home. We'll dance it to a gramophone.'

William walked on in silence.

She stopped suddenly under a tree and held up her little vivacious, piquant face to him.

'You can kiss me if you like,' she said.

William looked at her dispassionately.

'I don't want to, thanks,' he said politely.

'Oh, you *are* a funny boy! she said with a ripple of laughter, 'and you look so rough and untidy. You're rather like Jumble. Do you like Jumble?'

'Yes,' said William. His voice had a sudden quaver in it. His ownership of Jumble was a thing of the past.

'You can have him for always and always,' she said suddenly. '*Now* kiss me!'

He kissed her cheek awkwardly with the air of one determined to do his duty, but with a great, glad relief at his heart.

'I'd love to see you dance,' she laughed. 'You *would* look funny.'

She took a few more fairy steps.

'You've seen Pavlova, haven't you?'

'Dunno.'

'You must know.'

'I mustn't,' said William irritably. 'I might have seen him and not known it was him, mightn't I?'

She raced back to her father with another ripple of laughter.

'He's *such* a funny boy, Daddy, and he can't jazz and he's never seen Pavlova, and he can't talk French and I've given him Jumble and he didn't want to kiss me!'

Mr. Jarrow fixed William with a drily quizzical smile.

'Beware, young man,' he said. 'She'll try to educate you. I know her. I warn you.'

As they got to the door of Lavender Cottage he turned to William.

'Now just sit and think for a minute. I'll keep my promise.'

'I do like you,' said Ninette graciously as he took his departure. 'You must come again. I'll teach you heaps of things. I think I'd like to marry you when we grow up. You're so – *restful*.'

William came home the next afternoon to find Mr. Jarrow in the armchair in the library talking to his father.

'I was just dry for a subject,' he was saying; 'at my wits' end, and when I saw them there, I had a Heaven-sent inspiration. Ah! here he is. Ninette wants you to come to tea to-morrow, William. Ninette's given him Jumble. Do you mind?' turning to Mr. Brown.

Mr. Brown swallowed hard.

'I'm trying not to,' he said. 'He kept us all awake last night, but I suppose we'll get used to it."

'And I made him a rash promise,' went on Mr. Jarrow, 'and I'm jolly well going to keep it if it's humanly possible. William, what would you like best in all the world?'

William fixed his eyes unflinchingly upon his father.

'I'd like my bow and arrows back out of that cupboard,' he said firmly.

Mr. Jarrow looked at William's father beseechingly.

'Don't let me down,' he implored. 'I'll pay for all the damage.'

Slowly and with a deep sigh Mr. Brown drew a bunch of keys from his pocket.

'It means that we all go once more in hourly peril of our lives,' he said resignedly.

After tea William set off again down the road. The setting sun had turned the sky to gold. There was a soft haze over all the countryside. The clear bird songs filled all the air, and the hedgerows were bursting into summer. And through it all marched William, with a slight swagger, his bow under one arm, his arrows under the other, while at his heels trotted Jumble, eager, playful, adoring – a mongrel unashamed – all sorts of a dog. And at William's heart was a proud, radiant happiness.

There was a picture in that year's Academy that attracted a good deal of attention. It was of a boy sitting on an upturned box in a barn, his elbows on his knees, his chin in his hands. He was gazing down at a mongrel dog and in his freckled face was the solemnity and unconscious, eager wistfulness that is the mark of youth. His untidy, unbrushed hair stood up round his face. The mongrel was looking up, quivering expectant, trusting, adoring, some reflection of the boy's eager wistfulness showing in the eyes and cocked ear. It was called 'Friendship.'

Mrs. Brown went up to see it. She said it wasn't really a very good likeness of William and she wished they'd made him look a little tidier.

The
First Release

JOY ADAMSON

THE FIRST RELEASE

After raising Elsa from a cub the time has come when Joy
Adamson must take her back to the game reserve and encourage
the lioness to fend for herself.

It was after midnight when we had at last secured Elsa in her travelling crate and started off. In the hope of making the trip easier for her I gave her a tranquilliser; we had been told by the vet that the drug was harmless and that the effect would last about eight hours. To give Elsa all the moral support I could, I travelled with her in the open lorry. During the night we passed through country that is 8,000 feet above sea level, and the cold was icy. Owing to the effect of the tranquilliser Elsa was only semi-conscious, yet even in this state every few minutes she stretched her paws out through the bars of the crate, to assure herself that I was still there. It took us seventeen hours to reach our destination. The effect of the tranquilliser did not wear off until an hour after we had arrived. During these eighteen hours Elsa became very cold, her breathing was slow and for a time I feared that she was going to die. Luckily she recovered, but this experience showed us that one should be very careful with drugs where lions are concerned, for they are far more sensitive to them than other animals and individually they react differently. We had had previous experience of this when we had powdered all three cubs with an insecticide – one took it well, one became sick, and Elsa was very ill with convulsions.

It was late in the afternoon by the time we reached our destination: there we were met by a friend who is the Game Warden of this district. We pitched camp on a superb site at the base of a thousand-foot escarpment overlooking a vast plain of open bush country, through which a belt of dark vegetation marks the course of a river. As we were at an altitude of 5,000 feet, the air was fresh and brisk. Immediately in front of our camp lay open grassland sloping towards the plain, on which herds of Thomson's gazelle, topi, wildebeeste, Burchell's zebra, roan antelope, kongoni, and a few buffalo were grazing. It was a game paradise. While the tents were being pitched we took Elsa for a stroll and she rushed at the herds, not knowing which to follow, for in every direction there were animals running. As if to shake off the effects of the ghastly journey, Elsa lost herself among these new playmates, who were rather astonished to find such a strange lion in their midst; one who rushed foolishly to and fro without any apparent purpose. Soon, however, Elsa had had enough and trotted back to camp and her dinner.

Our plan was this; we would spend the first week taking Elsa, perched on the roof of the Landrover, round the new country, thus getting her used to it and to the animals, many of which belonged to species which do not live in the Northern Frontier and she had therefore never seen. During the second week we intended to leave her overnight, while she was active in the bush, and to visit and feed her in the mornings when she was sleepy. Afterwards we would reduce her meals, in the hope that this would encourage her to kill on her own, or to join a wild lion.

On the morning after our arrival we started our programme. First we took off her collar, as the symbol of liberation. Elsa hopped on to the roof of the Landrover and we went off. After only a few hundred yards we saw a lioness walking parallel to us downhill; she passed close to many antelope who took no notice of her, realising no doubt from her determined steady stride, that at the moment, she was not interested in killing. We drove closer to the lioness. Elsa displayed much excitement, jumped off her seat and, making low moaning noises, cautiously followed this new friend. But as soon as the lioness stopped and turned round, her courage failed and she raced back as fast as she could to the safety of the car. The lioness continued her purposeful walk, and we soon detected six cubs waiting for her on a small ant-hill in tall grass.

We drove on and surprised a hyena chewing a bone. Elsa jumped off and chased the startled animal, who had only time to grasp her bone and lumber away. In spite of her ungainliness, she made good her escape but lost her bone in the process.

Later we passed through herd after herd of different antelope, whose curiosity seemed to be aroused by the sight of a Landrover with a lion on it and allowed us, provided that we remained in the car and did not talk, to approach within a few yards of them. All the time Elsa watched carefully, but did not attempt to leave the car unless she spotted an animal off guard, grazing with its back towards her, or fighting; then she would get down quietly and creep forward with her belly close to the ground, taking advantage of every bit of cover, and thus advance towards her victim. But as soon as the animal showed any suspicion, she either froze to immobility or, if the situation seemed better handled in another way, she pretended to be uninterested, licked her paws, yawned, or even rolled on her back, until the animal was reassured. Then she would at once start stalking again. But however cunning she was, she never got close enough to kill.

The little Thomson's gazelles provoked Elsa, very unfairly, relying on the unwritten law of the bush that a superior creature will not attack a smaller one, except for food. They are the real urchins of the plain, most inquisitive and always busy with their tails. Now they challenged her, teased her and simply asked to be chased; but Elsa only looked bored, ignored them and, with dignity, put them in their place.

Buffalo and rhino were quite another matter. They *had* to be chased. One day, from the car, we watched a buffalo cantering across the plain. Perhaps his curiosity was aroused by seeing a lion in the Landrover. Quickly Elsa jumped to the ground and, using the cover of a bush, set out to stalk him. The buffalo had the same idea and also used this cover but starting from the opposite direction. We waited, and watched, until we saw them nearly collide. Then it was the buffalo who bolted, with Elsa bravely following him.

On another occasion, from her seat on the Landrover she saw two buffaloes asleep in a bush. Off she went; bellows, crashing, and a wild commotion followed, then the buffaloes broke through the thicket and galloped away in different directions.

Rhino too were most inviting; one day we came upon one standing fast asleep with its head buried in a bush. Elsa stalked him very carefully and succeeded in nearly rubbing noses with him. Then the poor beast had an abrupt awakening, gave a startled snort and, looking bewildered, spun round on himself and dashed into a nearby swamp. There he churned up the water and gave Elsa a shower-bath; she splashed on after him; outlined against high sprays of water, the pair disappeared from our sight, and it was a long time before Elsa returned, wet but proud.

She loved climbing trees, and sometimes when we had looked in vain for her in the high grass we found her swaying in the crown of a tree. More than once she had difficulty in getting down again. Once, after trying various possibilities, and making the branch she was on bend alarmingly under her weight, we saw her tail dangling through the foliage, followed by her struggling hind legs, till finally she fell on to the grass well over twenty feet below. She was most embarrassed at having lost her dignity before an audience, for, while she always enjoyed making us laugh when she meant to do so, she hated being laughed at when the joke was against her. Now she walked quickly away from us and we gave her time to regain her self-respect. When we looked for her later on, we found her holding court with six hyenas. These sinister creatures sat in a circle around her, and I felt rather nervous for her. But as though to offset her earlier clumsiness in the tree she now showed us that she was very superior to the hyenas who bored her. She yawned, stretched herself and, ignoring the hyenas, walked up to us. The hyenas hobbled off, looking over their shoulders, perhaps puzzled by the appearance of Elsa's strange friends.

One morning we followed circling vultures and soon found a lion on a zebra kill. He was tearing at the meat and paid no attention to us. Elsa stepped cautiously from the car, miaowing at him and then, though she did not get any encouragement, advanced carefully towards him. At last the lion looked up and straight at Elsa. He seemed to say, 'Don't you know lion etiquette? How dare you, woman, interfere with the lord while he is having his meal? You are allowed to kill for me, but afterwards you have to wait till I have had my lion's share, then you may finish up the remains.' Evidently poor Elsa did not like this expression and returned as fast as she could to the safety of the car. The lord continued feeding and we watched him for a long time, hoping that Elsa might regain her courage; but nothing would induce her to leave her safe position.

Next morning we had better luck. We saw a topi standing, like a sentry, on an ant-hill, looking intently in one direction. We followed his glance and discovered a young lion resting in the high grass, sunning himself. He was a magnificent young male with a beautiful blond mane, and Elsa seemed attracted by him. Just the right husband for her, we thought. We drove to within thirty yards of him. The lion looked mildly surprised when he saw his prospective bride sitting on top of a car, but responded in a friendly manner. Elsa, apparently overcome by coyness, made low moans but would not come off the roof. So we drove a little distance away and persuaded her to get down, then, suddenly, we left her and drove round to the other side of the lion: this meant that she would have to pass him in order to reach us. After much painful hesitation, she plucked up enough courage to walk towards the lion. When she was about ten paces away from him, she lay down with her ears back and her tail swishing. The lion got up and went towards her, with, I am sure, the friendliest intentions, but at the last moment Elsa panicked and rushed back to the car.

We drove away with her and, strangely enough, right into a pride of two lions and one lioness on a kill.

This was luck indeed. They must have killed very recently for they were so intent upon their meal that however much Elsa talked to them they paid not the slightest attention to her. Finally they left the kill, their bulging stomachs swinging from side to side. Elsa lost no time in inspecting the remains of the carcass, her first contact with a real kill. Nothing could have served our purpose better than this meal, provided by lions and full of their fresh scent. After Elsa had had her fair share, we dragged the kill back to the handsome young lion who had seemed so friendly. We hoped that if Elsa provided him with a meal he would have a favourable opinion of her. Then we left her and the kill near to him and drove away. After a few hours we set out to see what had happened, but met Elsa already half-way back to the camp. However, since the lion had shown an interest in her, we took her back to him during the afternoon. We found him still in the same place. Elsa talked to him from her couch as though they were old friends, but had plainly no intention of leaving the car.

To induce her to quit her seat, we drove behind a bush and I got out but was nearly knocked over by a hyena who dashed out of his cool retreat, in which we then found a newly killed baby zebra, no doubt provided by the blond lion. It was Elsa's feeding time, so regardless of the consequences, she jumped out of the car on to the carcass. We took this opportunity to drive away as fast as we could and left her alone for her night's adventure. Early next morning, anxious to know the outcome of the experiment, we set off to visit her, hoping to find a happy pair. What we found was poor Elsa, waiting at the spot at which we left her, but minus the lion and minus the kill. She was overjoyed to see us, desperate to stay with us, and sucked my thumbs frantically to make sure that everything was all right between us. I was very unhappy that I had hurt her feelings without being able to explain to her that all we had done was intended to be for her good. When she had calmed down and even felt safe enough in our company to fall asleep, we decided, rather sadly, that we must break faith with her again and we sneaked away.

Till now we had always given her her meat already cut up, so that she should not associate her food with living animals. Now we needed to reverse our system, so during her midday sleep we drove sixty miles to shoot a small buck for her. We had to go this distance because no one was allowed to shoot game near the camp. We brought her a complete buck wondering if she would know how to open it, since she had had no mother to teach her the proper way of doing it. We soon saw that by instinct she knew exactly what to do; she started at the inner part of the hind legs, where the skin is softest, then tore out the guts, and after enjoying these delicacies, buried the stomach contents and covered up the blood spoor, as all proper lions do. Then she gnawed the meat off the bones with her molars and rasped it away with her rough tongue.

Once we knew that she could do this it was time for us to let her do her own killing. The plain was covered with isolated bush clusters, ideal hide-outs for any animal. All the lions had to do, when they wanted a meal, was to wait under cover until an antelope approached down wind, rush out and get their dinner.

We now left Elsa alone for two or three days at a time, hoping that hunger would make her kill. But when we came back we always found her waiting for us and hungry. It was heart-breaking having to stick to our programme, when obviously all she wanted was to be with us and sure of our affection. This she showed very clearly by sucking my thumbs and holding on to us with her paws. All the same we knew that for her good we must persevere.

By now we realised that it was going to take us much longer to release her to nature than we expected; we therefore asked the Government if we could use our long leave in the country for the purpose of carrying out this experiment and, very kindly, they consented. After receiving this permission we felt much relieved since we knew that we should now have the time required for our task.

We increased the number of days on which Elsa was left on her own and we reinforced the thorn fences round our tents, so that they were strong enough to keep any lion out. This we did specifically to prevent Elsa from visiting us when she was hungry.

One morning, when she was with us, we located a lion, who seemed placid and in a good mood: she stepped off the car and we tactfully left the pair alone. That evening while sitting in our thorn-protected tent, we suddenly heard Elsa's miaow and before we could stop her, she crept through the thorns and settled down with us. She was bleeding from claw marks and had walked eight miles back, obviously preferring our company to that of the lion.

The next time we took her a longer distance away from camp.

As we drove we saw two eland bulls, each weighing about 1,500 lb., engaged in a fight. Elsa promptly jumped off the car and stalked them. At first, they were so engaged in their fight that they did not notice her, but when they became aware of her presence she narrowly missed a savage kick from one of them. They broke off the fight and Elsa chased them a short distance and finally came back very proud of herself.

Soon afterwards we met two young lions sitting on the grass in the open. They looked to us ideal companions for Elsa, but by now she was very suspicious of our tricks and would not leave the car, although she talked very agitatedly to them; as we had no means of dropping her off we had to miss this opportunity and went on until we met two Thomson's gazelles fighting; this sight caused Elsa to jump off and we drove quickly away, leaving her to learn more about wild life.

It was nearly a week before we returned. We found her waiting, and very hungry. She was full of affection, we had deceived her so often, broken faith with her, done so much to destroy her trust in us, yet she remained loyal. We dropped some meat which we had brought with us and she immediately started to eat it. Suddenly we heard unmistakable growls and soon saw two lions trotting fast towards us. They were obviously on the hunt and probably they had scented the meat; they approached very quickly. Poor Elsa took in the situation and bolted as hurriedly as she could, leaving her precious meal. At once a little jackal appeared, that up till now must have been hiding in the grass; he lost no time in taking his chance and began to take bite after bite at Elsa's meat, knowing that his luck was not going to last long. This proved true for one of the lions advanced steadily upon him, uttering threatening growls. But meat was meat and the little jackal was not to be easily frightened away; he held on to his possession and took as many bites as he could until the lion was practically on top of him. Even then, with unbelievable pluck he tried to save his meal. But size prevailed over courage and the lion was the winner. Elsa watched this scene from a distance and saw her first meal, after so many days, being taken away from her. In the circumstances it seemed hard that the two lions took no interest in anything but their food and completely ignored her. To compensate her for her disappoint we took her away.

While we were in camp we had some human visitors. Late one morning a Landrover drove up to camp containing a Roman Catholic missionary and a well-known Kenya personality and his young son. They had come to look at game. George asked them in and was just about to explain that we had a tame lioness in camp, when Elsa, hearing the car, came bounding in, full of curiosity and friendliness. With her usual good manners she made for the visitors, to greet them. They looked a little startled, to say the least of it, particularly the holy father, but I must say they took it very well. Then Elsa, having done her duty, flung herself down beside the table and went to sleep.

Then a Swiss couple, having heard that we had a lion cub, came to see it. I think they had visions of something small which could be picked up and cuddled, but seeing the three hundred-odd pound Elsa on the roof of the Landrover made them pause, and it was a little time before we could persuade them to get out of their car and join us at lunch. Elsa was courtesy itself, welcomed the strangers, and only once swept the table clear with her tail. After this, they could not have enough of her and had themselves photographed with her at every angle.

We had been in camp for four weeks and although Elsa had spent most of the last fortnight in the bush, she had not yet started killing for herself. By now, the rains had begun and every afternoon there were heavy showers. The conditions in this region were very different to those at

Isiolo; for one thing it was much colder, for another while the ground at Isiolo is sandy and dries within a few hours, here there was a black cotton soil which turns into a morass after rain; moreover, it is covered with waist-high grass, which prevents it drying for weeks on end. At home Elsa had enjoyed the rains and been invigorated by them, but here she was very miserable.

One night very heavy rain fell without stopping; at least five inches came down before daybreak and the country was flooded. In the morning we waded out often knee-deep in mud, and we met Elsa already half-way back to the camp. She looked so unhappy and wanted so desperately to stay with us that we took her home. That evening we suddenly heard a terrified galloping come past our camp followed by a stillness. What drama was happening outside? Next arose the hysterical chuckles of hyena mingled with the high-pitched yells of jackal, but these were soon silenced by the growls of at least three lion. We realised that they must have killed just outside the camp. What a chance for Elsa. But while we listened, fascinated, to the grandiose chorus of shrill, piercing staccato noises interspersed with deep guttural rumblings, she rubbed her head against us and showed how glad she was to be inside the thorn fence in our company.

After a few days the rain decreased and we renewed our efforts to turn Elsa into a wild lioness. But she had become so suspicious of being deserted again that we had great difficulty in inducing her to follow us into the plains.

She did, however, in the end accompany us and we met two lionesses who came hurriedly towards the car, but Elsa bolted from them and seemed more nervous than ever.

It was evident that in this place she was scared of lions, so we decided not to go on trying to force her to make friends with them, but to wait till she came into season again, then perhaps she would choose her own mate by mutual attraction.

Meanwhile we would concentrate our efforts on training her to kill her food and thus to become independent of us. Also, once she could kill, she would be a more suitable partner for a lion, should she decide to join one. The plains were still under water and most of the game had concentrated on the few bits of slightly higher ground which were drier. Elsa loved one little hillock which was studded with rocks, and we therefore chose this place as her experimental headquarters. It was unfortunately only eight miles from our camp; it would have been better if we could have moved off to a greater distance but, under the existing weather conditions, this was not practicable.

The First Release

We left Elsa for a week on her hillock but, when we returned, she looked so unhappy that it needed all my will power to harden myself sufficiently to carry on with her education. We sat with her during the midday lull until she dozed off with her head on my lap. Suddenly, in the bush, just behind us, there was a frightening crash and a rhino appeared. We both jumped up like lightning, and while I ran behind a tree, Elsa gallantly charged the intruder and drove it away. Most unfairly, during her absence we deserted her again.

Late that afternoon the atmosphere became heavy with moisture and the setting sun was spectacularly reflected against dark red curtains of cloud hanging out of a grey sky pierced by fragments of parallel rainbows. This kaleidoscope of luminous colour changed rapidly into threatening dark clouds loaded with rain which finally towered above us in one black mass. All was in suspense waiting for the firmament to burst.

Then a few heavy drops fell like lead to the ground and now, as if two giant hands had torn the heavens apart, a deluge descended with such torrential force that soon our camp was in the middle of a running stream. For hours the flood continued. I imagined poor Elsa alone in this icy night, drenched and shivering and miserable; thunder and lightning added to my nightmare. Next morning we waded the eight miles to the ridge where we had left her. As usual, she was waiting for us, overjoyed to see us and greeted us each in turn by rubbing her head and body against us repeatedly, uttering her moaning noise. But to-day, there was no doubt that she was miserable, indeed she was nearly crying. We decided that, though it would interrupt her education, we could not leave her out in such weather. Unlike the local lions used to this climate, she came from a semi-desert country and could not quickly adapt herself to very different conditions. Now she was pleased to walk back with us splashing in her familiar Isiolo way through the swamp and showing how happy she was.

Next day she was ill. When she moved she was in great pain, her glands were swollen and she had a temperature. We made her a bed of grass in the annexe to George's tent and there she lay, panting, listless and pathetic. I treated her with M and B, the only drug which I thought might help. She wanted me to be near her all the time, which, of course, I was.

The rains had now set in, even a car with a four-wheel drive could not plough through to the nearest place at which blood slides could be tested, so we sent a runner the hundred-odd miles with various samples. The reply, when it came, stated that Elsa was infected with hook-worm and tapeworm, from both of which she had previously suffered and which we

221

knew how to treat. But neither of these troubles could account for her swollen glands or her temperature. We believed that she had also become infected by some tick-borne virus. If this proved true it would suggest that an animal, immune to diseases in its own environment, when transferred to another, does not carry the same immunity to local strains, and might be one explanation for the often puzzling distribution of animals found in East Africa.

Elsa became so ill that for a time we did not think that she would recover. However, after a week the fever became intermittent, every three or four days her temperature would rise and then go back again to normal. She was rapidly losing her beautiful golden colour, her coat was dull, like cotton wool, and she developed many white hairs on her back. Her face became ash grey. She had difficulty in dragging herself from the tent into the sparse sunshine; the only hopeful sign was her appetite. We gave her as much meat and milk as she wanted although both had to be fetched from a long distance. We also succeeded in spite of the transport difficulties arising from the weather in corresponding regularly with the Veterinary Laboratory in Nairobi, but as no sign of a parasite was found in the samples we provided we had to treat her more or less by guess-work.

We dosed her for hook-worm and for Rickettsia, a tick-borne parasite, which had been suggested as a possible cause of her illness, but as it was impossible to insert a hypodermic needle into a gland in order to obtain the fluid from which her illness might have been diagnosed, all we could do was to keep her as quiet as possible and give her the affection she needed. She was very gentle and responsive to all we did for her and often hugged me with her paws when I rested my head on her shoulders.

During her illness, because she lived so intimately with us, Elsa became more dependent on us and tamer than ever. Most of the day, she lay across the entrance to our thorn-fence enclosure, in a strategic position, which enabled her to watch all that went on inside the camp and outside on the plain as well. At meal times she preferred to have the boys step over her as they brought in our food than to move from her place. The staff laughingly competed at running the gauntlet while balancing full soup plates, getting spanked by Elsa in a friendly way as they passed over her.

She slept in the tent with George but was free to come and go as she pleased. Late one night, he was awakened by her low calls and heard her trying to get out of the back of the tent. He sat up and saw a shape in the doorway of the tent. Thinking that Elsa could not have got around so quickly he switched on his torch and saw a wild lioness blinking in the glare. He shouted at her and she went off. No doubt she had scented Elsa and, reassured by the lion noises coming from inside the tent, had decided to investigate.

It was now five weeks since Elsa's illness had started, and her condition had only improved slightly. It was plain that the climate in this region was against her, also that she might not be immune from local infections such as ticks and tsetse, which vary according to localities. Beside this she was different in appearance from the local lions – much darker in colour, with a longer nose, bigger ears and generally much smaller. In every way she belonged to the semi-desert and not to the highlands.[1] Finally, being in a game reserve meant that not only did George have to go twenty miles by car to get outside the reserve to shoot meat for her, but also that he could not take her hunting with him and thereby give her the opportunity of being in at the kill and getting the feel of pulling down a live animal – an experience which, in her wild state, she would have gained from her mother. It was evident therefore that after having camped here for three months we must try to choose a better home for her.

It was not easy to find an area which has a suitable climate, permanent water, enough game to supply her with food, and no tribesmen or hunting parties; moreover, it needed to be accessible by car. Eventually we discovered such a paradise and received the Government's permission to release a lion there. As soon as the rains ceased we decided to go there.

Camp was struck, and everything loaded into the cars, except Elsa. She chose that very day to come into season and had disappeared into the bush. We had waited for two and a half months for just this to happen, but we knew now that we could not allow her to go wild in this area. During the day there was no sign of her. We hunted for her everywhere, in the Landrover and on foot, but without success; finally we became very worried in case she might have been killed by a wild lioness. However, there was nothing to do but wait for her to return. For two days and nights she kept away, except for one short visit during which she rushed up to us, rubbed her head against our knees and dashed off again, only to come back a few minutes later, indulge in some more rubbings, then make off a second time and as quickly return, as though to tell us: 'I am very happy, but please understand I *must* go. I just came to tell you not to

[1]There are two types of lions in Kenya:
  1. *Felix massaica* – buff-coloured with a yellow mane.
  2. *Felix leo somaliensis* – smaller with larger ears, more pronounced spots and a longer tail.
Elsa belongs to the *somaliensis* type.

worry.' Then she was off again.[1] When she finally returned, for good, she was badly scratched and bleeding from several claw marks and was very irritable when I tried to dress her wounds. It needed much patience to make her jump into the truck.

Thus ended the first three months of our experiment. We had failed this time owing to her illness but felt confident that given time and patience we would succeed.

[1]We often wondered why Elsa never produced cubs as a result of being with a lion while she was in season. Later I learned from a zoo authority that during the four relevant days the male sires the female at least six to eight times a day and that it is thought that it is only on the fourth day that the siring becomes effective. If this is so, it is obvious that Elsa never had sufficient opportunity, as the jealous lioness, holding guard over her male, would not be likely to tolerate too frequent love-making with a newcomer to the pride.

Black
Beauty

ANNA SEWELL

BLACK BEAUTY

When Black Beauty's owner, Jerry, is forced to give up his work as a cabman through ill-health, he tries to find Black Beauty a good home.

I was sold to a corn dealer and baker whom Jerry knew, and with him he thought I should have good food and fair work. In the first he was quite right, and if my master had always been on the premises, I do not think I should have been overloaded. But there was a foreman who was always hurrying and driving everyone, and frequently when I had quite a full load, he would order something else to be taken on. My carter, whose name was Jakes, often said it was more than I ought to take, but the other always overruled him.

Jakes, like the other carters, always had the bearing rein up, which prevented me from drawing easily, and by the time I had been there three or four months, I found the work telling very much on my strength.

One day I was loaded more than usual, and part of the road was a steep uphill. I used all my strength, but I could not get on, and was obliged to stop. This did not please my driver, and he laid his whip on badly. 'Get on, lazy fellow,' he said, 'or I'll make you.'

Again I started the heavy load, and struggled on a few yards. Again the whip came down, and again I struggled forward. The pain of that great cart whip was sharp, but my mind was hurt quite as much as my poor sides. To be punished and abused when I was doing my best was so hard it took the heart out of me.

A third time he was flogging me cruelly when a lady stepped quickly up to him and said in a sweet, earnest voice, 'Oh! Pray do not whip your horse any more. I am sure he is doing all he can, and the road is very steep! He is doing his best.'

'If doing his best won't get this load up, he must do something more than his best, that's all I know, ma'am,' said Jakes.

'But is it not a very heavy load?' she said.

'Yes, yes, too heavy,' he said. 'But that's not my fault. The foreman came just as we were starting, and would have three hundredweight more put on to save him trouble, and I must get on with it as well as I can.'

He was raising the whip again, when the lady said, 'Pray, stop. I think I can help you if you will let me.'

The man laughed.

'You see,' she said, 'you do not give him a fair chance. He cannot use all his power with his head held back as it is with that bearing rein. If you would take it off, I am sure he would do better – *do* try it,' she said. 'I should be very glad if you would.'

'Well, well,' said Jakes, with a short laugh. 'Anything to please a lady, of course. How far would you wish it down, ma'am?'

'Quite down. Give him his head altogether.'

The rein was taken off, and in a moment I put my head down to my very knees. What a comfort it was! Then I tossed it up and down several times to get the aching stiffness out of my neck.

'Poor fellow! That is what you wanted,' said she, patting and stroking me with her gentle hand. 'And now if you will speak kindly to him and lead him on, I believe he will be able to do better.'

Jakes took the rein. 'Come on, Blackie.'

I put down my head and threw my whole weight against the collar. I spared no strength. The load moved on, and I pulled it steadily up the hill, and then stopped to catch my breath.

The lady had walked along the footpath and now came across into the road. She stroked and patted my neck as I had not been patted for many a long day.

'You see he was quite willing when you gave him the chance. I am sure he is a fine-tempered creature, and I daresay he has known better days. You won't put that rein on him again, will you?' For he was just going to hitch it up on the old plan.

'Well, ma'am, I can't deny that having his head has helped him up the hill, and I'll remember it another time, and thank you, ma'am. But if he went without a bearing rein I should be the laughing stock of all the carters. It is the fashion, you see.'

'Is it not better,' she said, 'to lead a good fashion, than to follow a bad one? A great many gentlemen do not use bearing reins now. My carriage horses have not worn them for fifteen years, and work with much less fatigue than those who have them. Besides,' she added in a very serious voice, 'we have no right to distress any of God's creatures without a very good reason. We call them dumb animals, and so they are, for they cannot tell us how they feel, but they do not suffer less because they have no words. But I must not detain you now. I thank you for trying my plan with your good horse, and I am sure you will find it far better than the whip. Good day.' With another soft pat on my neck, she stepped across the path and I saw her no more.

'That was a real lady, I'll be bound for it,' said Jakes to himself. 'She spoke just as polite as if I was a gentleman, and I'll try her plan, uphill, at any rate.' And I must do him the justice to say that he let my rein out several holes, and going uphill after that, he always gave me my head.

But the heavy loads went on. Good feed and fair rest will keep one's strength under full work, but no horse can stand against overloading. I was getting so thoroughly pulled down from this cause that a younger horse was bought in my place.

I may as well mention here what I suffered at this time from another cause. I had heard horses speak of it, but had never myself had experience of the evil. This was the badly lighted stable. There was only one small window at the end, and the consequence was that the stalls were almost dark. Besides the depressing effect this had on my spirits, it very much weakened my sight, and when I was suddenly brought out of the darkness into the glare of daylight, it was very painful to my eyes. Several times I stumbled over the threshold, and could scarcely see where I was going.

I believe, had I stayed there very long I should have become purblind, and that would have been a great misfortune. I have heard men say that a stone-blind horse was safer to drive than one which had imperfect sight, as it generally makes them very timid.

However, I escaped without any permanent injury to my sight, and was sold to a large cab owner.

I shall never forget my new master. He had black eyes and a hooked nose, a mouth as full of teeth as a bulldog's, and his voice was as harsh as the grinding of cart wheels over gravel stones. His name was Nicholas Skinner, and I believe he was the same man that poor Seedy Sam drove for.

I have heard men say that seeing is believing, but I should say that *feeling* is believing. Much as I had seen before, I never really knew till now the utter misery of a cab horse's life.

Skinner had a low set of cabs and a low set of drivers. He was hard on the men, and the men were hard on the horses. In this place we had no Sunday rest, and it was in the heat of summer.

Sometimes on a Sunday morning, a party of fast men would hire the cab for the day – four of them inside and another with the driver, and I had to take them ten or fifteen miles out into the country, and back again. Never would any of them get down to walk up a hill, let it be ever so steep, or the day ever so hot – unless indeed, when the driver was afraid I should not manage it. Sometimes I was so fevered and worn that I could hardly touch my food. How I longed for the nice bran mash with nitre in it that Jerry used to give us on Saturday nights in hot weather, to cool us down and make us so comfortable! Then we had two nights and a whole day of unbroken rest, and on Monday morning we were as fresh as young horses again. But there was no rest, and my driver was just as hard as his master. He had a cruel whip with something so sharp at the end that it sometimes drew blood, and he would even whip me under the belly and flip the lash out at my head. Indignities like these took the heart out of me terribly, but still I did my best and never hung back. As poor Ginger said, it was no use; men are the strongest.

My life was now so utterly wretched that I wished I might, like Ginger, drop down dead at my work and be out of my misery. One day my wish very nearly came to pass.

I went on the stand at eight in the morning and had done a good share of work, when we had to take a fare to the railway. A long train was expected in, so my driver pulled up at the back of some of the outside cabs, to take the chance of a return fare. It was a very heavy train, and as all the cabs were soon engaged, ours was called for. There was a party of four: a noisy, blustering man with a lady, a little boy, and a young girl, and a great deal of luggage. The lady and the boy got into the cab, and while the man ordered about the luggage, the young girl came and looked at me.

'Papa,' she said. 'I am sure this poor horse cannot take us and all our luggage so far, he is so very weak and worn out. Do look at him.'

'Oh, he's all right, miss,' said my driver. 'He's strong enough.'

The porter, who was pulling about some heavy boxes, suggested to the gentleman as there was so much luggage, whether he would not take a second cab.

'Can your horse do it, or can't he?' said the blustering man.

'Oh, he can do it all right, sir. Send up the boxes, porter. He could take more than that!' And he helped to haul up a box so heavy that I could feel the springs go down.

'Papa, Papa, do take a second cab,' said the young girl in a beseeching tone. 'I am sure we are wrong. I am sure it is very cruel.'

'Nonsense, Grace! Get in at once, and don't make all this fuss. A pretty thing it would be if a man of business had to examine every cab horse before he hired it – the man knows his business, of course. There, get in and hold your tongue!'

My gentle friend had to obey. Box after box was dragged up and lodged on the top of the cab, or settled by the side of the driver. At last all was ready, and with his usual jerk at the rein and lash of whip, he drove out of the station.

The load was very heavy, and I had had neither food nor rest since the morning; but I did my best, as I always had done, in spite of cruelty and injustice.

I got along fairly till we came to Ludgate Hill, but there the heavy load and my own exhaustion were too much. I was struggling to keep on, goaded by constant chucks of the rein and use of the whip, when in a single moment – I cannot tell how – my feet slipped from under me, and I fell heavily to the ground on my side. The suddenness and the force with which I fell seemed to beat all the breath out of my body. I lay perfectly still. Indeed, I had no power to move, and I thought now I was going to die. I heard a sort of confusion round me, loud angry voices, and the getting down of the luggage, but it was all like a dream.

I thought I heard that sweet pitying voice saying, 'Oh! That poor horse! It is all our fault.' Someone came and loosened the throat strap of my bridle, and undid the traces which kept the collar so tight upon me. Someone said, 'He's dead. He'll never get up again.' Then I could hear the policeman giving orders, but I did not even open my eyes. I could only draw a gasping breath now and then. Some cold water was thrown over my head, and some cordial was poured into my mouth, and something was covered over me. I cannot tell how long I lay there, but I found my life coming back, and a kind-voiced man was patting me and encouraging me to rise.

After some more cordial had been given me, and after one or two attempts, I staggered to my feet, and was gently led to some stables which were close by. Here I was put into a well-littered stall, and some warm gruel was brought to me, which I drank thankfully.

In the evening I was sufficiently recovered to be led back to Skinner's stables, where I think they did the best for me they could. In the morning Skinner came with a farrier to look at me.

He examined me very closely and said, 'This is a case of overwork more than disease, and if you could give him a runoff for six months, he would be able to work again. But now there is not an ounce of strength in him.'

'Then he must just go to the dogs,' said Skinner. 'I have no meadows to nurse sick horses in – he might get well or he might not; that sort of thing don't suit my business. My plan is to work 'em as long as they'll go, and then sell 'em for what they'll fetch, at the knacker's or elsewhere.'

'If he was broken-winded,' said the farrier, 'you had better have him killed out of hand, but he is not. There is a sale of horses coming off in about ten days; if you rest him and feed him up, he may pick up, and you may get more than his skin is worth, at any rate.'

Upon this advice, Skinner, unwillingly, I think, gave orders that I should be well fed and cared for, and the stable man, happily for me, carried out the orders with a much better will than his master had in giving them. Ten days of perfect rest, plenty of good oats, hay, bran mashes with boiled linseed mixed in them, did more to get up my condition than anything else could have done. Those linseed mashes were delicious, and I began to think, after all, it might be better to live than go to the dogs. When the twelfth day after the accident came, I was taken to the sale, a few miles out of London.

I felt that any change from my present place must be an improvement, so I held up my head and hoped for the best.

At this sale, of course, I found myself in company with old broken-down horses – some lame, some broken-winded, some old, and some that I am sure it would have been merciful to shoot.

The buyers and sellers, too, many of them, looked not much better off than the poor beasts they were bargaining about. There were poor old men, trying to get a horse or a pony for a few pounds, that might drag about some little wood or coal cart. There were poor men trying to sell a worn-out beast for two or three pounds, rather than have the greater loss of killing him. Some of them looked as if poverty and hard times had hardened them all over; but there were others that I would have willingly used the last of my strength in serving – poor and shabby, but kind and human, with voices that I could trust.

There was one tottering old man that took a great fancy to me, and I to him, but I was not strong enough – it was an anxious time! Coming from the better part of the fair, I noticed a man who looked like a gentleman farmer, with a young boy by his side. He had a broad back and round shoulders, a kind, ruddy face, and he wore a broad-brimmed hat. When he came up to me and my companions, he stood still and gave a pitying look round upon us. I saw his eye rest on me. I had a good mane and tail, which helped my appearance. I pricked my ears and looked at him.

'There's a horse, Willie, that has known better days.'

'Poor old fellow!' said the boy. 'Do you think, Grandpapa, he was ever a carriage horse?'

'Oh, yes, my boy,' said the farmer, coming closer. 'He might have been anything when he was young. Look at his nostrils and his ears, the shape of his neck and shoulder. There's a deal of breeding about that horse.'

He put out his hand and gave me a kind pat on the neck. I put out my nose in answer to his kindness; the boy stroked my face.

'Poor old fellow! See, Grandpapa, how well he understands kindness. Could not you buy him and make him young again, as you did with

Ladybird?'

'My dear boy, I can't make all old horses young. Besides, Ladybird was not so very old – she was run down and badly used.'

'Well, Grandpapa, I don't believe that this one is old; look at his mane and tail. I wish you would look into his mouth, and then you could tell. Though he is so very thin, his eyes are not sunk like some old horses'.'

The old gentleman laughed. 'Bless the boy! He is as horsey as his old grandfather.'

'But do look at his mouth, Grandpapa, and ask the price. I am sure he would grow young in our meadows.'

The man who had brought me for sale now put in his own word.

'The young gentleman's a real knowing one, sir. Now the fact is, this 'ere hoss is just pulled down with overwork in the cabs. He's not an old one, and I heard as how the vetenary should say that a six months' run-off would set him right up, being as how his wind was not broken. I've had the tending of him these ten days past, and a gratefuller, pleasanter animal I never met with. 'Twould be worth a gentleman's while to give a five-pound note for him and let him have a chance. I'll be bound he'd be worth twenty pounds next spring.'

The old gentleman laughed and the little boy looked up at him eagerly.

'Oh, Grandpapa, did you not say the colt sold for five pounds more than you expected? You would not be poorer if you did buy this one.'

The farmer slowly felt my legs, which were much swelled and strained; then he looked at my mouth. 'Thirteen or fourteen, I should say. Just trot him out, will you?'

I arched my poor thin neck, raised my tail a little and drew out my legs as well as I could; but they were very stiff and sore.

'What is the lowest you will take for him?' said the farmer as I came back.

'Five pounds, sir; that was the lowest price my master would set.'

''Tis a speculation,' said the old gentleman, shaking his head, but at the same time slowly drawing out his purse. 'Quite a speculation! Have you any more business here?' he said, counting the sovereigns into his hand.

'No, sir, I can take him to the inn, if you please.'

'Do so, I am now going there.'

They walked forward, and I was led behind. The boy could hardly control his delight, and the old gentleman seemed to enjoy his pleasure. I had a good feed at the inn, and was then gently ridden home by a servant of my new master's and turned into a large meadow with a shed in one corner of it.

Mr. Thoroughgood, for that was the name of my benefactor, gave orders that I should have hay and oats every night and morning, and the run of the meadow during the the day. 'And you, Willie,' said he 'must take the oversight of him. I give him in charge to you.'

The boy was proud of his charge, and undertook it in all seriousness. There was not a day when he did not pay me a visit, sometimes picking me out from among the other horses, and giving me a bit of carrot or something good, or sometimes standing by me while I ate my oats. He always came with kind words and caresses, and of course I grew fond of him. He called me Old Crony, as I used to come to him in the field and follow him about. Sometimes he brought his grandfather, who always looked at my legs.

'This is our point, Willie,' he would say. 'But he is improving so steadily that I think we shall see a change for the better in the spring.'

The perfect rest, the good food, the soft turf and gentle exercise soon began to tell on my condition and my spirits. I had a good constitution from my mother, and I was never strained when I was young, so that I had a better chance than many horses who have been worked before they came to their full strength. During the winter my legs improved so much that I began to feel quite young again.

Then spring came round, and one day in March, Mr. Thoroughgood determined that he would try me in the phaeton. I was well pleased, and he and Willie drove me a few miles. My legs were not stiff now, and I did the work with perfect ease.

'He's growing young, Willie! We must give him a little gentle work now, and by mid-summer he will be as good as Ladybird. He has a beautiful mouth and good paces – they can't be better.'

'Oh, Grandpapa! How glad I am you bought him!'

'So am I, my boy, but he has to thank you more than me. We must now be looking out for a quite genteel place for him, where he will be valued.'

One day during this summer, the groom cleaned and dressed me with such extraordinary care that I thought some new change must be at hand. He trimmed my fetlocks and legs, passed the tar-brush over my hoofs, and even parted my forelock. I think the harness had an extra polish. Willie seemed anxious, half merry, as he got into the chaise with his grandfather.

'If the ladies take to him,' said the old gentleman, 'they'll be suited, and he'll be suited. We can't but try.'

At the distance of a mile or two from the village, we came to a pretty, low house with a lawn and shrubbery at the front and a drive up to the door. Willie rang the bell and asked if Miss Blomefield or Miss Ellen was at home. Yes, they were. So, while Willie stayed with me, Mr. Thoroughgood went into the house. In about ten minutes he returned, followed by three ladies. One tall, pale lady, wrapped in a white shawl, leaned on a younger lady, with dark eyes and a merry face; the other, a very stately looking person, was Miss Blomefield. They all came and looked at me and asked questions. The younger lady – that was Miss Ellen – took to me very much; she said she was sure she should like me, I had such a good face. The tall, pale lady said that she should always be nervous in riding behind a horse that had once been down, as I might come down again, and if I did, she should never get over the fright of it.

'You see, ladies,' said Mr. Thoroughgood, 'many first-rate horses have had their knees broken through the carelessness of their drivers, without the fault of their own, and from what I can see of this horse, I should say that is his case. But of course I do not want to influence you. If you incline, you can have him on trial, and then your coachman will see what he thinks of him.'

'You have always been such a good adviser to us about our horses,' said the stately lady, 'that your recommendation would go a long way with me, and if my sister Lavinia sees no objection, we will accept your offer of a trial, with our thanks.'

It was then arranged that I should be sent for by them the next day.

In the morning a smart-looking young man came for me. At first, he looked pleased; but when he saw my knees, he said in a disappointed voice, 'I didn't think, sir, you would have recommended my ladies a blemished horse like that.'

'Handsome is, that handsome does,' said my master. 'You are only taking him on trial, and I am sure you will do fairly by him, young man. If he is not safe as any horse you ever drove, send him back.'

I was led home, placed in a comfortable stable, fed, and left to myself. The next day when my groom was cleaning my face, he said, 'That is just like the star that Black Beauty had. He is much the same height, too. I wonder where he is now.'

A little further on he came to the place in my neck where I was bled, and where a little knot was left in the skin. He almost started, and began to look me over carefully, talking to himself.

'White star in the forehead, one white foot on the off side, this little knot just in that place.' Then, looking at the middle of my back – 'And as I am alive, there is a little patch of white hair that John used to call 'Beauty's three-penny bit.' It *must* be Black Beauty! Why, Beauty!

235

Beauty! Do you know me? Little Joe Green, that almost killed you?' And he began patting and patting me as if he was quite overjoyed.

I could not say that I remembered him, for now he was a fine grown young fellow, with black whiskers and a man's voice, but I was sure he knew me and that he was Joe Green, and I was very glad. I put my nose up to him, and tried to say that we were friends. I never saw a man so pleased.

'Give you a fair trial! I should think so indeed! I wonder who the rascal was that broke your knees, my old Beauty! You must have been badly served out somewhere. Well, well, it won't be my fault if you haven't good times of it now! I wish John Manly was here to see you.'

In the afternoon I was put into a low park chair and brought to the door. Miss Ellen was going to try me, and Green went with her. I soon found that she was a good driver, and she seemed pleased with my paces. I heard Joe telling her about me, and that he was sure I was Squire Gordon's old Black Beauty.

When we returned, the other sisters came out to hear how I had behaved. She told them what she had just heard, and said, 'I shall certainly write to Mrs. Gordon, and tell her that her favorite horse has come to us. How pleased she will be!'

Aftet this I was driven every day for a week or so, and as I appeared to be quite safe, Miss Lavinia at last ventured out in the small closed carriage. After this it was quite decided to keep me and call me by my old name of Black Beauty.

I have now lived in this happy place a whole year. Joe is the best and kindest of grooms. My work is easy and pleasant, and I feel my strength and spirits all coming back again.

Mr. Thoroughgood said to Joe the other day, 'In your place he will last till he is twenty years old – perhaps more.'

Willie always speaks of me when he can and treats me as his special friend. My ladies have promised that I shall never be sold, and so I have nothing to fear. And here my story ends. My troubles are all over, and I am at home; and often before I am quite awake, I fancy I am still in the orchard at Birtwick, standing with my old friends under the apple trees.

ACKNOWLEDGEMENTS

Grateful acknowledgement is made to authors, publishers and literary agents for permission to include in this volume the works listed below.

The National Trust and Macmillan London Ltd for THE CAT THAT WALKED BY HIMSELF.

Geoffrey Morgan and Collins Sons & Co Ltd for the extract from *Flip*.

Gerald Durrell, Granada Publishing Ltd and Curtis Brown Ltd for ADOPTING AN ANTEATER from *Encounters with Animals*.

Sheila Hocken, Victor Gollancz Ltd and Sphere Books Ltd for ENTER EMMA from *Emma and I*.

Richard Adams for THE RABBIT'S GHOST STORY.

Frederick Warne & Co Ltd for TUPPENNY AND THE TRAVELLING CIRCUS from *The Fairy Caravan* by Beatrix Potter.

MARY by John Collier is reprinted by permission of Souvenir Press Ltd from The John Collier Reader and A D Peter & Co Ltd.

Desmond Morris and Jonathan Cape Ltd for HIJACKING A TELEVISION STUDIO ISN'T EASY from *Animal Days*.

James Herriot, Michael Joseph Ltd and St Martin's Press, New York, for MONTY THE BULL from *All Things Bright and Beautiful*.

Christopher Lofting and Ralph Vicinanza for the extract from *Doctor Dolittle's Zoo*.

The estate of Richmal Crompton and Collins Sons & Co Ltd for JUMBLE from *Just William* and the Hamlyn Publishing Group for permission to use the original illustration by Henry Thomas.

The estate of Joy Adamson, Collins Sons & Co Ltd and Pantheon Books, Inc a division of Random House Inc for THE FIRST RELEASE from *Born Free*. © 1960 by Joy Adamson.